T0158331

THE WHITE TATTOO

A COLLECTION OF SHORT STORIES

THE WHITE TATTOO

William J. Cobb

THE OHIO STATE UNIVERSITY PRESS
Columbus

Copyright © 2002 by The Ohio State University.
All rights reserved.

Library of Congress Cataloging-in-Publication Data

Cobb, William J. (William James), 1957–
    The white tattoo / William J. Cobb
      p. cm.
    ISBN 0-8142-0901-7 (cloth: alk. paper)—ISBN 0-8142-5096-3 (pbk.: alk paper)
    I. United States—Social life and customs—20th century—Fiction. I.
Title.
    PS3603.O23 W48 2001
    813'.6—dc21

                                  2001006643

Text and Jacket Design by Jennifer Shoffey Carr.
Typeset in Abode Goudy By Jennifer Shoffey Carr.
Printed by Thomson-Shore, Inc.

The paper used in this publication meets the minimum requriements of the
American National Standard for Information Sciences—Permanance of
Paper for Printed Library Materials. Ansi Z39.48–1992.

9   8   7   6   5   4   3   2   I

FOR ELIZABETH

CONTENTS

ACKNOWLEDGMENTS

THE AUTHOR WOULD LIKE TO THANK all the people whose patience and savvy helped bring these stories to the page, particularly Steven Barthelme, Lucy Ferriss, and Heather Sellers. Rosellen Brown, James Robison, Mary Robison, Daniel Menaker, Ron Spatz, David Roberts, Bill Roorbach, Ken Hammond, David Carkeet, Robert S. Fogarty, and Fritz Lanham also deserve much appreciation. Much love and thanks also to Barbara Beaumont and Beverly Full, partners in climbs.

Additionally, great thanks go to the National Endowment for the Arts, the Associated Writing Programs, and the Texas Institute of Letters for their support and encouragement.

The stories, some in slightly different form, first appeared in the following magazines: "The Wishes" appeared in *The New Yorker*; "Letting the Dog Out" appeared in *The Sonora Review*; "The White Tatoo," "Why You?" and "Father Tongue" appeared in *Press*; "Marathon" appeared in *The Alaska Quarterly Review*; "Mergers & Acquisitions" appeared in *The Mississippi Review*; "Three Feet of Water" appeared in *Gulf Coast*; "The Atmosphere of Vienna" appeared in *The Literary Review*; "Motel Ice" appeared in *New Letters*; "For All You Dorks, Blah Blah Blah" appeared in *Puerto del Sol*; "The Decline of King Fabulous" appeared in *The Clackamas Literary Review*; "There's Nothing the Matter with Gwen" appeared in *The Antioch Review*; and "Dark Matter" appeared in *Natural Bridge*.

THE WISHES

L OPEY WAS TELLING HERSELF—in her mind's voice, of
course; she wasn't talking out loud—that if this were *her* planet,
she'd make it all rivers and mountains and forests and animals running every which way. Only all the animals, even the tigers and grizzly bears, would be vegetarians, so there wouldn't be any of the
ugliness you see on PBS. The moon would always be full. The air
clean. The days would be warm enough to swim, the nights cool
enough for sweaters. Sometimes it would snow, without warning.

It was Sunday morning in Boulder, Colorado. Weaver, the man
Lopey lived with, sat across from her at the breakfast table, but she
ignored him. Her 24½ birthday was the next day, and as this
anniversary ticked toward her, Lopey had been drifting. She was
unemployed. She'd had a secretarial thing but felt trapped; she had
trouble breathing in the office. She fainted twice. Her coworkers
avoided her, afraid of CPR, afraid they would fail to remember if it
was five breaths and one pump or five pumps and one breath. So she

quit. She didn't need money anyway, since Weaver had plenty for both of them. She had straight black hair with streaks of white, graceful posture, and super-white skin. Although she was born Penelope, her mother nicknamed her Lopey when she was five, the age when she waltzed around the living room in a tooth fairy outfit, wearing a tiny ballroom-dancer dress and small, shiny wings made of guitar-string loops wrapped in cellophane. She still talked to her mother on the phone at least once a week, and to her brother, Karl, in Idaho just as often. Her mother told Lopey she was worried about Karl, since he'd been fired from his job as a housepainter and he could really do so much better—what a waste. Her mother told Karl that she was worried about Lopey, because it just didn't seem right, her living with that man and admitting she wasn't even in love with him, and him so gaga about her. It was asking for trouble, she told Karl.

Opposite Lopey, wearing the reindeer sweater she had given him last Christmas (bought with his own money), Weaver folded his newspaper neatly in half, smoothed the creases down with his thumbs, and tried not to think. Although he pretended to read the Arts & Leisure section of the *New York Times,* he couldn't stop dwelling on the meeting he had had with his auditors the day before. They had changed the way they were figuring his company's revenue, and were forcing him to write off $1.5 million in ten-year notes his company had accumulated in the second quarter of this fiscal year.

As the CEO of a firm that manufactured solar water heaters, Weaver was used to arranging complicated tax shelters, loopholes, and dodges to market his energy saver, but this was different. This write-off was going to change his earnings-per-share figure from $1.07 to $0.76. Monday he would have to issue a press release about the change, which would look bad to investors. One is going to start selling, then another and another, and there goes the market capital. If only he hadn't issued that press release a month ago predicting an earnings increase. If only he hadn't agreed to those ten-year notes—

he probably could have gotten cash up front—maybe not the entire amount, but anything would have been better than this.

Weaver's hair was thin and brittle, his middle wide, and with his prostate gland swollen, urinating was slow and painful, full of hot splashes. He wondered if someday it would just stop working altogether. What would happen then? Would he swell up, lead a life of constant agony? He was older than Lopey's mother, Kay. He had deep grooves in his face from the wings of his nose to the corners of his mouth, grayish skin, and large pores. He was a man made for suits; in jeans and T-shirts he looked like a bum. The day after Lopey introduced him to Kay, they had a mother-daughter lunch together. Kay was concerned about her—that was all. Wasn't it a little early for them to be living together? Kay pointed out that Weaver would be sixty-five when Lopey would be forty. She didn't like that idea a bit. "What's the difference between him and your Uncle Fred?" she asked.

Lopey considered this. They were eating at a soup-and-salad café frequented by runners. Lopey watched an athlete walk by with a plate of watermelon. "What's the question again?"

"Uncle Fred and Weaver. The difference."

"Fred's in Cleveland?"

Kay sighed. She asked if Lopey loved Weaver. Lopey pursed her lips. "I can learn to."

Kay shook her head, ate her salad. "He certainly doesn't look very aerobic—that's all I know."

◆

Lopey had told Weaver bits and pieces of this conversation, since she didn't like to lie, and now he was very self-conscious around Kay. He wished he were her boss, so he could fire her. She was a symptom of something greater. Lopey's mother, the auditors, the traffic cop that pulled him over two weeks ago for speeding—they were out to get him. But now is not the time to panic. Now is the time to keep cool.

"You look lovely this morning, Lopey."

She squinted out the window. She didn't have her contacts in yet. "Or is that lopey this morning, Lovely?"

Weaver poured himself another cup of coffee and stirred it slowly. He watched Lopey put on her glasses and start working the crossword puzzle. He realized she'd be at it for hours. For a terrible moment he was keenly aware of the passage of time, and it occurred to him vividly—as it had several times—that he was allotted only so much time in his life, and that most of that time had already been used up. What did he have to show for it? Where was he now? Doting on a younger woman who didn't love him? He morbidly watched the second hand of his wristwatch marking off the moments until his death.

"Let's go for a drive today," he said. "Let's do something we've never done before."

Lopey kept at her crossword. After a minute or so, she said, "Did you say something?"

"Never mind."

She looked up and regarded him and his hurt feelings, his trying to spice up his life; it wasn't his fault he wasn't Marlon Brando. He refused to look at her. Rodin's *The Pouter*. She wobbled the table and spilled his coffee, made him catch her smile. "Come over here, you old dog," she said. He didn't like her to call him that, but he got up from the table anyway, to obey her, his tail wagging weakly.

◆

Kay was the only member of the entire family who was in love. She was dating a neurophysiologist named Leo Abruzzi, who was something of a star in Boulder because of his mountain climbing. He'd been on several trips to the Himalayas and Karakoram, and although he had never summited, he and his party had gotten as far as Camp IX on K2, at 26,050 feet. A storm hit when they reached that height, and they were forced to stay put for six days, shoveling snow off their tents, constantly in danger of avalanches, until finally they managed a heroic descent when the wind eased. He lost three of his toes to frost-bite, but the most serious effect was on his oxygen-starved brain. "I don't think I've ever been the same since," he told Kay once. He had trouble remembering things and would often fall asleep suddenly, sometimes in the middle of a sentence. "He sounds like one of those washer-dryers you get cheap at Sears because they have a nick or scratch on them," said Lopey, when Kay first described Leo—the new love—to her. Kay didn't care. She liked being with him, sleeping with him, talking to him. So he falls asleep sometimes. Is that a sin?

"It's not narcolepsy," she told Karl, who had said the word. "It's much more random than that."

Both her children were going to meet Leo for the first time on Lopey's 24½ birthday, Karl coming from Moscow, Idaho. At first he'd moved up there to take a job as a carpenter, but he'd been fired three times. He was fired from his last job, as a housepainter, because he got so stoned he spent all day on one wall of a house and wasted most of the time smoking cigarettes, playing with his radio, or checking him-self in the mirror. He was fired from his job before that, as a pizza deliv-eryman, because he would drive around town aimlessly, his dog, Butch, hanging his head out the passenger-side window. Lopey and Kay spent much of their time trying to figure out careers for Karl. Now he wanted to be a photographer. "I'm sure he has the talent for it," said Kay, when she discussed this new development with Lopey on the phone, "but I don't know. . . ." She bought him a Nikon F-3 anyway. Karl took after his father in looks, with his red hair and large freckles that thickly covered his body; at the beach, in trunks, he looked like an ocelot. Lopey took after Kay, especially in the way her dark hair was gradually paling with time. Kay always insisted her own hair had been completely white by the time she was thirty-two, and Lopey believed her, since she could only dimly remember her mother with dark hair, and that mainly from pictures. Lopey had only seven and a half years to go. Would her hair be all white by then, too?

Lopey was Kay's first child and, at least as far as Kay was concerned, the only thing her husband, Gavin, ever did right. Gavin was a lawyer who spent his free time and extra money big-game hunting in Africa, and populated the walls at home with heads of impala, warthog, gazelle, and rhino. Every day he drank martinis from the time he came home from work until he passed out. One evening, after Kay complained about his drinking, he said, "I don't need this." He stormed out of the house and drove the station wagon half a mile down the road and into a tree at seventy miles an hour. He flew through the windshield and into a froggy ditch. The police pulled him out later and found his mouth full of thick black mud and earthworms.

Kay never remarried. Lopey liked to say, "My mother—the widow."

Kay had a series of now-and-then boyfriends during the years after Gavin's flight through the windshield, but Lopey and Karl had always come first. But now Kay was a handsome woman of forty-nine, with an open, tanned face and pure-white hair worn short. Did she want to live alone the rest of her life?

◆

Before Weaver had time to issue a formal press release on Monday morning, a mole inside the accounting firm that had done the audit gave a group of morticians on Wall Street the word, and they got out their knives. The stock opened at 17 and down-ticked to 14. By afternoon it dropped to 12¼ and Weaver quit answering his phone. The company lost $23 million in market capitalization in one day. Weaver sat with his head in his hands and watched the phone ring. He twisted an entire boxful of large paper clips. He had no idea what to do. What are they going to do ten years from now, when the price of oil skyrockets again? Trust the Arabs? All that energy of the sun going to waste. What we need are solar panels on the roofs of homes, solar cars, solar panel collectors over shopping mall parking lots. We can make this a better planet. Plant a tree. Ride a bike. Use the sun. The stockholders would want answers. Or his head. There might be a class action lawsuit. What will Lopey do when she learns of this? Who's going to love a fifty-year-old bankrupt with a swollen prostate? In the tangly web of his depression, Weaver realized the pounding he was hearing was not his heart, but a migraine. He left his office and rummaged in the file cabinets behind his secretary's desk for Tylenol.

I hope it's poisoned, he thought. His secretary, Janet, tapped away at her word processor and watched him out of the corner of her Maybellined eyes. She wore a smart dark-gray wool skirt with a zipper at the side, and a sheer white silk blouse with throat ruffles. Mr. Greuze, the chief financial officer, warned her to keep an eye on her boss, in case he got too close to the windows. She finished the letter he had given her, in which he was asking his bankers for a $6 million extension on loans, and as she watched the laser printer slowly spit out the letter, she wondered what Weaver looked like naked.

♦

Kay drove to Leo's lab in the physiology department at the University of Colorado. They were supposed to go shopping for a half-year birthday present for Lopey, but Kay couldn't find him at first. The lab was a long, low room of eerie bright fluorescent light, with a white tiled floor and a kitchen-counterlike table in the middle dominated by a huge microscope. Another counter along one wall was cluttered with test tube racks, glass beakers, several centrifuges, Bunsen burners, and a sink with a dripping faucet. A young Asian student in a white lab coat was looking into the microscope, and when Kay asked where Dr. Abruzzi was, he pointed to the large aluminum-covered door of a walk-in cooler. She found Leo inside, doing sit-ups in his underwear. His body was enveloped in a sheen of his own vapor, but he didn't stop until he reached two hundred.

They went to a local shopping mall, and Kay lost Leo for a while, when she was looking at sweaters for Lopey, and found him by accident, adrift in a sea of bras. Leo was always disoriented in shopping malls; without being able to see the sky, he never knew which way was which. He followed Kay to the next boutique, where he sat down on the floor and was about to nod off, but he was in everyone's way, so the salesgirl made him move. They agreed to meet at the fountain in the middle of the mall later on, and he was already there, holding a brand-new ice ax in his arms, when Kay arrived. "This is something she can use," he said.

Kay took it awkwardly and smiled, then made chopping motions in the air. "Maybe we could scare away that boyfriend with this."

He nodded. "They're good for all kinds of things. On Nanda Devi, I once used one to—"

"Leo? Could I ask you a question?"

He shrugged and patted her white hair. "Always."

"Would you marry me?"

Leo ate his dinner slowly and methodically, in complete ignorance of the scrutiny of Lopey and Karl. He spoke directly to Kay about his plans for an upcoming climb of Annapurna, at 26,504 feet the eleventh-highest mountain in the world. They were all gathered at Kay's house, and Weaver was to join them as soon as he could. Leo described his previous treks through the blue forests during the monsoons, hiking with umbrellas in the constant rain, how the leeches covered your boots and socks, how the porters carried sixty-six-pound loads for a dollar seventy-five and two cigarettes a day, barefoot on cold mountain paths, nimble on their cracked and swollen, beastlike feet. And though he knew at fifty-three he was too old to be leading a climb up Annapurna, he was going anyway, because he would make up in experience what he lacked in strength. He also knew that as a climber, he had become more of a figurehead than anything else, that he was often described as a punch-drunk legend, and that he'd been chosen for this expedition for his political connections in Nepal, but it didn't matter to him, because he was going, and if he died at 24,000 feet that would be a good death. In the middle of describing something he lost his train of thought and stared vacantly at Kay. "What was I saying?"

"The avalanches," she said, and patted his hand. Poor Leo Abruzzi. Such a battered ram. Lopey wondered what it was like when those misshapen hands touched her mother's breasts. There were two fingers missing from each of Leo's hands. On Cho Oyu (26,750 feet), Leo descended during a snowstorm and lost his gloves in the seventy-mile-per-hour winds. By the time he'd reached Camp I, the fingers were yellowish and had no feeling in them. Knut Almass, the Norwegian climber, had rubbed them and struggled to get them warm, then loaned Leo his own gloves, which was the only reason Leo's hands weren't amputated later. In base camp the fingers thawed with a burning pain, as if they were simmering in boiling water. The tips of his ring and little finger on both hands started to rot and smell after a week had passed. In Kathmandu, all four were amputated at the knuckle, and this, coupled with the toes he'd lost on the other expedition, gave Leo the queer feeling that he was being dismembered piece by piece. Now he looked like a three-toed sloth. How could she ignore those stumps, thought Lopey. And look at those arms. All veins and muscle.

Karl wondered what was for dessert.

Leo enjoyed Kay because she had nothing to do with climbing. With her he could sometimes forget how much he resented those lucky bastards who published fat windbag books after each of their fat ego-trip expeditions—boring Bonnington and maniac Messner. What did they know about climbing? What did they know about struggle and failure and keeping that snowy peak in the back of your mind for years and working every day toward reaching it without someone so much as saying, "Hey Leo, keep it up, you'll make it." Well, this time he was going to make it. He would succeed. He would. He's swimming in snow at 26,000 feet. He's eating snow, and his mountain is a solid white pyramid floating in a sea of ketchup. If he falls he won't hurt himself, because the ketchup is soft. So soft and warm. . . .

The realization that Leo had suddenly fallen asleep at the dinner table passed from Kay to Lopey to Karl. Leo's head fell straight back, mouth wide open, so that Lopey—who sat across from him—could see the pink concave roof, bisected neatly by a darkish groove at the center. Karl quit chewing, looked at shiny-eyed Kay and mystified Lopey, and gave Leo a nudge. "Hey, man, you sleepy or something?"

"Leave him be," said Kay. "This happens all the time."

Lopey said she knew all about narcolepsy, and how usually it was a problem with circulation and body chemistry. "I had a friend whose father had that," she said. "They called him Dr. Nod, King of the Sleepyheads."

"It's not narcolepsy—I told you," Kay snapped. "And thanks for being so sensitive and caring."

"I'm just kidding."

"Other people have feelings, too, you know."

Lopey said she didn't mean anything by it and gathered the dinner plates from the table, stacking them carefully to muffle the sound of the china and silverware. She suddenly wanted to get out of the kitchen and leave her mother to deal with these damaged goods she called a boyfriend. And her so bent out of shape about Weaver, when at least he had some kind of presence. She rinsed the plates, stacked them into the racks of the dishwashing machine, and sat on the back porch to smoke a cigarette, since Kay didn't like anyone smoking in her house.

The lightbulb above the door of the back porch was burned out. Lopey sat on a tree-stump stool, and when she drew on her cigarette, the orange glow cast a faint pulse. Dim moonlight glowed over the backyard, but Lopey knew the place of everything by heart—the chain-link fence, the doghouse, the spruce tree. Lopey loved her mother's house, and for a moment hated the idea that it wasn't really hers anymore, and would be even less hers when Leo moved in, because even though Kay had complained about Lopey living with Weaver, she had not offered her the old room back. And should she? Of course Lopey knew why she didn't invite her back. Kay was afraid she and Karl would never make it in the real world and assume lives of their own. She didn't want to become like a mother cat who still lets her grown kittens suckle, whose teats become long and stretched out, who hisses when her erstwhile kittens come slinking up. Lopey brushed her bangs off her forehead and smelled the tobacco on her fingers. She remembered the times in high school when she smoked in the backyard up against the chain-link fence and dreamed of a house of her own.

She went back inside and found Karl and Kay eating what was left of an apple pie with scoops of caramel-buttercrunch ice cream on top. "Lopey, look," said Karl, and opened his mouth, his tongue covered in ice cream. Lopey could tell he was stoned again and hoped he hadn't smoked it in the bathroom, because Kay would be so disappointed to know the truth. She decided to finish cleaning up the dinner mess, and as she was wiping off the wooden tabletop with a towel, she stared at the inert figure of Leo Abruzzi. His body leaned to one side now, a spot of drool at the corner of his mouth. You know, he doesn't look so hot, thought Lopey, and she stepped closer. His eyes were rolled back in their sockets. When Lopey placed her hand in front of his mouth, she felt no breath. She looked at him closer for one more moment, then drew back. She walked carefully into the living room, keeping her arms at her sides, and stood in front of the sofa, where Kay and Karl were sitting, Kay with her legs folded under her.

"Mom?" She started to speak, and stopped. Kay stared at her.

Lopey felt like smiling but knew she shouldn't. She didn't know what face to wear. It would be snowing at the funeral, a row of black umbrellas dotted white.

"I don't think Leo's so alive anymore."

◆

Weaver walked out the double glass doors of his building's lobby and was standing on the steps leading to the parking lot when his mind went blank. He tried desperately to remember what he was doing and where he was going. Across the street from his building was a field of grass. Two dark-red cows stood in the center of it, face to face, under a pure blue sky, the eyelid of our oceans, reminding Weaver that three-quarters of the earth is covered with water. The parking lot's asphalt in front of his office was marked with freshly painted yellow caution stripes. How brilliant. We all need a plan. To the south of Weaver's solar water heater plant the same blue sky was tangled with power, criss-crossed by the transformers and electrical towers of Boulder Power & Light. His competition. Weaver turned around for a moment and start-ed to go back to his office, but he caught his reflection in the mirrorlike Lexan walls of the building and stopped. He looked so old and thick; his wispy hair, like an egret's plume, was lifted by a breeze. He felt himself sliding into past tense. The trout would rise to the mayflies on Snow-mass Creek tonight. The elk would come down to graze after the hikers were gone. After he was gone. He remembered—the roses for Lopey.

He drove to the florist's and stared off to the side, at the strip of Jiffy Marts, video rental stores, boutiques, Burger Huts, Barbeque Barns, pizza places; the smell of fried chicken was warm and soft against his cheeks. He paid no attention to the road or cars in front of him, driving entirely by reflex. The florist (man? woman?) rolled the long-stemmed roses, ferns intertwined, in green tissue paper (woman—long fingers, painted nails), then went back to answer a ringing phone Weaver had not heard. He looked at gladiolus, clay pots of daisies, Easter lilies, impatiens, marigolds, the floral arrangements behind foggy, tall glass doors of the cooler behind the counter, picked up the roses, and walked to the car. He had never stolen before, but he did it with middle-aged honor and dignity and the fear of death grip-ping him like a cold-handed prison guard grabbing his balls. If the police pull me over, I'll say I forgot. I've had a lot on my mind, Offi-cer—my company may go bankrupt, and if you'll excuse me I'm going to cry. The florist didn't have his name, did she? Thirty-six dollars a dozen. Twelve dollars a share and it will go lower tomorrow. I was on the phone, and I wouldn't make a fuss really, but it's the principle of the thing. Tudor-style bar/restaurant on the right. Parking lot in back, out of view. Welcome to Der Rathskeller. Hello, my name is Weaver Conroy, and I'm an alcoholic.

◆

Kay, Karl, and Lopey walked into the kitchen single file. Leo appeared to be leaning even more precariously than before. His mouth had closed somewhat, and his head twisted weirdly against his shoulder. A smell of excrement in the air. When Kay touched him, his body slipped out of its balance, one arm swinging heavily down, the two fingers and thumb clenched into a knuckleball-like curl. Kay caught his shoulders as he fell sideways out of the chair, his neck limp, and Karl helped her lug the heavy body out from under the edge of the table and into the open passageway between the dining room and kitchen, his sprawled legs pulling back the rugs. They struggled against his death weight and tried not to breathe in the smell. The phone rang. Kay cried now, even as they straightened Leo's body on the floor, and stroked his wrinkled face, misshapen as a mask. His brow seemed lower, lips fleshier. Lopey didn't know what to do, undid his shoelaces, and didn't realize until after the phone had stopped ringing that the sound had been irritating her. She placed his hiking boots by the side of his body and looked at Karl, who had his camera out. "Mom, could you move closer to Leo?" he asked. Lopey couldn't believe it. The flash blinded her for a moment, and when she could see again, she hissed at him. Kay flew about the room, her great wings beating, her hair a halo of shock.

◆

Weaver parked on the street in front of Kay's house, locked his keys in his car, and carried the white-boxed roses like a baby up the driveway, splashed by red flashes from the EMS van, and stopped in his tracks to watch two medics wheel Leo Abruzzi on a stretcher.

Weaver continued forward. Mother Kay (the bitch—he knew she was against him) stood on the porch, and brother Karl (dopehead) had his arm around her. Lopey lovely holds herself together, hugs herself, and starts to speak, but Weaver weaves and says, "Happy Birthday-half."

"It's Leo," she says. "Follow us to the hospital." She takes out her keys and wonders why he looks so sotty and shot. She'll tell him tonight. Just not working out. Now she knows what it feels like to date Broderick Crawford.

The ambulance and family drive off before Weaver grasps what has happened. After the siren dies away, the only sound Weaver hears is his ears ringing. The black trees, a moon, whose mailbox this is I think I know, his house is in the village though, he will not see me stopping here to watch his woods fill up with snow. Weaver searches for his keys, realizes they're in the ignition, with the door locked. He explodes the window with a brick.

◆

At the hospital, Lopey and Karl hold hands as they sit in the waiting room with Kay, whose face is red and haggard in the septic light of the room. Lopey is unusually aware of the oddness and old-lookingness of her mother's white hair. Karl stares at the tile floor and scratches the back of his knee. Lopey squeezes his hand, feeling sorry for him because he came all the way from Moscow and now this. Karl thinks it's kind of hot in the waiting room, and the ammonia smell of the freshly mopped floor really grosses him out.

Seems like they could afford to turn up the AC a little, I mean they charge an arm and a leg, ha ha. He wonders if Kay would notice if he slipped away to get high. She probably wouldn't care. She must have really liked the guy. Maybe Lopey would want to go with him. He looks at her beautiful streaked hair and pale arms. He wonders what it would be like to put his tongue in her ear.

Weaver sits in the waiting room, too, with the stolen roses on the seat next to him, being ignored by the family—Who is this pest? (The nurses think he's the grandfather.) Weaver wonders how he can phrase it—the knowledge that he isn't worth anything anymore. His life is over. He watches dully as two orderlies wheel a stretcher down the aisle past them, the sheet pulled over the face of the body, a tag on the toe. He lurches out of the waiting room, bounces off one wall, and walks to his car in the parking lot as if nothing had happened. I'm perfectly sober Officer watch. He brushes the broken glass off his seat and winces as something stings him. By squinting he narrows the double highway in front of him into one coherent, unified, infinite line. One hand is wet and sticky as he heads north for Alaska. Air rushes in the window, his hands grip the steering wheel, his heart pumps the time he has left with a vengeance.

Back in the hospital, Lopey wonders where he's gone: she sees the roses on the seat across from her and wants to thank him. He's really a sweet man—maybe not something you want to build your life around, but sweet. The thing to do now will be to move back in with Kay and make sure she doesn't get too depressed, suicidal, or anything, because she really did love this mountain-climber guy. What's a neurophysiologist anyway? He was nice, I guess. Not really a bad way to go. Softly, right in the middle of a conversation. Of course if I had my way, we'd all live forever. Well, except for the creeps and weirdos.

Letting the Dog Out

A FTER NICKY WON $3,000 in the lotto (he was always winning things: a Butterball turkey, a clock radio, a fake igloo filled with Eskimo Pies) his sister Rose—one of five, the third oldest one—called a few months later and asked him for $175 and he said I'd like to help really sis but I'm a little short right now. He felt bad about it after hanging up the phone, but really, the money was going fast and at this rate there'd be none left in a month or two. He wondered if he'd done the right thing. But just because he had a little money, he didn't want Rose to become dependent. Rose was known for that. Dependency was not a thing to encourage. You have to pull your own weight in this world!

Rose was the wacko one who had imaginary cancer for two years. She kept telling the family about the medication; you'd call her up and she'd say *I'm lousy today because of the chemo. My hair's falling out. I'm like a dog. I'm shedding!* she'd yell into the phone. *And my skin is splotchy.* Then it turned out she made it all up; she never had cancer at all. She was just snorting a lot of speed and needed an excuse for looking so trashed all the time. And a little sympathy.

Besides the two years of imaginary cancer, she had three ex-husbands and a five-year-old girl, Laney. Laney, Nicky's favorite little redheaded niece. She was going to be a showstopper, that one was. A heart stopper. It bothered Nicky that she had a mother like Rose. He always thought of that play, *The Rose Tattoo*. And tattoos were all wrong for Laney. She deserved better. She deserved the moon and the stars. She deserved a mother whose medicine cabinet was full of Band-Aids and cough drops, not Dexedrine and Darvon. But Nicky felt he couldn't do anything about it *I can't save the world, can I?* so he tried not to think about Laney. Besides, what did he know, anyway? Maybe Rose should be Mother of the Year. Maybe everything was going to work out just fine.

◆

Rose called Nicky up in the middle of the night later to complain how Mom cheated her out of Aunt Dinah's coin collection that she should have gotten. Dinah told her one night in Omaha she said Rosie, the coins are yours now don't let your mother deny you but what could she do? You know what they must be worth by now? All those silver dollars and Mercury dimes? Those Indian Head nickels? Thousands, I'm sure. More than $3,000. That's nothing. And by the way, thanks for the loan, *brother*. I guess it's hard to part with some of that cash, she said, and hung up.

Nicky wondered: So who told her about the lotto?

Rose called again and said my rabbit died. What rabbit? The hungry one, she said. Laney got this rabbit from school; they were going to put him to sleep but we saved him and nursed him back to health but we were broke and didn't have any money for food we'd give him some carrots now and then carrots are cheap but I guess it wasn't enough so he starved to death. Thanks to you. And by the way, we're being evicted tomorrow. We'll be out on the streets. Hope you're happy. Click.

One of Nicky's other sisters, Angie, called and told him, "Whatever you do, don't give Rose any money. She'll just spend it on drugs. It's not good to encourage that kind of behavior. And she'll never pay you back, either. You can kiss that cash goodbye."

"Maybe she's just down on her luck."

"She's been down on her luck since the word go. I'm just saying, watch out for that drowning man thing."

For the next few weeks, Rose sent Nicky postcards addressed *Dear Heartless*, signed *The Sister you're ashamed of*. She called to tell him how Laney used to look up to her uncle, now she doesn't even want to hear his name, after he let that rabbit starve to death. "Why did Uncle Nicky hate my bunny, Mama?" Rose says into the phone, mimicking Laney's little-girl voice.

◆

So Nicky goes to see Rosemary—to make amends. This is Wichita, Kansas. Nicky lives downtown, near the courthouse. Rose lives miles away. In the sticks. The boonies. It's a good half-hour's drive out there. He knocks on her door and no one answers. But her rusty Buick is in the driveway. He goes around to the back of the house to see if she's in the backyard and can't hear him. The grass is dead and brown, with blades like wet splinters. There are towels on the clothesline. Nicky steps over a coiled green garden hose. He finds the rabbit.

The good news is it's not dead. It's in a wooden cage stocked with a bowl of water and an aluminum pie pan of dark-green pellets. This rabbit is pure white, with long pink ears. Pink veins in pink ears. On a white fur backdrop. Like the veins in a leaf. It stares at him with its pink, frightened eyes, nervously chewing a piece of carrot in its cage. It's eating, huge and fat, and doesn't look as if it's missed any meals. He opens the cage door and is petting it when Rose warns him, "I wouldn't do that. He might bite."

"Rose. It's you."

Nicky gives her a big smile that he knows looks painfully fake. Rose is deadpan. She has a mess of dark hair crazy with split ends. Her face is speed-freak thin, her skin pale and freckled, as if she's just recovered from a long illness. Nicky remembers Rose as the least pretty of all his sisters. Her ears are too big, and she aggravates things by using them as a two-pronged hairband, by wedging her hair behind them. Nicky has even wondered if they've been misshapen by this habit, which is what Angie and Lila said. In high school Rose had always worn tube tops and miniskirts, and Angie argued it was to deflect attention from her monkey ears. God, Angie could be cruel, but Nicky always suspected there was an element of truth in that.

Rose steps onto the gray concrete of the back porch, a house robe the color of an old washrag pulled tightly about her. She's barefoot and her toenails are covered with chipped red polish. She used to be a topless dancer, before the illness or the pills kicked in. Her eyes are puffy. It's four in the afternoon, but for Rose, you would've thought it was seven, eight A.M., tops.

"Rose? Did I wake you up or something? I can come back another time."

"I wasn't asleep. What? You think I sleep in the middle of the day? That I'm some kind of lazy bum who can't even get out of bed?"

"I didn't mean that. Jeez, if I could sleep in the middle of the day, I would."

"I'm not you."

"I love sleep. I can't get enough of it. Every time I lie down to nap, the phone rings."

"No one ever calls here. I'd kill for a phone call."

"Okay." He holds up his hands. "Whatever you say. I didn't come here to fight."

Rose tightens the belt of her robe. "What *did* you come here for?"

"I'm here to make amends, Rose. I don't want to fight anymore. I want you to stop the postcards. And the phone calls. I've got feelings, too, you know. I want everything, all of this, to just stop. Just tell me what to do, and I'll do it."

"You've got feelings? Since when?"

"Rose."

She shakes her head and goes back inside, the door banging after her. Nicky is about to walk away when he hears her yell, "Don't just stand there. Come inside and I'll make you something to eat."

As he has grown older, Nicky has not seen Rose very often. He's become wary of her presence, and somehow feels that her sadsack life and losing streak is something best avoided. Secretly, although he would not have admitted this to anyone, he fears Rose's gloom and doom will rub off on him, that good fortune is something you were either born with or without, and there is nothing you can do to control it. He remembers the line of a song: "If it weren't for bad luck / I'd have no luck at all." That's Rose. And he wants to steer clear of that. Give her a wide berth. Keep that infection from spreading.

Her dinette is cheap and looks as if it belongs in a trailer park somewhere on the outskirts of Selma, Alabama, beside a louvered window looking out on the other trailers and a junkyard full of rusty scagheap cars where her husband's gone to find a water pump to get the El Camino running and inspected so they can drive to town for food stamps without being picked up on all their outstanding warrants by overweight southern deputy sheriffs who hate themselves, their wives, life itself. She warms up some Rice-A-Roni and meatballs, puts this in front of him with a bottle of Heinz ketchup, and says, "Eat."

Nicky says, "I didn't know you were a cyclist." He points at a pair of bicycle gloves on the top of the microwave. They are faded, knitted things with the fingers cut out, with palms made of padded leather, and no back on them. There's a Velcro strap across the back of the hands. "I've got some exactly like those. You like them?"

"They're not mine. They're Phil's."

"Oh."

"Yeah. Oh. You remember Phil, don't you?"

"You mean Phil the no-good-son-of-a-bitch that ruined your life?"

"The one," she says.

"I vaguely remember his name being mentioned."

"You know he's the reason I'm so screwed up, right? If I'd never met him, I'd probably be on easy street right about now. He set me back almost two years 'cause he never sent me any child support, and there isn't a damn thing I can do about it. Short of flying to Nome and chasing him down. I'm stuck."

"Maybe you should call *America's Most Wanted*."

She shakes her head. "Think it's funny, eh? Well, let me tell you about Phil. He had this thing, see. This game, sort of. Well, it wasn't really a game. I mean, there weren't any rules for it. It was just a thing he did, as a joke I guess. He called it 'letting the dog out.' Or he'd say, 'You don't want me to let the dog out, do you?' And we all thought it was a joke, at first. It started when he was playing with Laney, and he'd pretend to be a dog. He'd make like a dog, snarling and barking and chasing her around the house, but he was usually drunk when he did it, and it was just a little too, too *realistic*. Too much. So Laney started getting freaked out and crying. And hiding. She took to hiding in the closet whenever he let the dog out." Rose pauses to wipe the mouth of the ketchup bottle with a paper towel.

"He thought it was funny. Like you think he's funny."

"Listen, Rose. I didn't mean anything by it. A joke, okay?"

"A joke. Ha ha. The man beats the *shit* out of me, he puts me in the hospital, and you think it's funny."

"What?"

"Yeah. I guess you wouldn't know anything about that. It was one of those nights when he let the dog out. Laney was hiding in the closet and he's barking at the door and he was drunk so he wouldn't stop. I told him, Phil, cut it out, you're scaring her, and he wouldn't stop. So I grabbed an ashtray and hit him in the back of the head with it.

"I was trying to protect my kid. Is what I was doing." She shakes her head. "So he goes like this," she jerks her elbow back, "and punches me right in the face with his elbow, and then he's all over me saying he's sorry, he's so sorry, but my nose is bleeding, I still can't see out of this eye like I'm supposed to. The nerves are damaged."

"God."

"He really let me have it. The cheekbones were crushed. I had to have plastic surgery. Actually, I got a new nose out of the deal. Can you tell?" She turns her head, this way and that, for Nicky to get a good look at her nose. "Let me show you the pictures."

Rose opens one of the kitchen drawers, rummages around, and removes a pair of Polaroid snapshots. "Before and after," she says, and plops them down in front of Nicky. They are profile views of Rose— Rose's nose. In *Before* she has a black eye and a slightly irregular nose, a little bump in the middle of it; in *After* her black eye is gone, her nose is straighter, her profile better.

"Well," says Nicky. "Not to seem cruel or anything, but maybe there's a silver lining. That nose could win awards."

"At least we had insurance then. At least there was that. I'm on welfare now. The dole."

"Why didn't you tell anyone? I never heard this."

She stares at him, chewing a mouthful of ice. "You all thought I made that up about my cancer, didn't you?"

"Rose. Angie said she talked to your doctor."

"What does Angie know? Since when is she any authority on anything? I didn't see Angie taking chemotherapy for six months. Her hair falling out. Puking all the time. I was cured, okay? Would you believe me if I died, is that it?"

"Was the doctor lying, or what?"

"You wanted me to die, didn't you? You wanted me to just fade away, so the family wouldn't be disappointed."

"Mom was worried sick."

"You didn't answer my question."

"What kind of question is that? No one wanted you to die, Rose. You've been watching too much TV."

"I know what I know."

Nicky puts the cap back on the ketchup bottle and wishes he were dead, so he wouldn't have to be there.

"So how's the Roni?"

"The best I ever had."

"God, Nicky. You are one sarcastic son of a bitch, you know that?"

"I was being serious, Rose. It's excellent."

"*Excellent.* What kind of crap are you trying to feed me? When is Rice-A-Roni ever excellent? You are full of shit, you know that, don't you?"

"It's been pointed out recently. Twice."

"Third time's the charm."

"All right already."

Rose makes a face and says, "*Excellent.*"

"You know, I'm starting to sympathize with Phil here. I really am. To understand. Two sides to every story, right, Rose?"

She picks up his plate of food and throws it into the sink, where it clatters, rice and meatballs splaying across the Formica countertop.

"You want to see something Phil left me?" She starts untying the belt of her robe. "I'll show you Phil's side. The other side of the story."

"Rose."

She undoes the belt, turns her back to him, then yanks down the robe. She tucks her hair in by the side so he can get a good look at the back of her neck, her nape, the swell of her shoulders.

"See that scar? He did that to me."

Like the rest of their family, like Nicky, Rose's skin is fair, her hair dark and frizzy, Irish blood, freckled. Her back is mottled as the moon. He doesn't want to see this. But he forces himself to look. And there, right there high on her back, is a crisscross series of welts, of darker skin, faint and thin, like a mess of cat scratches. He reaches out one finger and touches them, touches the raised lines of skin, raised like embossed letters on a letterhead. He can think of nothing to say.

"You see them? The scars? They're more like welts now? Tell me you see them."

"I see them."

"He did that to me, and you think he's funny."

"I do not."

"Laugh. Go ahead. Ha ha ha. Hardy har har."

"Rose."

"My life. The joke."

"Can we stop now?"

"What he did was nothing special, really." She's putting her robe back in place. "He just let the dog out is what he did. All men have a dog inside them. He just let his out."

She finishes adjusting her robe as he sits there at the dinette, staring at a clock against the wall, a plastic black and white cat whose eyes tick-tock back and forth. "What can I do to help, Rose? Just tell me what to do."

"Nothing."

"I'm being serious here. Just tell me what to do. I'm going to give you some money for Laney, okay? Not for you. For Laney. Is that okay?"

"You know what you can do to help?"

"What, Rose? Just tell me what to do."

"Help me shoo a hummingbird out of my dining room."

Rose told Nicky how it had flown in the afternoon before, when she was calling Laney, telling her to get out of the driveway, to keep away from the street, telling her to watch out for cars. In came the bird, zooming and zigzagging through the air, going deeper into the house each time she and Laney had tried to coax it toward the open front door. Laney had begged her mother to leave it alone, it wasn't hurting anybody, why not just leave it there? But since Laney was taking a nap right now, maybe they could get it out. It was in the dining room, perched on the curtain rod at the top of a pleated length of beige curtains. Rose thought that it was getting tired, since it had quit flying and hovering, and for most of the morning had been perched in the same place.

If he had not been looking for it, if he had not had the thing pointed out to him, Nicky would never have noticed the hummingbird. It has a straight, thin bill, no bigger than a black toothpick. At its throat is a plait, a shimmering weave of iridescent aqua-green and royal blue feathers as a backdrop, with a blush of fiery scarlet, mauve, and violet hues atop the blue-green. It looks like a painted figurine, except there is the hint of life in its sheen of feathers, in the brief, quick movements of its neck and tiny black eye.

"You know these things migrate?" says Rose. "They fly all the way across the Gulf of Mexico, five hundred miles, straight across, without stopping. Isn't that amazing?"

"Oh, right."

"They do! I read it in Laney's kiddie encyclopedia. You guys never believe me. Why is that, Nicky? Why do you always think I'm lying?"

"Well, what about the rabbit? You told me it was dead. 'Why did Uncle Nicky hate my rabbit?'" he mimicked.

"Oh, that. That was just to get your attention."

"The girl who cried wolf."

"Ha. There could be a wolf in my kitchen, eating Laney, and you guys wouldn't help."

"Rose? I'll help, okay? I'll get this bird out of your house."

Nicky decides what they should do: pin a blanket over the passage to the hallway, because there's no door there, to block it from flying deeper into the house. Remove the screen from the outside of the window behind the drapes it's clinging to, get a broom and open the front door, raise the window, and try to herd it out.

At first it seems reluctant to move, even after Rose gently raises the window, until Nicky waves the straw end of the broom near it, at which it suddenly leaps to life, zooms into the air a few inches from the ceiling and hovers there, turning this way and that. Its wings are an oval blur, although it seems to lose its color in the shadows near the ceiling. Rose has turned off the lights so it will gravitate toward the sunlight of the open window and door. She waves her hands in the air and laughs as the bird zings toward her, swoops between the two of them and hovers for a moment near the window, then burrs away with an electric hum and lights upon the arch of a wall sconce near the front door. And it's in a swinging pat that Nicky tries to knock the thing out the door, but pins it instead, just seeming to brush it lightly with the broom, but it falls to the ground and buzzes there, like a wind-up toy fallen on its side.

Rose crouches beside it and tries to nudge it with one long polished fingernail, but it twists and squirms against the carpeted floor. "We better not let Laney see this."

"I just meant to coax it out the door," says Nicky. "How could I hit the thing? It seemed so fast."

Rose leaves the room as Nicky stares at the hummingbird, afraid of what is happening to him. With the tip of his finger, Nicky reaches out to touch it. He strokes its chest gently with his finger, petting it, wishing it would get up and fly, feeling its faint heartbeat, feeling the softness of the pearl gray feathers on its underside. There's a thick droplet of blood on its beak, like a black syringe, and while one of the wings beats wildly, the other just twitches back and forth.

"Let me see that." Rose takes the broom from Nicky and sweeps the buzzing thing onto the dustpan, carries it out the door and off the porch. She crosses to the side of the yard, stepping carefully in her bare feet, and drops it gently into the shadows of some hedges. Nicky follows behind. She returns to the house and he kneels there, looking at it, as it begins to move slower, and the droplet of blood grows larger at its beak. He knows he should wring its neck, but doesn't have the heart. He goes back inside. Rose is smoking a cigarette, watching TV.

"This is not my day," says Nicky.

Rose shrugs. "Baby Huey doesn't know his own strength."

He nods and sits there, staring at the TV.

"Listen," says Rose. "I think I have some vodka and lime juice left over from the last time Phil came to visit. You want a drink, maybe?"

Nicky says that's a good idea. The best idea he's heard all day. They each have a glass, talking about the bird for a moment, then they change the subject. Rose complains about her doctors, how they can't figure out what's wrong with her, how they make all that money and still don't know what they're doing. In the middle of the second drink Laney comes in, wearing a pair of corduroy overalls, tiny Converse sneakers, and a plastic banana barrette in her hair. She tugs on her mother's robe and smiles at Nicky.

"What is it, honey?" says Rose.

"Hey, Laneyhead. Looks like somebody around here just woke up."

She smiles and whispers in her mother's ear.

"She says you look different."

"I do? Why?"

"You didn't use to have that," says Laney, and points at Nicky's dark brown mustache.

"Oh, this? I guess this is the first time I've seen you since I grew it. You like it?"

She shakes her head and hides her face.

"Well, I guess I'm going to have to shave it off, then. Hey. I almost forgot. I've got something for you."

Nicky goes out to his truck and comes back while Laney is still clinging to her mother's robe. He's got something behind his back. "If you can guess which hand it's in, I'll give you whatever I've got behind me." She points to his left and he goes, "What a lucky girl! You guessed!" He holds out a stuffed animal, a monkey, by its huge rubbery ears, its long floppy arms hanging down and swinging back and forth as he walks it toward her. She smiles and takes it from him, as Rose says, "Well, look at that. A monkey. Laney loves monkeys, don't you, Laney?"

She nods her head and puts her hands on the monkey's rubbery face, its pug nose, feeling it like a blind person trying to recognize a long lost someone. Rose asks her *What do you say? What do you say?* And finally she shyly gives a begrudging *thank you* before she runs off to play with it. Rose makes them another drink after Laney leaves. When she brings it back, she says, "You should see this dress I'm making Laney for her first communion. It's so cute. I got the pattern and material from this friend of mine who has a little business in her house, some tailoring and dressmaking and stuff. She was going to make this dress for somebody who canceled the order but paid for the materials, so I get it, free. It's really cute, all pink and white and lacy. I mean, this dress would cost maybe two hundred bucks if I bought it in the store. You wouldn't believe."

Laney was always Nicky's favorite niece. At birth her skin was so fair it looked almost translucent, almost blue. When he first saw her, visiting with his mom at Rose and Phil's place after she came home from the hospital, he thought there was something wrong with her. "She looks like an albino," he said.

"Nicky," said his mother. "Be nice."

"Yeah, thanks a lot, little brother," said Rose. "You weren't much to look at when we brought you home from the hospital, either. You looked like an ugly old bald guy, only really small."

As she'd grown up, Laney had retained her fair, pale skin, but the bluish hue had been replaced by a faint rosy blush, and as Rose never cut her hair, it had grown thick and complicated, in heavy twisting curls the color of Irish setters. Nicky could still remember those first few months when Laney had just been born, how they would make him hold her, how delicate and mysterious she would seem, how her tiny fist would clutch onto one of his fingers and squeeze it fiercely, though she was no stronger than a shrew or a star-nosed mole. He would baby-sit for them during this first year of Laney's life, when Rose and Phil still lived in the city, and if Laney was sleeping and he was watching TV, Nicky would get up during commercials to check on her. He would stand over her, watching the shadows from a mobile of plastic stars and quarter-moons play across her face, listening to her breathe, her baby mouth open, moist and crumpled, her nose small as a rhesus monkey's.

If she woke and began to cry, he learned to cradle the back of her head lightly, morbidly aware of the plates of her fragile skull, that soft tympanum below her ghostly white hair. That unformed spot of her skull frightened him. He feared he would jab his thumb into it accidentally, ruining her forever. He touched the cranial gap lightly, using just the tips of his fingers, awestruck that he could lightly feel her pulse that way, amazed at the vulnerable brain beating below. Holding her, his face close to her pink ears and white curls, he smelled her mixture of milk and talcum powder, of soap and saliva.

And here she is, five years old now. Everything is changing. He can't help but think that Rose isn't a good mother for her. He feels terrifically confused. And what's the deal with all these animals? Rabbits and hummingbirds? It's like a zoo around here. Anarchy is loose! There must be order!

After they finish their fourth drink, Nicky is feeling a little woozy and says he has to go. While Rose goes to get Laney to say goodbye, he takes out his wallet and counts out ten twenty-dollar bills and leaves them under an ashtray on the coffee table, just one edge of the bills visible. Rose comes back and says she doesn't know where Laney is at the moment, that she's probably gone next door to see her little friend Brandy. "She really loves that monkey, though. Thanks, Nicky. I'm sorry about what I said earlier. Things have just been so lousy lately. I guess I was projecting, right?"

"Forget it, Rosie. It's all my fault."

They hug and Rose is standing in the doorway, smiling. Nicky weaves and stumbles against nothing as he walks toward his truck and gets out his keys. He feels awkward, with her watching him, as he climbs into the truck. He senses that something is wrong. Has the truck grown taller? It's like he needs a stepladder to reach the cab. He latches his seat belt and waves goodbye one last time. But Rose doesn't see it. She's wearing that same ugly robe but isn't looking at him now; she's pulling letters from the mail slot on her porch. And Nicky? Nicky doesn't see his niece, little Laneyhead, playing with her monkey doll, sitting on the white concrete driveway, right behind the truck's bumper. He pauses to push his hair out of his face and exhale, his last motions in this first half of his life—the lucky half—a vortex of guilt and remorse hurtling toward him in the quiet air, before he drops the truck in gear and backs up.

THE WHITE TATTOO

THERE WAS NO SUCH THING he knew that we all know that but still once the idea the image of it took hold it was impossible to shake like a scar like a something burned into his own skin or something you want burned there to become your very own special marking that signals Desire and Longing. The white tattoo. Katherine's. Katey's. No one trustworthy had ever seen it, only Adrian (the asshole), but still, it was said to exist. A small legend, like a tiny frog you can clutch when your hands are cupped together to form a warm cage, and feel the thing inside, wet and squirming. A white tattoo in the perfect form of a swan in flight. Owen imagined it in profile, graceful wings swept forward, neck raised aloft, tail wings spread like a fan. It was said to be there, right there, at the top of her bottom, the wimple of her cleft, that sheltered spot where small of back meets sacroiliac. And no matter what he did, Owen would never be worthy of seeing it.

"Oh, get out of here," said a female friend he told about it. "She's a woman, right? Not a statue. She has hunger. You just need to catch her at the right moment."

It was his luck that when the moment arrived, Adrian was in the way. (His problem: the world was full of Adrians.) And Adrian was not only there, he was deliberately provoking him. He'd come to accept this, but you can only take so much.

For instance, the first time Adrian called him a rat, Owen took it as a joke, of course. He was just kidding. We don't want to be too sensitive, now, do we? Paranoia is not a pretty picture. Besides, if you believe everyone is out to get you, they probably will. Adrian didn't mean Owen actually was a rat. No, he meant that Owen had some rat-like tendencies. And, well, you know: his nose *was* sharply pointed, his eyes *were* black and beady. Given gray fur, whiskers, a long pink tail . . . he could see the resemblance. Owen could laugh at himself. That's the point. He's not laughing *at* you, he's laughing *with* you. But then Adrian called Owen a rat again, and . . . well, it was hard to explain the second time so easily.

◆

That particular late February New York Big Apple in winter center of the universe day began in intense radiance and disquietude. Owen Kelly woke as usual at seven, hit the snooze button, crawled from the cocoon of blankets to pad—groggily, hair a mess—to the bathroom. The medicine cabinet mirror was unclean. It reflected a sallow face Owen would have paid great sums of money to refigure if he had it but he didn't so oh well you do your best and it's never good enough. The toothpaste tube was empty. With scissors from the first aid kit, he cut the tube in half and scraped a bit of blue-colored tartar control gel from one half, saving the other for later. After swallowing his vitamins, he could find no clean socks. He pulled on some dirties anyway, reasoning that once inside his shoes, unpleasant odors would not escape. Dressed in gray slacks, dark sport coat, white shirt, and tie, he patted his pockets to check for keys and wallet and left his townhouse, dark eyes still thick and cloudy with sleep.

Overnight it had snowed, hushing for a moment the ambulance sirens, police chases, and honking taxicabs. Now the sky was clear as god, shaded a pale morning saffron. Tires hissed on the wet and salty asphalt of the street. Pigeons flapped heavily. As he donned his gloves, Owen noticed a remarkable sight. A black cat crouched in a field of snow. The whiteness and purity of the snow was dazzling. This was in a small fenced parking lot beside Owen's townhouse. It had the untrammeled smoothness of a fresh fall. And in its center, the black cat. Crouched low, it was worrying something, and as Owen enjoyed the beauty of the scene, he saw the thing held down by the cat give a start and flop briefly, its brown wings flashing, before being pinned for the final time by the cat's sharp claws.

He thought of Katey, of course, and Katey's tattoo, though the cat/bird thing made him queasy, the symbolism of it.

On his way to the building, Owen had stopped by the deli where he bought his morning coffee and bagel and, as a treat and surprise of sorts, bought a cranberry muffin for Katey. They worked in the same office, she being the coworker he loved madly and secretly. She had once said, "I'm a sucker for a gift," and Owen remembered it.

◆

Katey was at her desk when Owen walked up. "You're looking chipper today," she said, smiling. Her hair was gorgeous, dark brown streaked with silver, lapdog bangs in her eyes, straight and shoulder-length otherwise—very Audrey Hepburn. She wore a white wool turtleneck and dark suede skirt with dark stockings, and Owen would have swooned if she had kissed him—once, just once—at that moment, but he wasn't a fool, after all, and there's a time and a place for everything.

"Look what I've got," he said, and pulled the cranberry muffin from its paper sack.

"For me?" Katey lifted it to her nose and inhaled. "Fresh, even."

"You said they were your favorite."

"You're a prince, you know that?"

When Owen related the incident with the black cat and brown bird to Katey, she said, "Stop." She made a gross-me-out face. "Owen? Why do you tell me these horrible things? You know how long that gruesome scene will be in my mind?" She closed her eyes so hard Owen dizzily watched her quivering eyelids, her trembling lashes. "It's still there," she said. "It's not going anywhere."

He tried to change the subject. Win her with small talk. "Have you ever noticed how much the doorman downstairs looks like Danny DeVito?"

"Now that you mention it, no."

"I swear, you see him in the right light, and he could be DeVito's double."

"I'll take a look next time I go for coffee."

While they were talking, Adrian arrived and sat on the table beside Katey's computer. "Who looks like Danny DeVito?"

Owen was immediately put off. He didn't like Adrian and felt he was always trying to get the best of him, playing some kind of game with him, a cat-and-mouse thing. When Katey explained Owen's comment, Adrian shook his head and, lifting the muffin from Katey's desk, slowly began pulling away the accordion-shaped paper wrapper. "Too tall. DeVito's almost a midget, and that guy must be five-six, five-seven."

"Adrian? Do you mind?" Katey held out her hand, acting injured. Adrian returned the half-unwrapped muffin.

"He looks a lot like DeVito, if you ask me," said Owen. "I guess it depends on how you look at things."

"Well, sure," said Adrian. "But what if someone said you looked like a rat? Would that be the same thing?"

"What do you mean?" Owen felt himself blush.

"Would you still say it just depends on how you look at things?"

"I'd probably tell him to take a flying leap."

Adrian raised his eyebrows and made a silly, mock-frightened face.

"Now that's a scary picture."

"So what's your point?"

Katey pushed Owen away gently. "Hey. If you two want to duke it out, choose someone else's office to do it in, okay?"

"Who's fighting?" said Adrian. "I'm not fighting."

"Whatever. I need to get some work done, okay?"

Owen walked away without saying a word to either one, and when he reached his desk, had to feign reading the morning paper, his eyes burning with angry tears.

As he left Katey's desk, Adrian made a face behind Owen's back, both hands held inches from his cheekbones, clawing the air as if at a hunk of cheese, nose scrunched, lower lip sucked beneath uppers to appear buck-toothed, eyes glittering: The Rat.

◆

At his desk, Owen tried to blot out the clutter in his mind—Katey's frown, the black cat in white snow with brown bird, red blood, his odorous socks, the toothpaste shortage, the evil Adrian—and concentrate on work. He had to review a proposal for asbestos removal, but his heart was not in it, still fuming over Adrian's slight.

Adrian was Katey's ex. He had thrown away the woman, the lovely that Owen would have killed for. He was not a gentleman. Once, standing in line at the Xerox machine, Owen heard Adrian tell Wallace or Emory or one of those nobodies on the nineteenth floor, "She moves around a lot, if you like that sort of thing." Did he mean Katey?

"Who moves around a lot?" Owen had asked, trying to seem cool.

Adrian smiled and blinked, tapping his stack of copies against the machine's glass top. "Private con," he said. "My lips are sealed."

After getting little work done on the asbestos project, Owen went to the coffee shop in the lobby of their building for his break. Two of them he hated, Adrian and Lenny, were talking about women when

Owen sat down, which Adrian didn't bother to notice. He grinned across the table at Lenny, ignoring Owen, and said, "What they want are the two Cs. Compliments and cunnilingus."

Lenny nodded. "That always reminds me of the genus species name of a really clever mammal. Like, 'We'd been stalking the cunnilingus for days before sighting it in the veldt.'"

"Yeah, or maybe an entree. Like, 'How did you find the cunnilingus, sir?'"

Adrian and his smart-aleck buddies always talked like this, like they were auditioning for an episode of *Seinfeld*, but Owen felt they got it all wrong somehow, like they were taking a trip and using the wrong map, like they were heading for Klever and ended up in Snyde.

Owen stirred his coffee and tried not to wobble the table. "I like the word wombat, myself. I'd like to have a wombat for a pet, just because it's such a cool word."

"What's a wombat?" asked Lenny.

"Some kind of South American rat," said Adrian.

"Not quite."

"Yes it is."

"It's an Australian marsupial. Like the duck-billed platypus."

"Now that you mention it, you wouldn't be related to a wombat, would you?"

Back at his desk, Owen thought, I can wait. I can be patient. I can watch the bird swing wide its wings in a graceful arc to alight on the graveled path near the scattered seed, its wing-beat shadow slight as an unfounded suspicion to its side, linked by a delicate line to its talons, their dark forked feet. I can stay extremely still. No part of me will move. I will wait, watch, listen. Some night, he will trudge drearily, wearily out to his car, half drunk perhaps, filled and frolicking with a bellyful of bubbly, celebrating a promotion or some award of sorts. He'll never see it coming. He'll get in his car and put the key in the ignition. The bomb will crouch like a cougar on a cliff. In the shadows, I'll raise my hand, pointing at him and showing him the way to grace. At that moment he'll see me, frown, turn the key to start his car . . . then blooey!

◆

When he rode the E train to the job site, a blonde woman with a broad Slavic face sat reading passages from a children's book titled *The Stinky Cheese Man* to a three-year-old who would not sit still. They sat beside Owen on the plastic subway seats. He stared at the book's cover, an illustration of a thin cartoon figure with a head made of Swiss cheese. Cheese. Rats. Owen realized his fears were absurd, but that realization did not stop them. His teeth were unpleasant, and he knew people talked about this. Katey would never go out with him, no matter how much he loved her. He was a loser. What good was a love like that? Loser love? It was good for nothing at all. But did love need a purpose, a payoff? Adrian probably thought so. But Adrian was a winner, and that was the difference. The unruly child stared at him, and Owen made a face, trying to smile. The child burst into tears, causing his mother to rock him in her arms, saying, "Now come on. Come on, now. The man was just trying to be nice. He's not going to bite. . . ." Owen shut his eyes and tried to block out the world; his mind became cloudy and cluttered. He composed several witty replies to Adrian's comments. He imagined the quips.

I may look like a rat, but you smell like one.

No, that wouldn't work. What if they somehow removed his shoes and tossed that back at him? Wearing dirties to work was strictly verboten.

Adrian would say, "O-ho, Owenbo! I think *you're* the stinky cheese man."

◆

The asbestos removal job site was a dilapidated public school building in a ragtag area of the Bowery. The sidewalks were a tunnel of plywood and scaffolding to protect against falling debris from the buildings under construction overhead. The plywood ramps wobbled and made a racket when Owen walked across them, and they smelled strongly of urine.

Between the blackened, sooty buildings were slots of white sky, and between the plywood tunnels of sidewalk scaffolding were patches of chain-link fences topped with barbed wire. The world here was much different than the busy hustle and shine of Forty-fifth and Lexington, where Owen now worked. Here he remotely felt as if he were walking through a theme park replicating either Gangland USA or the Warsaw ghetto of World War II.

At the job site, Owen needed to verify the layout of certain classrooms so that the instructions concerning remodeling his firm gave were correct: they had contradictory information, and the best way to get the straight dope was an on-site look-see. He arrived a little after noon and everyone was gone. Lunchtime. In the main hallway of the old elementary school, Owen clicked open his briefcase and took out the clipboard and blueprints he needed. With no one to stop him, he passed through the entryway with a large sign above it: ASBESTOS REMOVAL IN PROGRESS: DO NOT ENTER. What if he brought Katey a present, perhaps a dozen roses? Would she like that? Women like flowers. Compliments. But maybe it would seem cliché. He knew she hated clichés. She often said it. "How cliché" was one of her favorite expressions.

Without thinking, he passed through a doorway completely blocked with thick plastic, with a slit down the center that overlapped, then, a few feet later, another similar barrier. Inside that area, the air seemed a bit dusty. He found the classrooms in question and noted the correct information on his clipboard. While he was there a pair of workers arrived, dressed in what looked like spacesuits: white coveralls, white gloves and boots, white helmets with clear plastic visors. They started shouting at him, their voices muffled and odd-sounding, distorted by their decontamination helmets. "What is it?

What's wrong?" he asked, moving close enough to them to hear the muffled sounds. They hustled him to an exit, and after a moment, Owen realized they were saying he was crazy, there was asbestos in the air, get out, now.

Confused, Owen didn't know where to turn, where they were leading him, although one of them had him by the elbow and led him in a different direction than where he came, saying this was the fastest way to safe air. They passed through double doors and another plastic partition into a basement room. Without taking his helmet off, the worker told him how to reach the street level via the rear maintenance entrance. Owen tried to tell him that he was from the firm responsible for the redesign of the building, but the worker pointed to the side of his helmet as if he couldn't hear, then shouted, "You can't breathe it!" Shaking his head at Owen's stupidity, he then headed back up the stairs.

Owen gazed around the dank basement and shivered. He had just inhaled friable asbestos, the kind that causes lung damage with even slight contact. He remembered now; they had warned them about it early in the project, though he didn't need to pay much attention because he generally wouldn't visit a job site, as some of the engineers did regularly. Inside the basement, it was dark and wet. The concrete walls were sweating. Most of the room was filled with old wooden school desks and folding chairs, and much of it lay in shadow, a naked bulb the only light. Owen wormed his way through the clutter and jumbled equipment—chair legs in the air, upside down atop knife-scarred desks—to the back door. He heard a faint crepuscular rustling, a squeak. And when he pushed open the back door—thank god—he caught a quick glimpse of a huge and loathsome rat. It seemed to have been nearing him in the shadows, but in a blast of sudden though pale sunlight, scurried away, dragging last its long pink tail.

✦

The second time Adrian called Owen a rat was after lunch, when Owen returned from breathing the asbestos. He shuffled self-consciously down the main hallway of the architectural design firm where he worked, passing Katey's desk with a concerted, determined effort not to glance her way, which was successful, if just barely. She was on the phone when he passed by, and felt a twang of sorrow for him, a flicker of pity mixed with irritation, because she knew he was in love with her, or thought he was in love with her, perhaps not her but some idea of her, but though she liked him, she would never love him or want to touch his skin. There was something about him, something lumpy and coarse. Not vulgar, because at times he was polite to a fault, misshapen. His mouth was all wrong, thin and nervous. He had a tendency toward bitterness and suspicion. Overall the world he lived in was darker and gloomier than Katey's, and sympathy is one thing, infection another. Still. Adrian muscled him unfairly, showing his true nature. Knowing Owen was depressed and upset over this morning's slight, Katey had decided to cheer him up. On her lunch break she'd stopped at Macy's and bought Owen a new sweater. Gray wool. Crew neck. Simple and attractive. As well, it did that two-birds-with-one-stone thing: It would cheer him up, and repay all the gifts he'd bought for her. So after she got off the phone, she took the gift-wrapped package to his desk.

Years later, Owen would remember that moment. Katey placed the package on his desk and said, "For you," half smiling. There was a piece of Scotch tape in her Audrey Hepburn hair, and when he pointed it out, she said, "How'd that get there?" She looked so clean and crisp in her white turtleneck, dark suede skirt, like a stylish clothing advertisement for Bergdorf Goodman in *The New Yorker*.

At first he tried to unwrap the box carefully, turning it upside down and sliding his thumb along the sealed flaps, but the same Scotch tape that had clung to her hair held the paper tight. He pawed at the Disney wrapping with the cartoon *101 Dalmatians* on it, black-and-white dogs in a field of baby blue, until Katey said, "Oh, just rip it already! It's not gold or anything."

Owen realized he was blushing and, for a moment, was suffused with feelings of confusion, embarrassment, and happiness as he tore away the paper, the ripping sound louder than he wished, lifted the lid of the blue rectangular box, unfolded the white tissue inside, and removed the soft gray sweater.

"What is this?" he asked, trying to keep from smiling too widely and showing his crooked teeth. "My birthday's not for two months yet."

"I just saw it and thought it had Owen Kelly written all over it."

Katey's office was a cubicle: four walls with a narrow doorway, the walls only five feet high so that if you wished, you could lean over the desk and peek into your neighbor's cubicle to see what was going on. The firm was filled mainly with young architects and designers of some sort—interior or graphic—and there was an unwritten rule not to make too much noise and disturb your coworkers: besides, whatever you say can and will be used against you. Adrian said it was so that you didn't get too cozy and start giving each other blow jobs in your offices, but that was typical for him. His kindness was infinite. As his cubicle abutted Katey's, he leaned over the wall and watched as Owen pulled on the new sweater self-consciously. His hair was a mess when his head poked through the crew neck, spiky and weird, full of static electricity, and he quickly ruffled it with his fingers. He then held his arms out and caressed the wool. "It's so smooth," he said.

"Like a rat in sheep's clothing," muttered Adrian, winking at Katey.

"Pardon me?" said Owen.

Adrian held up one hand, smiling, and shook his head.

"No," said Owen. "You said something. Why won't you repeat it?"

"I didn't say a thing."

"Yes, you did. What? Are you a coward?"

Katey said, "Cut it out, you two."

"He started it," said Owen.

"Okay, I said, 'A rat in sheep's clothing.' Satisfied? It was a joke, okay? I was kidding."

"No you weren't. What kind of joke is that? Why is insulting me funny?"

Adrian made an exasperated face and drummed his fingers along the top of the partition separating his cubicle from Katey's. "Forget I said it, okay? I'm sorry. You win." He backed away and Owen stood there, foolish in the gray wool sweater, his face flushed a deep red. "I don't win," he said. "I never win."

Katey patted his arm and said maybe it was best if they all got back to work. After he returned to his desk, Owen remembered that he'd never thanked her for the gift, and thought to tell Adrian if he were going to get even with someone a car bomb would probably be just the thing—only kidding!

◆

Owen needs a new start a breath of fresh air a second chance for Chrissake that's all I'm asking for with Katey so he buys two tickets to the Moscow Classical Ballet's touring production of *The Nutcracker* knowing that Adrian would probably smirk when he heard about it well fuck him and the horse he rode in on. He doodled an elaborate invitation on his office stationery FROM THE DESK OF OWEN ROBERT KELLY with tiny dancing figures and the flags of the Lincoln Center, stick-figure crowds with men in stick bow ties and women with stick lorgnettes, secreting it onto Katey's desk when she was away for a moment, and logging onto his Mac to check e-mail an hour later he got a message from her that said simply, "Yes, I'd *love* to! You are a Prince!"

Owen smiled to see that Katey had placed "love" in italics.

When he arrived to pick her up and saw Katey dressed for the evening, Owen knew he was unworthy. She wore high heels, a long, silky black skirt, and a sleeveless charcoal-gray blouse. Everything about her *flowed*. With her straight hair grazing her shoulders and bangs in her eyes, she looked like a black-and-white mermaid with a daring haircut. As soon as she opened the door, she headed back to the kitchen, telling Owen she was in the middle of getting ready—and everything had gone wrong so far, so don't expect much. He followed her into the living room, everything blurred, his world bedazzled.

"You look gorgeous," he said.

"I do not." She stared into the refrigerator and asked if Owen wanted a drink. He said he'd take a rain check. She removed a jar of olives, blowing the bangs off her forehead in an exasperated sigh, slouching, the temperamental beauty in full swing. "This skirt does not fit and I don't have anything else to wear. I must be getting my period. I feel so bloated. And these shoes are killing me." Owen watched as she speared a trio of green olives on a fork and put them in her cocktail glass.

"Oh, come on. It can't be that bad."

She sipped carefully from the martini, then nodded elaborately.

"No. It's not that bad. It's worse." She picked up a hand mirror and looked at herself. "I'm twenty-eight years old and I look like I'm going to my junior prom."

"I never went to my prom," said Owen.

"Well, I did. And don't worry. You didn't miss anything."

Katey told Owen she'd be ready in just a moment, went to her bathroom, and locked the door. Staring at herself in the mirror, she examined a life of failure and big fat regrets, hotel rooms and airport lobbies. She smoothed a coat of gloss on her lower lips, thinking I should not be doing this. This is a mistake. But it's too late to back out now so let's put on our game face. Get it over with. She opened her eyes wide and planted a phony smile dead in the center of the mirror, slipped three tampons in her purse just in case, and went out to meet her doom.

The Lincoln Center was ablaze with light, ingenues in evening gowns, TV anchormen in tuxedos, the air thick with colognes and hullabaloo. Owen knew he didn't belong there and now and then clutched the expensive tickets (they set him back two months, at least) in his sweating fingers. Everyone seemed to know each other but

them. He overheard someone say, "Didn't we see each other last down
on the Vineyard?" Owen realized he might be the only one in the
crowd who had never been to Martha's Vineyard, and even more
embarrassingly, didn't even know exactly where it was. And who was
Martha anyway? In the lobby lurked policemen, dark blue uniforms
fitting too tightly, enormous belts. What were they prowling for? Cat
burglars? Jewel thieves? Pickpockets? Owen had a sudden image of
Deputy Dawg, one of his cartoon heroes, and grinned. He considered
holding Katey's hand, but instead, just clutched her coat sleeve with
the claws of his right paw, and did his best not to growl at the other
K-9s. When the throng clogged at the entryways and his wet black
nose thrust into the cascades of Katey's fashion model hair, he struggled to keep his tail from beating a happy tattoo against the elegant
socialites behind them.

Their seats weren't in the closest rows; he couldn't afford the best.
Even these balcony jobs cost arms and legs. He strung a series of words
together and Katey shook her head no, no, no. "They're fine," she said.
She wished to god he would please please please just lighten up and
accept himself, considered whether she should change her tampon
before the performance started, and wondered if Owen would try to
kiss her at the end of the evening, imagining his too-eager tongue
worming against the drawn drawbridge of her brilliantly white teeth.

Owen buried his nose in the playbill as he figured you are supposed
to do at these things. He didn't read start to finish, but read and reread
particular passages.

*Once upon a time, Pirlipat's father, the King, had killed many of
Queen Mousilda's relatives. An evil mouse creeps up to the lovely Pirlipat.
The mouse touches the lovely face and watches as it becomes wrinkled and
ugly. A handsome Prince bravely and victoriously attacks Queen Mousilda. The Princess changes back into a lovely young girl, but the evil mouse
scratches the Prince. He then turns into an ugly Nutcracker with a huge
jaw and enormous teeth, which makes the Princess turn away from him in
disgust.*

After the lights dim, Owen forgets himself and the performance is mesmerizing. The costumes, the swirl of colors, the graceful figures, the close and allure, the scent and the slightest touch of Katey serve to put him in another world, another zone where he's not an oaf of only mediocre intelligence and talents, where he's the magical Mouse Prince and Katey the Queen of Mice, where a dazzle of snowflakes will surround them in the night beneath a hush of stars, the swoosh of owls, the promise of gifts, fruit, spice. Afterward, after the curtain calls and clapping till his palms are sore, when the lights return, Owen feels sadly Cinderella-like, as if he can see the carriage turning into a pumpkin before his eyes, the fabulous horses returning to their lives as mice, his glass slipper lost, and he himself returning not to the soot-streaked and ragged girl of the cinders, but to the rat that Adrian pegged him to be.

◆

And he was right. At the office the next day, Katey was sweet, but said she had plans for the next weekend—some friends were coming in from out of town. Adrian seemed better looking and more arrogant than ever. At five o'clock he heard several of his coworkers talking about whether they should have a drink or not before heading home, a thank-god-it's-Friday kind of thing, and Owen decided he would not budge from his cubicle unless one of them invited him to join the crowd. He listened to their laughter as he read a report on asbestos removal, his vision blurring with emotion once again.

He listened as they wandered to the elevator, Katey's voice faint among them, Adrian's rich and mocking. He even thought he heard his name, followed by a hush, laughter. The elevator bell dinged. A hustle of coats and boots. The doors hissed shut.

◆

Katey sat beside her answering machine, watching it as Owen's voice wriggled through, not making a move to lift the telephone.

"If you get this message later on, give me a call, okay?"

Katey sighed, blowing the sheepdog bangs off her forehead. "Oy," she said. "Oy and Helen o' Troy."

She remembered when Owen had kissed her, what it had felt like—slugs in the garden.

◆

Two months later, Adrian got a better job at a more prestigious firm, and everyone whispered of his enormous salary—the lucky stiff. Katey moved to San Francisco and got a job designing graphics for a CBS affiliate, then moved to Seattle, then . . . who knows? Owen lost track of her. He coughed often and his lungs vaguely ached sometimes, especially in the cold weather of winter, but never again did he see a black cat in a field of snow, though he did glimpse rats scurrying in the shadows of the subway rails. Now and then, during the December Christmas season, he remembered her, their date at the Lincoln Center, *The Nutcracker*. He kept the playbill as a memento; occasionally he leafed through it, loser that he was. He loved particularly the line, "The Mouse Prince leads Masha through the Pink River." He wasn't sure why.

He was not a happy man. He was a clerk, a drudge, a doorman. He considered jumping off the George Washington Bridge, but no one would have cared.

◆

Three years pass until one day, while walking down Third Avenue, he happens to meet one his ex-office mates, a woman, Stacy Melter— Stacy who had been good friends with Katey. They exchange long-time-no-sees, you're-looking-greats, that's-good-to-hears. He casually asks whatever happened to Katey, she was always such a nice person.

"Oh, Kate's back in town. She's been here for a couple years now. I talk to her all the time."

"Really? I thought she was in Canada or somewhere."

"No. She's here, hanging out. She works freelance, mainly."

"Could you give me her number? I'd love to call her."

Stacy bobbed her head—not a nod, not a shake. A bob. "Well . . . I don't know about that. You know, some people are pretty touchy about that kind of thing. Why don't you give me yours and I'll make sure she gets it."

He does, but something about the way Stacy writes it down makes him wonder. She doesn't say that Katey has been trying to find him all this time, that she often asks about him. She says nothing, just takes the number. And won't give him Katey's. He's not worthy.

That he would never have the secret of Katey's white tattoo revealed to him had increased the pain of it, that scar of longing, and made it itch now and then, when he thought of her, when he considered it, when he wondered. How can one score a tattoo of white into a young woman's skin? Especially into that whitest of skin, that softest, silkiest reach that nestles the base of her spine? (For a moment he envisioned her fulsome bottom, but banished the thought from his mind as slightly puerile, pornographic.) What ink would equal, surpass such whiteness? But if it did exist, how beautiful it must be! And the thought of it only seen by the privileged few, the Adrians of this world, made a foul and bitter taste rise in Owen's mouth. He wanted to spit. She would never call. It would be one more disappointment and loss in his life. Why don't people *like* me, he wondered? Why?

◆

All through Christmas Owen waits for the call, eyes his answering machine as soon as he gets home, feels the pressure increase and crush his lungs as if he's descending into the atmosphere of Jupiter.

On January 3rd, the phone rings while he's taking a bath, soaking in hot water because he doesn't have the gumption to shower; he grabs a towel and trundles sopping wet across the bath mat to the hallway. When it should hit the third ring, there is silence. He reaches the phone in his bedroom, but the rings are not coming any longer. He picks it up anyway, and stands there, dripping in the cold room, listening to the dial tone.

MARATHON

WHEN I FIRST STARTED TRAINING for the marathon, I was married to a quiet woman with perfect calves and lovely skin. She laughed at my jokes. She was almost six feet tall. We slept in a clean room full of windows, and outside the windows were marigolds, a yard of St. Augustine grass, a white toolshed, an elm tree, a clothesline, and blue sky. I looked up out of my bed in the mornings at patches of the blue sky, the green leaves of the elm, the white toolshed.

My wife slept nude, and if she were lying on her side and the sheets were tossed off the bed, she looked like that Velazquez painting, *The Rokeby Venus*. She had Italian hips and the longest, most beautiful hair you can imagine. It changed color in different light. Sometimes it was walnut, sometimes auburn, sometimes oak or coffee. She had dark brown eyes that matched her hair, that also changed color in the light.

I remember a waitress who sighed as she came up to take our order, and said, "You have such beautiful hair," and she touched it, envious.

Jealous, but in a nice way. My wife smiled graciously and said, "Thank you." After the waitress walked away, my wife noticed the table wobbled slightly, because the legs weren't all the same length. She took a book of paper matches out of her purse and asked me to fix the wobble by putting the book of matches under one of the legs.

When I first started training for the marathon, my life seemed simple and clear, as if there was nothing wrong that a book of paper matches couldn't fix.

◆

It was summer, when I started training for the marathon, summer in a hot and humid city. There were frequent thunderstorms. It often flooded after the storms. Two small hurricanes came through that summer, and the people who lived to the north of our city, in Liberty County, were flooded out of their homes by the rising waters of the Trinity River. You saw them on the news every night for a while there, canoeing through their backyards or taking outboards to look in their soggy living rooms, their kitchens full of frogs. I felt sorry for them at first. What a mess! Can you imagine? Four feet of water in the living room! The TV! The stereo!

I worked freelance, which meant I slept late, wore sloppy clothes, and rode my bicycle around the city. I took hours to read the newspaper, did the crossword, drank coffee, and sat down to read a novel whenever I felt like it. A woman delivered Federal Express packages to my door every morning that had something to do with my work. She always came at nine o'clock and I answered in my boxer shorts with tiny French horns on them, my hair sticking straight up, eyes puffy, and signed here, right here, as I squinted and said, "Hot out there, isn't it?" The Fed Ex woman smiled at me, nodding. "You're telling me."

We always said this, when I was training for the marathon.

It was so hot, when I began training for the marathon, that you weren't supposed to leave the house, much less run six miles or eight

miles at a time. I'd get dizzy, at first, when I didn't realize how important it was to drink lots of water. Sometimes I weaved down the street
and felt like I was going to pass out, but I kept going. Later, I realized
that many times I was near death.

"It's not good for you, this running thing," said my wife. "What are
you trying to prove?"

"It's a goal," I said. "Everybody needs goals, right?"

I came up with the idea of running the marathon after reading
about a seventy-three-year-old grandmother who did it. I figured, if
she can do it . . . (I was thirty-two at the time.) I thought that by
running 26.2 miles my life would be richer, more meaningful. I'd be
able to start sentences with phrases like, "Last year, while I was training for the marathon . . ." People would admire my perseverance,
my strength, my fortitude.

I started out running nine miles a week, then increased to fifteen,
then twenty, and so on. When I reached thirty-five miles a week, I fell
in love with another woman. Sometimes I ran past her house, wondering what she'd be doing at that moment. And then again, sometimes I purposely didn't run by her house, because I was afraid I'd see
her, afraid of seeming a pest. Or simply afraid of being too obvious.

I was in love with her so much that as I ran, I carried on imaginary
conversations with her, telling her how I felt, and she was touched.
Have you ever wondered what people think about when they run?
Maybe they're carrying on conversations with the people they're in
love with. I was in love with her in the worst, the most painful way. I
won't tell you her name, because she's an actual person. If I refer to the
woman I loved, you'll know it's her.

She's like Katherine Hepburn. Charming and elegant. Brilliant in
a subtle way. Not flashy brilliant like she's brilliant and she wants
everyone to know it, but subtle brilliant like she's brilliant and she
wants it to be a secret. And beautiful? You wouldn't believe. Fistfuls of
copper-red hair, and fair skin with freckles. Enormous green eyes. An
inconspicuous nose. Everyone was in love with her, a little. You'd love

her, too, if you saw her. Her face, I'd stare at it and she'd say, "What are you staring at me for? Is there something wrong?" I loved her so much! Maybe I still love her. Maybe I don't want to love her anymore. Maybe I want to hate her. Or her hate me. Maybe.

But the most beautiful thing about the woman I loved is that she was born with only one hand. I loved her with a fierceness, and I think this fierceness hinged on that missing hand. Imagine losing one of your hands! Where would it go? Where would it be? I loved that missing hand. The end of her left arm is shaped like a bell pepper, but the skin is as pink as a baby's ear. She can't hold things with that arm, but she pins things with it. She carries her purse on her left arm. I remember watching her open it, and her arm was like the thin snout of a ferret nosing into a rabbit's nest. She slugged me in the stomach with it once. Hard. I fell to my knees, gasping for breath, almost blacking out. I had told her that her hand looked really beautiful that day. She slugged me, and shouted, "Shut up about my hand, okay?"

"You only love me because I'm different," she said. "You only love me because I'm a freak."

◆

I went to a party with my wife, and I saw the woman I loved. We were in the kitchen of someone's house, and her missing hand filled the room and the very air we breathed. Everyone in the room wasn't looking at her missing hand. Someone was talking about dolphins raping people. They joked about it. Someone else said, "Can you just imagine it, though? The dolphin's there, struggling in the water, thinking, If only I had hands!"

Someone asked if there was any champagne left.

Someone else said that snakes had penises. We all thought this was funny. Madcap laughter! "Snakes have penises, really?" said the hostess. "I mean, isn't that kind of redundant?"

◆

While I was training for the marathon, my wife began to feed a litter of wild cats that lived under the house next door. She sat on the back steps and tossed pieces of cheddar cheese to them, and at first they wouldn't come very close, but before long two of them came close enough for her to pet them, and they all had names, and personalities. Booty, Brownie, Blackie, Spooky. Her favorite was Spooky, an affectionate runt, and he disappeared. After he'd been gone a couple of days, I found her crying in the living room, and when I asked what was wrong she said, "I don't want to talk about it," but I kept bugging her, and finally she admitted, "I was thinking about Spooky. He probably got hit by a car, and maybe he's in pain somewhere. Maybe he needs me."

"Don't worry, darling," I said. "He's probably just roaming around somewhere, seeing the world." And I hugged her, touched by her compassion.

"You don't care," she said. "You don't care about anyone but yourself."

"That's not true. I care about Spooky. Why don't we go drive around and look for him?"

"Just forget it," she said. "Just go for a run or something."

◆

There were two hurricanes that summer. Some people said this was unusual, that there had never been two hurricanes on the same coastline in the same summer. They said it was because of the ozone layer; the clouds over our planet were haywire. I don't know. The first flood was in June, and during July the flood victims who lived to the north of our city, in Liberty County, dried out their carpeting and bought new TVs and stereos with their insurance money. By August I was running forty miles a week and was in love with the other woman. The second small hurricane came through and whipped up the palm trees on our avenues, rain blowing slantwise. Supermarkets sold out of bottled water and flashlight batteries. The newscasters went out into the storm and reported live from flooded streets, water up to the apartment balconies, Vietnamese people sitting on the roofs of houses.

The Trinity River flooded again. That second time I didn't feel sorry for them, the people who lived near the river, when I saw them motorboating to look in their living room windows. They had used up all my TV news compassion. I just thought, Why do they keep living there? Why don't they move or something?

◆

Everything in this story is true.

◆

The woman I loved read me poetry over the telephone. I wondered how she was holding it. In the crook of her neck? With her missing hand? I idealized her missing hand. It became the Platonic form of a hand for me, the fingers graceful and elegant, like Bernini hands. Not hard and curled as marble, but soft and dry and warm. Sometimes I imagined her missing hand reaching up and pushing the hair out of my face, or brushing its fingers gently down my neck.

The woman I loved read Gerard Manley Hopkins over the phone. I remember her reading this:

> The world is charged with the grandeur of God.
> It will flame out, like shining from shook foil.
> It gathers to a greatness, like the ooze of oil
> Crushed. Why do men then now not reck his rod?
> Generations have trod, have trod, have trod;

And all is seared with trade, bleared, smeared with toil.
And wears man's smudge and shares man's smell: the soil
Is bare now, nor can foot feel, being shod.

The woman I loved said, "Isn't that beautiful? Isn't that the most amazing poetry you've ever heard?"

"I love you," I told her.

"No, you don't," she said. "You just think you do."

There was a pause, because there was nothing I could say, or think, or feel.

"But you really don't," she said.

◆

In November I was running fifty miles a week. "Don't do this to us," she said. "You're going to ruin everything."

◆

The woman I loved only wanted to be my friend. "We're just friends," she said. "If we touched each other, it would ruin everything," she said. "Believe me," she said. "I know what I'm talking about."

My wife still loved me, but I had lost the feeling somehow, maybe like a leg that falls asleep. You know it's still there because you can see it, connected to your body there, and you can walk on it, awkwardly somehow. But you feel nothing.

Gradually I realized, through the many rooms of stupidity in my mind, that the woman I loved didn't love me. Her feeling for me wasn't like a leg fallen asleep, one that could awake and walk again. It was more like her missing hand, something essential and graceful and beautiful that had never been, and never would be.

◆

The morning of the marathon, I drove downtown to the starting line alone and parked in a parking garage. There was an empty Styrofoam cup in the middle of the black sooty asphalt of the garage. Who had left it there? I thought about picking it up and putting it in a litter basket, but I didn't. The parking was free, and I felt like I was getting away with something. The mayor and Terry Bradshaw—ex-quarterback of the Pittsburgh Steelers—gave speeches, wishing us well.

"The whole city is proud of you!" they said.

There were over five thousand of us, all with white plastic banners with black numbers safety-pinned to our chests, and we ran together, close enough to touch, as thick as the soldiers on D-Day or Guadalcanal. We ran over bridges and through Hispanic neighborhoods. People played trombones and tubas and cheered as we passed, waving American flags, throwing confetti, and I imagined telling the woman I loved that this was all for her; this was life, the sheer amazement of it; this was what she was passing up. We ran past fountains and parks and local DJs from radio stations calling out our names and rock bands playing songs just for us, for the runners of the city.

We ran under freeways, under overpasses, where homeless people lived in cardboard boxes that smelled of urine, and the homeless people stared out at us and urged us on, clapping, bearded and hungry and caught up in the absurdity and magnificence of it.

I talked to the runners beside me. We became close. I told them I was in love with a beautiful woman who had only one hand, but she didn't love me. I told them she only wanted to be friends.

"I've heard that one before," said a man running beside me.

"Maybe she's right," said a woman on my left. "Maybe you would ruin everything."

We ran past cheerleaders with pom-poms and mariachis in sombreros, playing guitars; we ran past Girl Scout troops and a group of overweight middle-aged women tap dancing in frilly skirts at the entrance to a drive-through bank.

By the last few miles I didn't see the point of anything anymore. Why did I love the wrong woman? Why did I want to run 26.2 miles? What was I trying to prove? For over a mile I ran next to a beautiful girl who was crying, in pain, and I realized that I could love her, too, maybe; it was just that I didn't know her.

I was struck with the randomness of life.

When I crossed the finish line, grimacing, someone came up to me and asked, "Are you okay? Can you walk?" I said I was. They tore the number off my chest and put a space blanket around my shoulders, pointed to the pavilion beyond the finish line, where you could get bananas, cola, bottled water, and muffins. I got a banana and a paper cup of Gatorade and sat down on a folding metal chair, thinking that nothing was really worth it, and I was so weak I couldn't peel the banana to eat it. I shivered, wrapped in a blanket that was the color of aluminum foil but as thin as Kleenex, aware that even though I had just run 26.2 miles, it meant nothing. The pavilion was full of people just like me, sore, aching, too tired to even eat a banana or drink a cup of Gatorade, who had also run 26.2 miles. I could be anyone.

Mergers & Acquisitions

As SHE TIED HER RUNNING SHOES, Lael spaced out for a second, and suddenly found herself staring at a rain puddle the shape of Africa. She was sitting on the steps of her row house, and it—the Africa puddle—was there in the yard, by the end of the steps. Reflected in it were the twisted arms of a tree, green-black leaves, and an opaque sky. How weird and portentous, she thought. And for a moment, she wondered what it signified, but not for long, because she had ten million different things on her mind. Like Brian. Like law school. Like how someone was trying to take over her dad's company. She knew it's not good to worry too much, because it probably causes all kinds of diseases, but when your world is in jeopardy, what else can you do? The Saturday morning sky was close and hazy—a real greenhouse effect kind of day. Brian said it would be perfect for a run. But you couldn't trust him, of course. What did he know about running? What did he know about anything?

Lael was all freckles and wavy blonde hair. Right now, she kept it out of her face by a black hairband. Brian sat on the top steps of the porch, thinking how marvelous she looked in her Lycra tights and sleeveless T-shirt. But he didn't say anything. He believed it's not good to compliment beautiful women too much, or they'll walk all over you. He learned this inside the projectionist's booth at the cine octoplex where he worked. You don't see Bill Hurt or Bobby De Niro gushing over their women. They just smile. Or sometimes a gesture says it all. Like that scene in *Broadcast News*, when Bill Hurt sees Holly Hunter walking into the black-tie dinner and she's wearing this strapless evening gown that's like death, sequins and everything. And when their eyes meet, he leans back as if he's been hit by something, her beauty, bowled over, and he grabs his heart as if it's hers now, or as if he's trying to hold it back, because she's so gorgeous she's wrenching it out. Brian closed his eyes and concentrated, trying to hold that image in his mind for a moment.

Lael finished tying her shoelaces and stood up, dusting off her bottom. "It was a wonderful company before it went public," she said. "I mean, aluminum bicycles! That's a brilliant idea."

"Maybe a miracle will happen," said Brian. "Maybe Kubelka will get hit by a bus."

"Sure," said Lael. "And maybe you'll stay sober for more than a day."

Brian looked at her, dropping his mouth open. "And where did that come from?"

"Sorry, honey," said Lael. "Just kidding."

Brian walked toward the street, shaking his head, and saw their cat rolling on his back on the cracked sidewalk by the mailbox. He squatted down to scratch the cat's chin, and said, "Hello, Hokey Mokey."

Lael came up and sat on the concrete beside the cat, rubbing his face and passing her thumbs over his closed eyes and stroking his ears. She had adopted Mokey when he'd been a stray with gunk in his eyes and an urgent meow. "He just wants to be loved," she cooed. As Brian petted the cat, he thought about seventeen-year-old Carol Johnson. The popcorn girl. He thought about how he had kissed her neck and cupped her breast after the final show last night. Goose pimples had stood out on her arms, and they had ground their hips together in a miasma of popcorn-butter smell, pressed hard against the glass counter of Milk Duds and Junior Mints. When they heard the doofus usher coming, she whispered, "If Derek sees us, he's going to die."

Lael said something about Mokey not coming home the night before. "I bet there's a girl-kitty in heat somewhere," she added.

Brian smiled and scratched Mokey's head. Just above his eyes. "You rascal."

"Rascal nothing," said Lael. "I think we should get him fixed."

◆

Myron Levin, Lael's father, rowed his shell down the middle of the Schuylkill River and tried to think positively. But this wasn't easy. For one thing, he was afraid of the water. Although he could see other rowers off to his left and right, as he passed through the bluish shadow beneath the arc of a stone bridge, he suddenly feared that he would capsize and be attacked by snapping turtles. He'd seen one eat a baby duck once, at a pond in the Adirondacks, and always feared dark lakes and rivers after that. Any water where you couldn't see the bottom.

As he rowed, he concentrated on keeping his body tight and symmetrical, and watched the river receding behind him. The vee of his wake spread out and rippled on the river's surface under the stone bridge. Above him, pigeons that nested on the black underside of the bridge flapped and fluttered. Myron couldn't see in front of him, but could only stare at the swells of murky green water that held up his boat.

Maybe it's greenmail he wants, thought Myron. Maybe if I offer him $28 per share, he'll sell the 12 percent and I can go on with my life. That would mean a $6.7 million profit for Kubelka, for nothing more than ruining my life. I should blow his brains out is what I should do. Put the barrel in his mouth and watch his blood splatter all over his Mercedes' upholstery. Or hire someone to do it. We'd have to make it look like an accident. Like drop a Xerox machine on his head. Or an elephant.

Although Myron Levin was the president of Arapaho Bicycles, he could remember when his father ran the company, when he was young and he'd go into a hardware store and see a row of candy apple red or turquoise blue Arapahos back behind the Briggs & Stratton lawn mowers and the rows of shovels, picks, and ax handles. They'd been sturdy bikes with welded frames, whitewall tires, and the name ARA-PAHO spelled vertically along the down tube. Their logo had been in front, below the handlebars, a capital A with a tomahawk above it, on a metal plate brazed to the bike.

Now the bikes were made of aluminum, because it was lighter and hip, and they came in colors like emerald, lobster, and periwinkle. When sales skyrocketed for three years in a row, everyone told Myron what a genius he was, but the company had been highly leveraged to fund the new factory and technology, so it went public in 1986 to pay off the debt, and traded as high as 21 until the Crash of October 1987, when it fell to 5¼. In came Arthur Kubelka. Rumor on the street was Arapaho might go into play, that Kubelka was planning to offer share-holders a fantastic price to buy up controlling interest, then dump Myron.

That afternoon Myron was supposed to meet Kubelka for the first time. At eight o'clock he'd been so nervous he couldn't eat breakfast, and although he hadn't rowed his shell in over a year, he decided he needed to work off some energy and toughen himself up. Myron was as nervous as when his wife Stella didn't return from her trip to New Hampshire, eight years ago. She was driving back alone, and was sup-posed to arrive by early afternoon, but didn't. As soon as it got dark Myron called the police. They asked him to hold. He and Lael ended up sitting all night by the telephone. She kept trying to find a reason for her mother being late. "Maybe she just lost track of time." But she didn't look like she believed it.

A police officer finally called, on a dull, cloudy dawn, to say there had been a head-on collision north of Allentown, and did he own a late model Buick, tag number ADA 577? He did. And they had Stella's body, covered with a sheet.

◆

After Lael took off running, Brian drank two Bloody Marys for breakfast while he read film reviews in the *Philadelphia Inquirer.* He knew you can't trust what anyone says these days, but he liked to keep his feelers out. He wondered how people got started as film reviewers. You probably have to know someone. Maybe live in New York. Of course, that wasn't impossible. He could move to Manhattan with Lael, when she left to start law school at NYU. But that would be kind of low, wouldn't it? Just moving to New York with Lael because it was convenient?

This thing with Carol was anything but convenient, though. Brian felt kind of sorry for her, actually, because her mother was hardly ever at home. She was a teenage latchkey girl, a latchkey popcorn girl, and her mother—who owned a couple of rundown Laundromats—seemed eager for her to move out. Carol was tall and skinny, and when Brian first met her he asked, "Do you play basketball or something?" "No. Why?" she'd answered.

"Never mind." She had sex with Brian in the projectionist's booth after they'd known each other for only a week. Later she told him that she didn't have any friends at her high school, and he had felt creepy about their affair, if that's what you could call it. She seemed to think it was "cool" that he was twelve years older than her. After reading the paper and having one more Bloody Mary, Brian drove to her apartment.

◆

When she opened her door, Brian said, "Hey, Carol," and took both of her hands in his, leaned forward to kiss her lips, but she turned her face at the last moment and he only grazed the wick of her mouth and her cheek, while Carol's lips smacked the air beside his face. Now she wouldn't stop talking about a movie that had just opened at the octoplex.

"It was all murky and dark and set in the future. One of those sets that looks like a chemical plant. You know, with pipes and girders everywhere and steam hissing out at the characters for no apparent reason? Just mood, I guess. Very Robocoppy. Very Batmanny."

Brian was thinking if I was smart I'd open a separate bank account now and start dropping my deposits in it, write a check for half of what's rightfully mine from the joint checking, and make a clean break. That's what Jack Nicholson would do. That's what Kevin Costner would do. Carol was still going on and on about this movie (will she never stop?) when Brian interrupted her and said, "You know, last night I was having the nastiest thoughts about you."

Carol smiled for a moment and poked his stomach. "But the lighting was horrible, all pastels and gun metal blues. A direct rip-off of *Blade Runner*. I mean, does everyone think the future is that dark? I just don't buy that 'apocalypse now' stuff. I mean, look at Poland. Look at Czechoslovakia."

"Look at you," said Brian.

Carol rolled her eyes. "Oh, please."

"I mean it. You're gorgeous today."

"Would you stop?"

"And I was thinking about what it'd be like if we got a place together."

"What about Lael? I can just see you telling her you're leaving her for a popcorn girl."

Brian shrugged. "Lael who?"

◆

After her run, Lael picked up her little brother Todd and took him to buy an eight-hundred-dollar bird. Todd had dyslexia, and although Lael tried to be understanding about it, she secretly believed he used it as an excuse to be lazy. He dropped out of Penn in his first semester and now just hung out with his friends, playing Nintendo baseball and smoking pot. He still lived at home, in the pool house, where he could party all night without waking up Myron. All his friends mooched off their parents, and Todd didn't even own a car; that's why Lael had to taxi him around. Lael wondered why anyone would spend eight hundred dollars on a bird. What if it dies?

"It's not an investment," said Todd. "It's a Moluccan cockatoo. And besides, it's on sale."

They drove home from the pet shop carefully, trying not to scare the bird, with a blanket over the cage. "What should I name him?" asked Todd. Lael had no idea. Back at the pool house, she watched the cockatoo as Todd tried to figure out where the best place would be to put the cage in his room. It had a huge black beak, which it used as a third claw to grab the bars of its cage and climb upside down, in a kind of slow motion somersault, over and over.

"I don't think they're supposed to do this constantly," said Lael. "That's forty-seven somersaults since I started counting."

"He's just getting adjusted to his new cage, man. Give him a break."

"All right, *man,* but I think you bought yourself a neurotic bird. And where'd you get the money for Mr. Cockatoo anyway? You're still jobless, aren't you?"

"I hope so," said Todd. "I get some cash from Dad now and then, and you know, I don't really need money, except for tapes and stuff."

"Well, I wouldn't count on him indefinitely. You know that someone's trying to take over the company, don't you?"

Todd hooked a plastic cup of seed onto the black iron bars of the cockatoo's cage. "They can't do that. Don't we own the company?"

Lael looked at him and shook her head. "I can't believe you," she said. "You are so totally out of it."

◆

Myron combed his gray hair and straightened his tie, standing in front of his bathroom mirror in his black socks with garters and boxer shorts. He remembered how he would strut around in front of Stella like this. Hike his boxers up and tell her this was his favorite look. He'd tell her just how lucky she was. And she would roll her eyes and laugh. But Myron would know who the lucky one was.

He decided to wear his expensive charcoal gray suit, but it had been tailored back when he weighed 205, and now, at 227, the waist button popped off as he was trying to fasten it. Rather than change to another suit, he safety-pinned them together. I'll be sitting down, he thought. No one will ever notice.

He shuffled out to his Lincoln and wondered if he should check those directions to the restaurant where they were meeting, but decided against it since he was late already. He simply drove in that general direction. After he'd circled the block where he was sure it was supposed to be, he finally pulled into a service station. The clerk was an East Indian man in a bullet-proof booth. It had a stainless steel slot to pass money through, and a small circular mouth of metal to speak into. Myron was ten minutes late and the clerk had never heard of the place. "Try the Yellow Pages," he said. He gave Myron directions to the nearest pay phone down the street, because the gas station's phone had been ripped out by vandals.

At the next intersection, Myron waited for the light. A street person walked up and started wiping his windshield with a dirty rag. Myron rolled down his window and said, "That's not necessary. Please. I don't need that." But the man quickly rubbed the glass as if he didn't hear. The cars behind began to honk as Myron looked for change, couldn't find any, and sped away. He saw the squeegee man shouting in his rearview mirror. His heart didn't calm down until he had run a yellow light and was completely lost.

The street was so narrow it seemed almost an alley. On either side of him were tenements spiny with fire escapes. He drove through block after block, randomly. Old women pushed shopping carts down the streets, and he had to weave to avoid the potholes. When he finally reached a wide avenue, he turned right and had to stop at the next intersection for a light. As he stared at the shop signs beside him, he realized that the restaurant was just ahead.

Inside the dining room, Kubelka was talking with a waitress and laughing when Myron walked up. They shook hands awkwardly as the waitress asked if Myron wanted anything to drink. Lunch was served. Kubelka was a stocky man with a broken nose, and looked more like a prizefighter than a businessman. They discussed the company, and Myron offered to buy Kubelka's block at five dollars per share over market price. Kubelka raised his eyebrows and was silent for a moment.

"The problem with you, Levin," he began, dipping his boiled shrimp, speared on a tiny trident, into the cocktail sauce, "is that no one *believes* in you anymore." He popped the shrimp into his mouth and chewed, staring straight at Myron. "For all intents and purposes, you might not even exist. Can you imagine that?"

"Sometimes I pretend I don't exist," said Myron. He forced a weak and nervous smile. His eyes were focused on Kubelka's sleeves, which showed an inch and a half of bone-white cuff and gold cufflinks. For a moment Myron wondered if Kubelka was part of the Mob.

"What would happen to Arapaho Bicycles if you weren't there tomorrow? Imagine that. Picture that."

"Are you threatening me?"

Kubelka laughed. "Of course not, Levin. I'm just trying to make you visualize the future. You won't be here forever, you know. Before you know it," Kubelka snapped his fingers, "you'll be gone."

"Well, I know I won't be here forever," said Myron. I bet those cuf-flinks cost three hundred dollars. "I'd get tired of watching you eat shrimp cocktail after about fifty years."

Kubelka stared at Myron and cleared his throat. "I didn't mean you wouldn't be *here* forever. I meant you wouldn't be alive forever."

Myron nodded. Three hundred dollars at least. Maybe more than that. "I know what you meant. I try not to think about it."

"Well, for the sake of argument, just imagine what would happen to Arapaho Bicycles if you weren't there tomorrow."

"I think Judith, my secretary, would be upset. She hates taking messages."

"Okay. Judith's life would be in shambles—"

"I didn't say that."

"Okay, a mess. Phones ringing off the hook. What else?"

"My daughter Lael might wonder what happened to me."

Kubelka sighed and rubbed his face with both hands. "You're miss-ing the point, Levin." He told Myron that Arapaho Bicycles wouldn't miss a beat. They'd hire a new president. And if they were smart, start making some real money. He outlined how the quarterly earnings should improve, while Myron became more and more depressed, thinking about the inevitability of his death and the meaninglessness of everything we do and the universe in general. Why not give up the company? Did anything really matter?

After a moment Kubelka quit speaking. He could tell Myron wasn't really listening. And, in fact, he looked as if he were about to cry. Kubelka rubbed his broken nose and sighed. He signaled the wait-ress for the check. Myron's face was so downcast he seemed to be star-ing at his half-eaten plate of linguini Alfredo and Italian sausage. Kubelka found himself also staring at it. "You wouldn't catch me eat-ing all that fat in a million years," he said. Myron didn't respond. Kubelka cleared his throat. "Levin, I'm going to make you an offer."

◆

Through the windows of a bar, Brian saw that dark had fallen outside. Purple neon lights were shining across the street, and he guessed it was later than he thought. He knew not calling Lael was stupid and cruel, but as he sat across from Carol Johnson in a post–happy hour haze and listened to her go on and on about those changes in Eastern Europe— "Like you were saying Russia's going to have a stock market I mean isn't it incredible?"—he stared at her huge green eyes and nose that was just a little too big but gave her face an exotic, ethnic look, pale hair in a ponytail, lapdog bangs to her eyebrows, cardigan sweater and blue jeans, and he told himself if you're afraid to take any risks in life you might as well be dead. He was on his twelfth drink of the day by then. Full of risk. Carol was wearing a white blouse with a row of black buttons down the front. He wanted to unbutton them. There. Right there. In the middle of the bar. And bury his face in her breasts.

"Wouldn't it be cool to go to Moscow? Or, I don't know. Budapest or somewhere."

Brian nodded and took out his wallet, unfolding it open to show Carol he was out of money. "The worst fate," he said.

"I know where we can get some more."

They drove to one of her mother's Laundromats to take the quarters out of some of the machines. As soon as they got there, Brian climbed inside one of the dryers. Carol told him to quit fooling around. But he closed the door and blinked at her from behind the porthole like a passenger on the *Titanic*.

"Whatever you do, don't touch that dial," he said, pointing to the coin slot.

"You know I think you've got a drinking problem," said Carol. "I mean, Wednesday you were drunk and Friday you were drunk and in fact you were drunk Tuesday, too."

Brian opened the door a crack and whispered, "Nag."

"I should take you home and leave you there. Maybe move and leave no forwarding address."

The blue-white glow of fluorescent lamps filled the Laundromat, and for a moment, as Brian climbed out of the machine, he felt as if he were in a slow-motion rinse cycle, washing machines spinning around him, the air full of detergent. He tried to compose himself, leaning against the fat box of a washing machine, noticing the burned end and speckled brown filter tip of a cigarette butt someone had ground with their heel on the floor. "It's those kind of people who make this world the mess I am," he said, pointing at the cigarette butt. Then he wrinkled his eyebrows and weaved, unsteady there, trying to figure out just exactly where that sentence went wrong. He banged against the glass doors of the exit and couldn't get out, until Carol came up and said, "Wait a second, spazmo."

In the front seat of her VW Rabbit, Carol had to lean over Brian to pull the shoulder strap between the door and seat to buckle him in. She felt the warm smear of a sloppy kiss on her neck and shrank away, pinching her chin to her shoulder. "Would you behave?"

The drive was a roar of freeways with Brian's window rolled down ("I need the air") and a dizzy heartbeat of street. Bands of flashing streetlights gave way to one red eye as they reached Brian's neighborhood. Carol pulled up at the curb in front of Brian and Lael's house. Her headlights reflected off the taillights of Myron's Lincoln and shone directly into Lael's eyes, who was standing in the driveway behind her father's car. She shaded her eyes and frowned until Carol turned off the headlights. Carol got out and left the engine running. She went around to open the passenger-side door. Brian was leaning back in his seat, head against the headrest. "I don't think I can walk," he said.

She folded her arms and walked up to Lael, who was standing in the driveway, calling, "Hokey! Hokey Mokey!" and making kissing sounds into the darkness. "Mokey didn't come home for dinner," she told Carol. "I'm afraid something's happened to him."

Carol looked into the darkness of black trees in dark yards, white sidewalks faintly visible as breaks in the lawns. "He's probably just tom-catting around. Do you have company?" she asked, pointing to the car.

"Just my dad."

Carol nodded. "You know, this is totally embarrassing, but Brian's in my car and he's really drunk."

"That's nothing new."

"But I don't think he can walk."

Lael shrugged, and for a moment looked into Carol's eyes to see if there was a real person there. "What do you want me to do about it?"

"I don't know." Carol put her hands in her blue jean pockets. "He's in my car."

Lael walked away, calling Hokey's name again. Carol walked back to her car. The night was so dark she touched the fender to feel her way along. "Brian, you're home." He looked like he was asleep. She had to shake his shoulder. "If you're going to sleep, you should get in your bed, Brian. You can't sleep in my front seat."

He opened his eyes for a moment and looked at Carol uncertainly. "I'm not asleep," he said, then closed his eyes again. "I'm thinking."

"Goddammit. Get out of the car, Brian. I've got things to do." She opened the car door and finally managed to get him to walk out and stand beside the maple tree near the mailbox. He leaned over to get some air, and he wasn't aware of how much time had passed before he was alone. He didn't know how he'd gotten there or where exactly he was for a moment. He stared at the yellow light over the side door and the two cars in the driveway before he realized he was home.

He decided to head for the side entrance where the light was and felt the yard slam him in the face. He smelled dirt and grass, tasted something gritty in his mouth. It reminded him of the snails he would put in his mouth when he was five years old and played in the flower garden. He remembered his mother forcing his mouth open and shouting, "Spit it out! Spit it out!" Somewhere a woman's voice called, "Hokey! Hokey Mokey!"

Lael walked into the light of the driveway and looked at him. He managed to raise himself up on all fours and say, "I think I'm going to be sick."

She nodded. "Good. Think of it as a learning experience."

In the kitchen, her father sat at the small dinette table with Todd, stirring a white china cup of black coffee. Todd was uncharacteristically glum and gloomy. He turned around an empty Pepsi can in his hands. "Any sign of the Moke?"

"No, but Brian's in the front yard."

"What's he doing there?"

"Crawling, I think."

Myron shook his head and clucked his tongue. "And this you call a significant other?"

"Don't worry, Dad," said Lael. "He's getting less significant day by day." She leaned against the back of his chair and put her arms around him from behind.

"That's good news," he said. "I think it's time this family took a long hard look at itself. Maybe Kubelka's buyout proposal isn't so bad."

Lael toasted bagels for all of them, and for a moment they were full of life. She argued that Myron should stick with the company and not sell out, even if Kubelka bought up controlling interest and deposed him as CEO.

"But if this guy does buy us out, how much are my shares going to be worth?" asked Todd.

"Just forget it, Todd. We're not selling."

"What's this? Queen Lael has spoken? I don't know. Maybe we should take the money and, like, screw it. Who needs the hassle?"

Myron stirred his coffee slowly, the spoon ringing against the inside of the cup. His back was sore and his hands blistered from the rowing he'd done earlier. He felt heavy and weak, and he could hear his own breathing. Maybe I should travel. Take a train through Morocco. Camels and sand dunes. Wicker baskets of dates. A sad middle-aged man with gray hair and ridiculous luggage. In a fleabag somewhere in Marrakesh, the maid finds me dead, wrists agape, a puddle of blood on the Islamic tiles of the bathroom floor.

His voice suddenly rose as he spread a layer of cream cheese onto one of the toasted bagels. "And you kids have to learn how to handle your own finances. I won't be around forever, you know."

Lael frowned and shook her head. "Don't be *silly*. Of course you won't be around forever. But neither will we." She looked at her gray-haired father, at the deep grooves in his face and his fleshy lips, at the bluish shadow of beard down his jaw and around his mouth, and she wondered how long it would take to get Brian out of her life. There's plenty more where he came from. But is this what it comes down to? You care for something all your life just so some rat fink can come and take it away? The best thing to do is not to feel or care. The best way to walk is chin held high, arms swinging. Look busy. Act like you know where you're going. If anyone asks for directions, keep moving.

THREE FEET OF WATER

ISABELLE WAS PACKING WHEN Aunt Roberta called and said that if they didn't mind, she was going to join them at the beach house for the weekend. "I'll stay out of your way, though. You won't even know I'm there."

Isabelle felt as if she had been sucked out the door of a 747. She fell through clouds, saw snow geese fly past, watched her luggage swirl around her in the sky. "Of course we won't mind," she said. She was so dizzy she had to sit down, holding the phone with both hands. "You'll love Zack," she said. It turned out Roberta's Audi was in the shop, so she needed a ride, too. "Maybe I should just rent a car. That's what I should do."

"Don't be ridiculous," said Isabelle. "We'll pick you up at six."

So okay, I can handle this. I can cope, thought Isabelle. She drove. Roberta sat in the front seat, smoking menthols and brushing out her hair, which was the color of motor oil. She cracked the window to let the smoke out, and the air rushing in made a heavy, buffeting sound.

"Is that too much wind for you, Zack?" she asked.

"Not at all. It feels good," he said loudly, from the back seat.

Roberta cleaned the matted hair out of her brush and let that slip out the open window, too. She read travel brochures to them. "Tell me where I should go, Zack. Ixtapa? Corfu?" She twisted around and held out the brochures to Zack, holding them fan-shaped, like a poker hand. "Pick one, any one. Give my life some direction."

Zack looked into Isabelle's aunt's blue eyes. With her eyeliner and powder blue eye shadow, she looked like a nightclub singer. "I think you should look for adventure in your own backyard," said Zack.

Roberta frowned, and propped her chin up on the back of her seat. "You're no help."

"London, then. Or Paris. Somewhere nicely cliché."

"Izzy's never been to Europe," said Roberta. "Have you, Izzy?"

"Not yet," said Isabelle. She kept her eyes on the road. "I've always wanted to, but I've never had the chance."

"That's sad," said Roberta. She made a pouty face, pooching her lips out at Zack. "I think Louise was always a little too protective of her. Too mother-hennish."

"I'll take you to Europe," said Zack, looking at Isabelle in the rearview mirror.

"All three of us should go," said Roberta, brightly. "I can be your chaperone. But no funny stuff. Or I'll tell my big sister."

Isabelle sighed and punched a tape into the cassette deck, keeping her eyes on the road. "Is it going to be like this for the rest of the weekend?"

Roberta stared at her. "Is what going to be like what?"

"You know."

"No, I don't. I think we're going to have a wonderful time."

The inside of the car was quiet for a moment, except for the roar of the wind coming in through the cracked window. Roberta had quit brushing her blue-black hair, and now she was letting it hang out the window, trailing behind the car like thick black exhaust.

◆

Roberta was Isabelle's mother's little sister. She was forty-three, but looked thirty-five, and had been married four times. Her first husband, Bill, was a washout. "I hung him out to dry," she used to say. Her second husband, Mitch, made a killing in real estate for a time in Texas, and with that money bought the beach house, a Hobie Cat, and a metallic green ski boat with twin black Mercury outboards that went forty-five miles an hour. At the helm, he looked like Jack Lord in *Hawaii Five-O*, with his dark tan, strong jaw, and thick black hair on his chest and back. Isabelle remembered when he used to parade around the beach house in his bikini bathing suits, calling Dallas and Houston on business deals, his hairy chest smelling of coconut oil.

One afternoon Roberta was pulling him with the ski boat and he was slaloming, cutting back and forth across the white crests of the boat's wake, the wind pinning Roberta's hair away from her face as she steered to avoid the fishing piers in Tornado Bay, Mitch leaning back and shooting rooster tails and wings of spray into the air. He made her stop so he could put on his trick skis, then, as she gave the engine full throttle, they passed a floating wooden ramp used for ski jumping. Mitch had never jumped. He swung over to the ski jump and launched himself into the air, his legs spread in an awkward V shape, the skis splayed out like giant paddles, and he hit the water in an ugly tumble, legs and skis tangling until Roberta killed the engine.

He had not been wearing a life vest, because, of course, they were for wimps. Roberta circled back to where he had been, waves slapping against the hull, the ski rope cutting a line through the water behind the boat. His skis floated on the surface. She fished them out, and shouted across the rippled gray water. "Mitch, this isn't funny!" she yelled, thinking he was hiding somewhere beneath the waves. She called his name until her voice was hoarse, until finally she lit a cigarette and just sat there, in the cushioned seat over the ice chest, as the ski boat drifted. A pair of gulls glided above her. Sunlight glistened on the swells. Roberta flicked her cigarette butt and watched it float. After a while, staring at the water, she realized she had no idea where Mitch had fallen, so she returned to the marina and called the police. Three days later his body washed up on Pineapple Beach, his blue limbs tangled in seaweed and jellyfish, several of his fingers bitten off, his eyeballs plucked out by the sea.

Her third husband was a lawyer she met while working out the details of Mitch's estate. They divorced in two years, three months. The fourth husband was one of her third husband's friends (seven months, two weeks). "Love is just a matter of timing," Roberta told Isabelle after the last divorce. "And remember, Precious. Now is as good a time as any."

◆

The beach house was stuffy and mildewy when they arrived. Isabelle and Zack offered to clean things up a bit. She was dusting and he was vacuuming the living room when Roberta decided they needed a bag of ice for daiquiris. She asked if Zack would drive her to the store. "I bet you're a stock car driver or something, aren't you, Zack."

"I'm a carpenter," said Zack, still holding the vacuum cleaner.

"Carpenter. Stock car driver. What's the difference?"

"It's okay, Zack. I'll finish up here."

Isabelle vacuumed the living room and mopped the kitchen. As she cleaned the cobwebs off the ceiling of the screened porch, she tried to decide if she was in love with Zack or what. She had met him on a flight from Dallas to Portland. He struck up a conversation with her, and explained what he was going to do in Oregon. They had been in the air for over fifteen minutes by this time, when Isabelle interrupted him and said, "But this flight is going to Portland, Maine."

He looked at her for a moment. "You're kidding, right?" He got out his crumpled ticket and smoothed it with his fingers, spreading it atop the tray that folded down from the back of the seat in front of him.

She was right. He smiled stupidly and said, "There must have been some mix-up with the travel agent." Isabelle laughed so hard she had to cover her face with her hands. Zack grinned, shaking his head. "You think maybe I should have checked the ticket, right?"

That was two years ago. They had been seeing each other off and on ever since then, but had never slept together. At first Isabelle had been dating a pharmacist, and then Zack was involved with some person named Tiffany whom Isabelle never met but knew she wouldn't like. Only recently both of them had become free. Now Isabelle could tell something was going on, because Zack had begun to drag his feet when he left her door at night and often seemed to be staring at her for no reason. She didn't know what to think of this. She knew love should be like a sledgehammer or an anvil that falls from the sky, something that suddenly hits you and knocks you out, but that was just one kind of love, wasn't it? Wasn't there another kind that develops like a slow pneumonia or the latest flu—the Asian, the Hong Kong love—where you meet someone and they breathe on you at a party or something and gradually you start sneezing and coughing, your eyes watering suddenly, people saying Bless You and Gesundheit; then comes that delicious achy feeling when you know this is for real; this is really sickness, with all that entails—the bowls of tomato soup on TV trays, the *Days of Our Lives*, the Saltines—and the next thing you know you're bathed in sweat, tossing and turning in a bedroom with the blinds pulled dark, moaning. Wasn't this how greater loves develop, gradually, over years, an accumulation of café lunches, matinées, telephone calls?

She was standing on a chair, holding a broom upside down, cleaning the cobwebs off the ceiling. They looked like gray thread matted onto the yellow straw of the broom, giving off a wet dusty smell, like old rain you find in a box. A dark spider scrabbled out from one corner, heading down the wall, until Isabelle smashed it with the raspy torus of the broom, fearing black widows. Through the open door behind her, which led into the main part of the beach house, she heard someone knocking on the front door. Isabelle realized that love seemed like a good idea, and she wanted it—really, she did—but she felt as if she had no clue how to begin. She went to get the door.

It was a tall man with gray hair and a cinnamon-brown tan, who asked if Roberta was home. He was dressed in a tennis outfit, with sunglasses hanging from a loop around his neck. "Who are you? I've never seen you around here before."

"Roberta is my aunt."

"You look like her little sister. Well, anyway. I'm Tim. Can I make myself a drink?"

"Help yourself, Tim."

He knew where the bar was. He twisted a blue plastic tray for some cubes and filled up a glass with two fingers of bourbon. I know I shouldn't be doing this, he thought. This is not something I should be doing. But what the hell. It's a free country. "She called and told me she was coming. But she didn't mention you."

Isabelle squirmed up on a barstool. "Should she have?"

"No. I'm not surprised, come to think of it. Why wouldn't Roberta mention that her gorgeous young niece was coming with her? Go figure."

He was on his second bourbon when Roberta opened the door for Zack, who was carrying two brown paper bags of groceries. "Sorry we were gone so long," said Zack. "It's all Roberta's fault."

"Want to go for a swim?" asked Isabelle.

Zack said he just needed time to change. Roberta hugged Tim and they kissed. "Maybe I'll join you later," she told Isabelle.

"Hey, Bobbie, you didn't tell me you had a gorgeous niece. I think I'm going to marry her."

"Don't listen to him," said Roberta, kissing the back of Tim's neck. "He's girl crazy."

"I'm dead serious," he said, and winked at Isabelle.

When Isabelle and Zack were out of sight down the hallway, Zack grabbed her by the belt loop and whispered, "Who's the geezer?"

Isabelle shook her head. "The beach boyfriend, I guess. But doesn't he look exactly like Richard Crenna?"

◆

It was late afternoon on the beach. A flock of curlews culled the shoreline for the small yellow clams that lived in the wet sand at the end of the waves. Isabelle lay on a straw beach mat, on her side, her head propped up by her left hand, watching the curlews. Zack sat on his mat next to her, scraping beach tar off his feet with a piece of driftwood.

"Where does all this gunk come from? You think this is from an oil spill or something?"

"Who knows?" Isabelle pulled her straight, dark-brown hair off the back of her neck to keep from getting a funny tan, and absentmindedly held it up to her nose and inhaled, filling her lungs with its shampoo smell of vanilla and lilacs.

"Aren't they goofy?" said Zack.

"What?"

"The birds."

"Curlews, sweetheart." Isabelle rolled over onto her stomach. Her skin was white in the sunlight, although the small of her back was carpeted with tiny hairs. "My mom always thought there was something hopeful and sweet about them. She figured any world that tolerated a bird with such a ridiculous beak couldn't be all bad."

Isabelle was twenty-seven years old and still lived at home with her mother, who had divorced Isabelle's father fifteen years before and never remarried. Isabelle secretly believed that her mother envied Roberta's frequent affairs, and that she lived vicariously by talking to her sister often on the phone. And Izzy sometimes wondered if she had too much of her mother's blood. She'd been a history major in college and was thinking about going back to graduate school, but she just couldn't muster the enthusiasm for being a student again. She dreaded the thought of the classrooms full of dweebs, professors with blackboard chalk on the backs of their jackets, research papers on the Dreyfus affair or Catherine de' Medici. She spent most of her time reading, going to restaurants with Zack or other friends, and watching movies on her mom's VCR. She lived on the second floor, had her own balcony and stairwell, and a swimming pool with snorkel, mask, and fins. What else could she ask for?

"Did you know that I've had these sneakers since 1983?" said Zack. He picked up his leather Nikes and tapped them upside down, trying to get the sand out. "They're my buddies. My pals."

"You're a fascinating man, Zack McCloskey. One might even say brilliant."

Zack thought for a moment, then nodded. "This is true." He continued to stare at her, because of her eyes. Her irises were amber, and because she had taken off her sunglasses, her pupils had shrunk to tiny black dots in the center, showing the crystalline radii inside, like topaz.

"Why are you looking at me like that?" asked Isabelle.

"Nothing," he said. He stretched his legs out and wiggled his toes, leaned back on his arms, and looked in the direction of the beach house. "Mayday, Mayday," he said, in a low voice. "Aunt and midlife crisis at ten o'clock."

Isabelle tied her bikini strings, sat up, and put her sunglasses on. Roberta and Tim were coming toward them, carrying towels, Tim carefully holding a drink. They walked up without saying anything, until their shadows stretched over Isabelle and Zack.

"We just came down here to watch you two make love," said Tim.

Roberta slapped his shoulder with the back of her hand, and shook her head. "His idea of humor." She spread out her towel and took off her robe. She wore a black one-piece; her body was muscular and slim. Zack shaded his eyes from the sun, holding his calloused hand above him, and watched Roberta. I bet she's a volcano in the sack, he thought. And I gotta lotta lava love locked up inside me.

Roberta pushed her long black hair off her shoulders and said, "I love the ocean. It reminds me of Marlon Brando in *Mutiny on the Bounty*."

"I'm going for a swim," said Isabelle. She stood up and pinched her bathing-suit bottom, pulling it into place.

"Watch out for sting rays," said Tim. "Step on one of those babies and they jab their tail right into you." He took a sip of his drink. "Then you ride twenty miles screaming to the hospital with that barb in your leg."

Isabelle took off her sunglasses and tucked them into her towel. "I'll keep my eyes peeled," she said, then walked toward the water.

"And don't forget," said Roberta. "Most shark attacks occur in three feet of water."

But instead of going into the water, Isabelle walked down the beach. The sun was low in the sky behind her, its light faintly orange on the whitecaps of the waves. She watched seagulls catching wind and hovering in it, watched them as they glided to the sand, with their beady black eyes and their spread webbed feet. She walked in the shallows, where flecks of floating sea foam cast shadows on the brown sand beneath. After about a mile, she came upon a sea turtle stranded at the end of the waves. It was motionless, and its eyes were closed. The shell had a heavy ridge down the center, and a fluid pattern of hexagrams flowed out to the sides. She sat and watched it for several minutes, until Zack came up behind her. She waved to him to kneel down, not to scare it, and put one finger on her lips. "Shhhh," she whispered. "It's sleeping."

They sat quietly, and Isabelle softly told Zack that sea turtles lived incredibly long lives, over two hundred years maybe, and this one had probably swum thousands of miles to get there and was probably bushed. Didn't it look like a dinosaur or something?

"I think he's dead," said Zack. "He's not moving."

"He's not dead. He's just sleeping, isn't he?"

"I don't know. Seems pretty comatose to me." Zack reached over and touched the shell with one finger. When it didn't respond, he moved closer and pushed the turtle, rocking it. "Wake up, Mr. Turtle. Time to go to work."

They both sat there for a moment on their haunches, looking at the dead turtle. "I wonder if we could perform mouth-to-mouth resuscitation on it," said Zack. "I heard of someone doing it to an iguana once."

"This is terrible," said Isabelle. "Doesn't he just look like he's asleep? Couldn't he just be taking a nap?"

"I don't think so."

Isabelle didn't speak when they walked down the beach. Zack put his arm around her and kissed her temple, shook her a little bit to try to get her to look at him, but she wouldn't take her eyes off the sand. She concentrated on following their line of footprints, paralleling the crisscross tread of a Jeep that had driven by after them. Roberta and Tim were gone. The flock of curlews was still near the spot of beach where their towels lay, picking at the shoreline, while seagulls floated smoothly on the currents of hazy air above the salt grass, which grew like thinning hair upon the dunes.

◆

They ate at Captain Billy's, the same dockside seafood restaurant that Isabelle had been going to since she was fourteen, when her Aunt Roberta had first bought the beach house. Its sign was a huge facade of a sailing ship, with the name Captain Billy's written across the bow, with clumsily painted blue and white waves splashing up at the waterline, and dolphins jumping out of the curly plywood sea.

The wind had come up during the evening. Isabelle and Zack sat on the back deck area, where colorful, triangular flags upon the railing popped in the stiff breeze. The sailboat docks of Mustang Island were behind them, and the light along the docks and on buoys glittered and wiggled in wavy lines across the water. A huge butterscotch moon hung low on the horizon. Ropey brown nets with green glass balls were stretched across the back wall of the restaurant, and seashell wind chimes clonked heavily in the wind. Isabelle made Zack promise not to order shrimp, because the nets killed the turtle. He couldn't use Heinz ketchup either, because Heinz owned Starkist, and Starkist was one of the main killers of all the dolphins caught in the tuna nets of the Pacific.

Zack looked lost for a moment, staring at the laminated menu spread before him. "Jeez," he said. "I hope the french fry and cole slaw companies didn't do anything wrong."

"This is serious, Zack. I think you need to become more environmentally aware."

While they were eating, a sleek white cabin cruiser pulled up to the dock, with Roberta at the helm, and after Tim tied it off, they walked up to Isabelle and Zack's table. "Mind if we join you?" asked Roberta. "We're being horrible bores, but we can't help it. You know how I love their snapper, Izzy."

"I think they're mad at us," said Tim.

Isabelle said that was all wrong. They weren't mad, and yes, of course they could join them for dinner. "Only you can't order shrimp or use ketchup."

"Great," said Tim. "Is that so we can look crustaceans in the eye without feeling guilty?"

"I wouldn't use ketchup anyway," said Roberta. She lit a menthol cigarette and blew an icy blue cloud of it into the air. "It's low-class."

"I think we need a drink," said Tim. "To loosen up our bones. Hear this?" He flapped his hand above the table, wagging it back and forth from the wrist. "Hear that rattle?"

"Like a duck chewing dominoes," said Zack.

"That's the spirit. A couple more drinks and maybe you'll come up with something original."

"Timothy. Precious. Would you try to be sweet, for once?"

Tim was wearing a pink polo shirt and khaki shorts. His tanned jaw and chin looked clean-shaven and braced with aftershave, but the rest of his face sagged, his lower eyelids drooping to reveal a rim of red skin and inflamed capillaries in his eyes. The grooves around his mouth and nose were as deep as battle scars. He looked around in an exaggerated manner at the other tables on the deck and said, "Where's our waiter? Where's our food? I'm starving."

"We haven't ordered yet," said Roberta. "Would you cool it?"

He stared at her for a moment, breathing heavily. A dense purple fog filled the air in front of his face. He tried to think his way through it. Whistlestop Whistlestop. *I knew a man Bojangles and he'd dance for you. For drinks and beers.* Lord hold on here the deck is spinning, spinning. Turn the music up I know that song. *Silver hair and baggy pants and something something. His dog up and died. Up and died.* Tim burped loudly. He rubbed his eyes with his thick, squarish fingers. His face turned a deep red. "I don't feel so hot," he said.

Roberta stood up and took her purse off the back of her chair. "Tim, I think you need to go home."

"Thatsa good idea," he mumbled, and tried to stand up, but staggered, brushing his hand across his face as if he'd walked into a cobweb, then he lurched, one meaty arm jolting the woman sitting behind him, and grabbing the tablecloth, he fell backwards, overturning the drinks and knocking plates and silverware onto the wooden floor, scattering a wicker basket of plastic-wrapped Melba Toast crackers across his chest. Someone cursed for a moment, then everyone whispered as Zack and Roberta got out of their seats, and Isabelle watched, stunned, as a spilled glass of iced tea dripped onto her white dress.

"Tim? Are you okay?" asked Roberta. He started retching weakly. His legs were tangled in the chair. A waitress came up and struggled to move the table back and free him from it, but the people at the table next to them were staring and slow to scoot back. A busboy squatted beside Tim and Roberta and said, "Hey, man, what's going on?"

A few of the other diners stood to get a better view of Tim's body, but no one got up to help. Roberta told the busboy to call 911 and held her hand against Tim's forehead. "I think he just had too much to drink," said Zack. Isabelle noticed the glass windows of the inner dining room were full of staring faces, their lips moving without sound. For a moment all she could hear was the sickening sound of Tim's retching. As they waited for the ambulance, the waiters brought out food to the other tables. "How are we supposed to eat?" someone asked. After a moment, they heard the sound of a siren wailing. A vein bulged down the middle of Tim's livid forehead as he breathed roughly, his chest heaving. "I think you better go on the wagon, buster," said Roberta. The ambulance people arrived and loaded him onto a stretcher, having to move the tables out of the way to make space. As he was being carried away, Tim said, "Where's Isabelle? Isabelle, are you there? I want to marry Isabelle." Some of the other diners laughed and clapped.

Isabelle, Zack, and Roberta drove home to the beach house. Roberta apologized the whole way, insisting that nothing like that had ever happened to her before, that it had been possibly the most humiliating episode in her life. She knew they must think she's a terrible person to associate with drunkards and dissolutes like that Tim person.

"It's not your fault," said Zack. "You didn't make him drink. We're all responsible for our own actions here."

"Exactly," said Isabelle.

They turned on the ten o'clock news in time for the weather and sports. Roberta called the hospital and was told that Tim was already asleep, and tomorrow morning they were going to run some tests on him. Isabelle sank back into the soft cushions of the living room couch. "What a catastrophe," she said. "I hope he doesn't die or anything. He looked awful."

"We'll visit him in the morning," said Roberta. She opened the refrigerator door and brushed against Zack as she looked in. The beautiful thing about men is they all want the same thing, she thought. At least the ones that are worth their salt. If salt is the right word. Maybe not. Maybe sweat. Izzy has no idea who she's playing with. This ape

will scream and throw his bowl at the bars by the time I'm finished
with him. Sorry, Charlie. Starkist want tuna that taste good, not tuna
with good taste. Roberta pushed her hair out of her face, making it
stand stiffly away from her forehead and temples, and yawned. "I know
this doesn't sound appropriate, but I need a drink after that."

"Me, too," said Zack.

Isabelle closed her eyes and sighed. "I feel like I've been hit by a
truck," she said. Her skin was deliciously warm from sunburn, and still
smelled of Noxzema. By the time the late show started, she was asleep.

Roberta and Zack finished a bottle of Stolichnaya they found in
the freezer and started in on the Cutty Sark. They leaned close to each
other when talking, to keep from waking Isabelle. Zack chipped at the
bag of ice with a butter knife and Roberta said, "Shhhh," softly, putting her hand on his waist. "Let's go outside to look at the moon," she
whispered.

They held hands as they left the house and passed through the
deep sand to the sea. The wind blew in off the waves. Zack stood
behind Roberta and cupped her breasts. Her hair, whipped by the
wind, wrapped his head in a black cocoon.

◆

Later, Isabelle woke and sat up on the couch. She pushed her hair out
of her face and blinked, trying to remember everything. The TV screen
hissed. The lights were still on in the kitchen, but someone had turned
off the lamps in the living room and had put a blanket around her. The
hallway to the bedrooms was dark. She stood up and walked dreami-
ly—barefoot, in her strapless white calf-length dress—to the sliding
glass doors, which were closed, with a swatch of batik curtain caught
in the crack.

She slid the door open and stepped onto the wooden deck. The
wind had died and she could hear the waves. She left the deck and
walked through the deep cool sand to the beach, thinking about Zack,

what she felt for him. She knew this: she knew that sometimes she couldn't help but smile when he was around; she knew she told her old friends, who lived in other cities, all about him, and insisted they had to meet him; she knew the sudden feeling of recognizing his voice on the answering machine, the way he would start talking without saying Hi or who he was, and how she would rewind the tape and listen to his message a second time, just to hear his sound again. If this wasn't love, what did the word mean?

The moon was high, full and white in the sky, its light shining on the waves. Suddenly Isabelle noticed, in the damp sand near the wave's end, scrape marks on the beach, as if they had been dug by some heavy creature scrabbling in the sand. She realized it must have been a sea turtle, a beautiful sea turtle dragging its heavy armored body up the beach to lay its eggs, and she stood there, smiling, digging her toes into the cold wet sand, wanting to find Zack, wake him and tell him, *Look. I tried to tell you earlier but I couldn't say it, couldn't find the words. But look at this, look all around you. The world is really a beautiful, beautiful place.*

THE ATMOSPHERE OF
VIENNA

WHAT HE BROUGHT HER TODAY was the face of the moon. He explained that the dark patches resembling eyes and nose are not craters but areas of blacker rock, compared to the whiter mountains, and these dark patches have names, like the Sea of Rains, the Sea of Clouds, and the Ocean of Storms. Apollo XI touched down in the Sea of Tranquility. But Vienna didn't seem to be paying attention. She stared into the sky—a yogurt white, bruised blue around the edges—and wondered if her class would have a Japanese vocabulary quiz on Friday. What did she care about the moon? After all, she was only twelve years old, and Michael Bering was what, thirty-two? Thirty-two! Her principal was younger than that.

Vienna and Michael sat on a slatted bench, near a slide and swings, and behind them, a flock of Canada geese preened themselves on a knoll. Gray tombstones and a black, spiked iron fence lined one side of the park. Michael hobbled out there every afternoon so that Vienna could sign another name on his cast as she stopped by on her way home from Montessori school. Every day he brought her something worth knowing, because he was afraid they were brainwashing her.

For instance, after a recent photo safari to Africa, he'd told her about dwarf mongoose, forest bushbucks, and Goliath herons. He explained how lions often rest in trees, to hide from biting flies and elephants; how when a lioness is in estrus, she mates every fifteen minutes for a period of ten days; how a baboon's canines are as large as a leopard's; how a single flock of flamingoes at the Ngorongoro Crater in Tanzania can number half a million and fill the sky with a brilliant pink cloud; how a Thomson's gazelle can run seventy kilometers an hour; tickbirds drink giraffe's saliva; and the scaly anteater or pangolin is extremely rare. Africans believe if you see a pangolin, you will be rich and have many children.

He brought her something every day because he loved her more than water and Oreos, he told her. More than ketchup and comets. "I wonder if you and Krista would get along," she said. Krista, her mother, was divorced, and Vienna had told Michael she thought her mom was "looking for a mate."

Vienna's eyes and hair were both pecan pie brown, with her hair cut in what she called "an Egyptian." Her arms and legs were thin, she was taller than most of the sixth-grade boys, and she had a small birthmark on her cheek. Michael said he thought it was bigger than usual today.

"Krista says I should have it surgically removed. But what *I* want is a tattoo."

"Over my dead body," said Michael.

He and Vienna had met in September on a windy day in the park. It was right after Michael had broken his leg and had to take a sabbatical from Bell Labs, where he was a research physicist. He'd been hit by a taxi, although it was really his fault, since he explained that he had walked right into traffic—"Stupid me"— and the taxi just happened to be there, providing transportation. In telling the story, he'd zoom with his face and pantomime being knocked down, grabbing his leg in vivific agony.

Vienna sometimes walked home through MacArthur Park, and found fifty-nine dollars there the day before she met Michael, unmarked fives and ones. How did she know they were unmarked? She didn't, but she liked the sound of it: unmarked. They had been in a wallet underneath the slatted wooden bench she sat on now, that was polka-dotted with old pigeon droppings.

She promptly took the wallet home that day and put it in her sock drawer. But two hours later, in the middle of watching her favorite Gary Cooper—the one where he belts the snobby poets—for the umpteenth time, she gave a shout, ran upstairs, and yanked the wallet out of her drawer to inspect it. She had suddenly feared that maybe a slug had been hidden somewhere and was now crawling around in her socks. You could never be too sure. Vienna believed the world was in danger of being taken over by slugs. At night she saw their slimy trails across the front door and the welcome mat of their house. Vienna hated slugs more than anything in the world. Slugs! Just the thought of them made her sick. She brushed her hair in front of the mirror and thought of things she loved: aquariums, igloos, wooden back-scratchers, shoe trees, weather. Especially the weather. Like tornadoes and gales.

◆

The next day she walked by the bench and met Michael, the wind blowing his hair in his face. "What is this?" he asked. "A hurricane?"

She wondered if he were from the FBI. Is fifty-nine dollars a felony? "No way," she said. "Hurricane season is over." They became pals. That's when he first learned about Krista, her mother, the Heartbreaker. "She's a bigwig in her office at Manny Hanny. The phone never stops ringing, all for her."

"I'm jealous," said Michael.

"Me, too."

He held her hand as they shared a taxi home, his yellow pine crutches on the floorboards. She thought it was weird, but went with the flow. He liked to hold people's hands, and didn't see anything wrong with it. What's wrong with two people touching each other? he wondered. The world needs more physical contact. They stared out the window, at the tangled skies of New Jersey. "In the future," said Michael, "there won't be any poles or power lines visible on our streets, because all the phone lines and electricity will be either underground or passing through the air in microwaves."

"I don't know if I like that," said Vienna. Her palm was sweaty. She pulled her hand away and wiped it on her skirt. "I bet you can feel it, somewhere. Like in your follicles or something."

Three weeks had passed, and now Michael saw Vienna almost every day. He was beginning to daydream about her. He imagined what she would say each time he brought her something special, like the Japanese poem about cranes, the wildlife of Africa, or the face of the moon. She was so open! She didn't seem to have her mind made up about everything. Michael liked that, the same way he liked his work at the laboratory—the ammonia smell of the white tile floors, the distorted reflections in all the stainless steel, the hum and whir of big science in the works. The way he liked his colleagues, like Stuart Tearme, who wrote science fiction novels in his spare time and did a column for *Cryptozoology* magazine; Oki Yumiko, who set aside five waking hours of each day for total silence; Trudy Singer, who wrote him sexually confessional letters and passed them via her home modem to his computer screen. The way he enjoyed his work on superconductivity, the superchilled vials of liquid nitrogen, the idea of electricity without resistance. Michael reasoned that Vienna had joined these things as an element of his life. But his secret, private dream—his version of finding a planet with nine moons and a pale green sky—was the waterbike.

Already there were some working models of the waterbike, but it needed fine-tuning. It was a bicycle mounted on pontoons, with the pedals turning a crank connected to a propeller in the water below, which drove the machine forward. Below the pontoons, in the water, were the blades of a hydrofoil, and when the waterbike gained enough speed, it would rise up in the water, lifting the pontoons above the surface and reducing their drag, which made it faster and easier to pedal.

Michael believed the waterbike would change the world. He envisioned thousands of commuters lined up on the shores of New Jersey, all mounting waterbikes and pedaling across the Hudson to their jobs in the city, avoiding the diesel fumes of buses and sooty murk of the Port Authority. Thousands of men and women, pedaling across the river and into the maelstrom, waves splashing onto their black leather shoes, lemon yellow ties waving in the wind. A better world! And the waterbike was just a first step, of course. He had a genetic engineering friend who dreamed of designing the chromosomes for winged humans.

But his hero and role model in his obsession with the waterbike was Chester Carlson, inventor of the photocopier, also a former employee of Bell Labs and graduate of Cal Tech. He had patented his idea in 1936, but no one believed in him or would back the project; he offered it to IBM, but they turned him down, saying it had "no future." For months he experimented with photoconductivity, using burned sulfur, and the halls of his apartment building smelled like rotten eggs. He discovered that the element selenium holds an electrical charge, but only in the dark, and that when light is shined on a charged piece of selenium, the dark parts alone hold the charge.

He kept at it, through the many drums of dry ink, the first photocopy on a piece of wax paper, rough prototypes like the Ox Box, which was made up of three different machines—until 1960, when the Haloid Xerox 914 was finally perfected. What did it matter that Chester Carlson became a millionaire from his invention, or that he later became fascinated by poltergeists and séances? He changed the world. He improved it. That's what Michael wanted to do. But it wasn't until he met Vienna, when his leg was broken, that he felt something was wrong. Even Chester Carlson had been married. Twice.

◆

Soon they began to plot how to get Krista to fall in love with him so that they could become a family and never be apart. Michael was always a little hazy on the matchmaking part of the story, and tended to skip over that to the more important aspect of what kind of honeymoon they would have. Vienna would, of course, join them. They would travel, most likely all around the world, because there's so much to see and you never know when you might just drop dead tomorrow. First, Mexico. Michael said he knew of a secret, beautiful village in the mountains of Oaxaca that would sweep Vienna away. Tell me about the village, she said. Is it hot and dusty, or what? Michael described the narrow streets, where orange peels and corn husks littered the slate gray cobblestones, how the sidewalks were smooth and swept, faintly revealing the faded rose and ocher shades of old tile, worn by barefoot peasants, how the orphans slept outside the wrought iron gates of the hotel at night and begged to run errands for nothing in pesos, how the courtyards of the white plastered colonial posada were filled with shadows and pichicatas, a brilliant fuchsia-colored flower, how the fog at night drifted down like a slow-motion waterfall over the red tile roofs held in place by stones, and how the cathedral bells could be heard from anywhere in the village, and only the black-winged grackles in the ceiba trees in the zocalo competed in sound. It was a spiritual place. Michael thought it would be a good idea if all three of them went to church and tried their hand at praying.

"I've never been baptized," said Vienna. "Can you believe that? Someone asked me the other day what religion I was and I panicked. Told them I was Lutheran." She crossed her legs, and leaned dramatically against the back of the park bench. "God, I wish I had a cigarette."

◆

Michael dreamed one night he was watching Vienna get dressed, except she really didn't look like herself. In the dream, she had curly black hair, moon-white skin, and full breasts. In the dream, he was sitting on a chair beside his bed, while Vienna was actually in the bed, with her legs crossed. It was windy and rainy outside, and tree branches scratched against the bedroom window. Michael kept asking her where she was going, but she wouldn't answer. She picked up a black bra and put it around her waist, backwards. She fastened the clips. As he watched, she twisted it around her ribs until the snap was in the back, and wriggled into the cups and straps, not looking at him. It was as if he were watching her from a distance.

All morning he felt slightly shocked and guilty. He shook his head as he drank his morning's coffee, wondering where *that* came from, absentmindedly staring at his leg cast with all the names Vienna had decorated on it in the last few weeks: Natasha Badonov, "Natalya" in quotes, Oona O'Neill, Crazy Jane, Debbie the Ridiculous, Juanita Dark, Michael Jordan, Albert Einstein, and William Shatner. All in different color felt-tip pens with precise doodles, like purple hearts, blue stars.

The next time they met, Michael tried to be especially funny. "I like this park because of the cake in the rain, the sweet green icing flowing down."

"Say what? Are you speaking English? Or Japanese? You know *domo arigato?* That means 'thank you,' in Japanese. In a few years we'll all be speaking Japanese, because they're going to become our rulers." Vienna scratched the back of her knee self-consciously as Michael smiled at her.

"That's probably true. Notice how many people sleep on futons? And all those sushi bars? Next thing you know, our coffee tables will be four inches high."

"You be Michael san. Me Vienna san."

"*Hai.*"

Vienna squirmed on the bench, slouched, then put her hands beneath her legs. She wished he'd quit looking at her like that.

"I told my mother about you and she says she's not interested. She says there's no room in her life for another man. She has enough men, she says. She needs more time, is what she needs, she says."

"Don't we all."

"All what?"

"Need more time."

Vienna bent over and grabbed a handful of maple leaves, then started slowly ripping them apart. She had no idea what he was talking about.

"This is just like that movie with Jack Lemmon and that blonde actress," said Michael. "What's her name? I don't know. She was famous in an obscure way. But he's a documentary film maker, and he meets this girl in Central Park named Gladys Porter. And she starts renting billboards all over the city advertising her name, Gladys Porter. And Peter Lawford is this millionaire playboy after her, remember that one?"

"Never seen it."

"Oh, yeah. I forgot. You're only twelve years old. You haven't seen anything."

"I have too! I've seen *Alien* nine times. We have the tape. I hate it when that thing comes out of his stomach. Double retch."

They made more honeymoon plans, even though Michael struggled to shake a secret hopelessness, a feeling he was making plans never to be realized, as if he were drawing up patent designs for absurd machines never to be built. This time they chose Spain and Greece. Vienna hated the cold weather, except for snow. Tell me about it again, she said in November, tell me about how hot it is. In Greece, said Michael, the people paint their houses bright white, a whitewash, but doors and wooden window frames and shutters are painted blue as gel toothpaste or brown as peanut butter. Everything has dignity in the islands of Greece. Even wooden shutters are beautiful in the pure sunlight, light so bright it hurts your eyes in midday, and you have to hide from it by sitting in little outdoor cafés. And in the shade, the flagstones of the cafés are cool and feel good if you slip your feet out of your sandals and rub them on the stones. Brightly painted fishing boats are moored in the harbor, and squiggly lines of light bounce off the sea and curl about the hulls of the wooden boats or the stone embankments of the harbor. Cats fill the streets. Cats eat fish heads in shadows of the harbor, or sleep curled up on the check-in counter of your hotel or pension, licking themselves clean on the register, and the clerk shrugs when you go to sign in, as if to say, What can I do?

"I want to pet that cat," said Vienna. "I'd let him sleep there, too. I want to rub my bare feet on those stones and go out with fishermen in one of those pretty boats, while you and Krista visit all the little shops in the village, buying neat things, all for me."

◆

Michael had no one to talk to about Vienna. His mother lived alone in Orlando, but he certainly couldn't tell her, although she phoned almost every week. She was worried about her "genius son," as she called him. After Michael's father died, she planted palm trees for his soul, and in the wind and rain of what passed for winter there, she liked to think that her husband's soul was planted in her front yard, waving lustrous green fronds at her through the window. She worried that Michael would never marry and have children to worry about, or a wife to mourn for.

Michael's mother had been overprotective ever since his brother Matthew died of wasp stings, twenty-four years ago. Michael was nine then, and Matt only seven. He'd been playing in the pine woods behind their house and had stumbled into a giant nest of yellow jackets, where he was stung 341 times, everywhere, in his nostrils, ears, tongue, between his fingers. At the hospital, they sat beside Matt's bed, and Michael held his mother's hand. Matt had an IV hooked into his arm. They sat quietly, the three of them, their mother stroking Matt's forehead, as he, in a small, faraway voice, said he hoped this wasn't going to put off their vacation plans for Michigan, because he really wanted to see Lake Superior. He recited vocabulary words and multiplication tables, his voice growing fainter and fainter, nine times nine is eighty-one, six times seven is forty-two, three times eight is twenty-four, nine times twelve is, nine times six is, forty-three? Thirty-nine?

And as he quit speaking and slumped upon his pillow, their mother squeezed Michael's hand harder, as if that would stop her other son's life from evaporating, while Michael continued the progression of Matt's multiplication tables, and had reached the square root of 289, seventeen, when he began to cry.

Now she was concerned about his lack of faith; as far as she could tell, he believed in nothing. What kind of person didn't believe in anything? Was her son a heathen? She called after he broke his leg, and asked lots of questions. Did he have trouble concentrating? Was he prone to violent mood swings? Did he often give evasive answers to questions about his life to his loved ones? After questioning her motives, Michael found out this was a magazine drug abuse quiz.

"You're not smoking crack, are you, Michael? Tell me you're not. Oh, please Lord, that's the last thing I need."

"You've really flipped, Mom. You're totally ridiculous. You know that, don't you?"

"I just worry about you, darling. You never tell me what you do with your life. You never tell me about your job."

"It's too complicated, Mom."

"What about children, Michael? Don't you want a family?"

He sighed. "You know, I was thinking of adopting a highway."

◆

He called Vienna and Krista answered. He hung up. He called again later and got Vienna. Her voice was birdlike and full of energy. He was the first boy to ever call her, did he know that? What was he doing? Nothing? Nobody does nothing. You have to be doing something!

"I'm calling to tell you that the world won't be the same without you. I'm calling to tell you we're all going to miss you when you're gone."

"Michael." She was silent for a moment. "We who? Gone where? Speak English! *Domo arigato!*"

"*Hai.*"

She told him that Krista would be back soon, and that she wasn't sure if he was supposed to be calling. "I know," he said. "I should let you go."

On another day at the park, Michael brought Vienna an expensive coffee table book on meteorology, beautiful glossy photographs of funnel clouds in Kansas, lightning in Colorado, and rain in Sumatra. She held the big book in her small hands, thinking that she'd have to hide it from Krista because she'd kill if she found out, after what she said and everything. But Vienna turned the pages of the book and said, "Where'd you get this? I love photographs of rain. It must have cost a bundle."

Michael noticed she didn't hug him or kiss him on the cheek as she had done before, and wouldn't lift her face up from the page to look at him, to thank him. All he could stare at was the straight part of her fine brown hair, the strands, the roots, the scalp beneath.

◆

He didn't see her for several days, and when he did, it was only because he ran into her at the drugstore on Bergen Avenue, where she was shopping for a birthday card. She hated all of them because they were so uncool. "I've got something for you," he said, "but it's not with me."

"Michael? You can't keep buying me presents. Really. My mom doesn't want me to accept them. She's getting all weirded out about this." He nodded, leaning on his crutches in the shampoo aisle. "Sure. No big deal. It's nothing, really. Just a sheet of commemorative stamps. Sea mammals. Like killer whales and manatees."

"Oh, how sweet," she said, picking up a bottle of perfume and sniffing it. "But I never write any letters. Isn't that weird?"

He started calling every afternoon, and at first Vienna would talk to him, in her soft and high voice, but after a while he kept getting their machine. He was too afraid to leave a message. Finally, one night she answered and told him Krista said he shouldn't call her anymore. "Okay. Sure. Fine," he said. "I guess I'll see you at the park."

"I guess," she said.

Thirty minutes later, he called back. Krista answered. He told her who he was, and asked if he could take the two of them out to dinner Saturday night, that he'd always wanted to meet her. Krista said she would have to discuss it with Vienna, and could I call you back?

When she did, an hour later, Michael waited until the third ring to pick up, to learn that Friday would be fine.

◆

It was a Chinese restaurant: red booths, red tablecloths, small pagoda-shaped candles on the tables. On the walls hung bamboo scrolls of horses and birds. Vienna's mother held the door for Michael—"Thank you, I can't wait to get rid of these things"—as he swung his left leg forward, putting his weight on the crutches, and keeping his right leg, in its cast, slightly off the ground, his toes visible. "You're a lot faster than you used to be," said Vienna. As they waited for Michael to maneuver himself into the booth, Vienna told her mother how Michael's leg used to itch all the time, but he couldn't scratch it. Wouldn't that drive you crazy?

"Yes, it would," said Krista.

Michael was breathing hard by the time he got settled into the booth, his hair in his face again. Vienna propped his crutches against his seat and sat down. He refused to look at Krista. He saw only bits and pieces of her. Veiny hands. Fingernail polish. A string of pearls. She was feminine and pretty in a department store way, and he felt like he had muscular dystrophy, with his cast stretched out in the booth, compared to her.

As soon as they sat down, for some reason—too much coffee, nervousness—Michael's ears blushed a newborn pink. From the expressions on Vienna's and Krista's faces, he knew they thought there was something wrong with him. He pointed out a man across from them and said Doesn't he look like someone familiar? I swear to god I've seen him somewhere before. Eli Wallach! That's who it is! It must be him. When is that waitress coming back? The service isn't usually so slow here. What would Eli Wallach be doing in Weehawken? Maybe he grew up here. Do you want coffee? What are you going to have to eat? Am I talking too much?

"What are you going to eat?"

"Michael? You already asked that."

"Sorry."

"I feel so strange," he said. "Do you feel strange? Maybe it's something in the air, or in the food. Maybe I'm coming down with something."

Krista (who was she? where was she? he wouldn't look at her but felt her as some vague nebulousness in the booth across from him) said nothing. Vienna shrugged and said, "It's kind of hot in here, isn't it?"

They ordered. Soup came. Bowls of rice. Soy sauce. Michael stared at his chow mein and wondered why he'd ordered it. He never ate chow mein. How ridiculous. First thing he saw. "But don't you feel strange? Maybe it's just me."

Krista said something he didn't catch.

"What?"

She shook her head. "Never mind." She was thinking she really needed to have a talk with Vienna about strangers again. I mean it's one thing to be precocious and outgoing, and it's another to pick up nutty men at a public park. Is he really a physicist? How do I know? He might have invented the whole story. You never know. Really. He could be anyone.

Michael babbled. You remember Eli Wallach, don't you? He was in *The Good, the Bad, and the Ugly*. The one where Clint Eastwood turns him in to get the bounty money, then shoots the rope when they try to hang him, and they ride away. That great Civil War battle scene, where he makes Eli Wallach dig up the grave full of money? But of course it was all ridiculous and futile. What did he want with this businesswoman? Can she figure the price to earnings ratio of her daughter? And the hopelessness of his life struck him with such force that he put his chopsticks down and wiped his mouth with his white cloth napkin. No, he wasn't in *A Fist Full of Dollars*. You're thinking of Lee Van Cleef.

When the check came, Krista put out her Visa card.

"No," said Michael, "I want to get this."

He took out his wallet and reached for the check, but Krista had picked it up. "I'm the one who invited you two out."

"It's my treat," said Krista. "Besides, I'm sure Vienna owes you all kinds of favors from those presents you bought her."

"Well, I just did it because I wanted to."

"I didn't say you didn't."

As they waited for the waiter to come, Michael divided all the leftover rice on his plate into two equal sections, curved into the yin and yang symbol. Everything was suddenly different. What had he been thinking?

"I guess this means we're not having a big wedding, huh," said Vienna.

"It's a joke, Mom."

Krista nodded, keeping her eyes on the candle in the middle of the table. "Ha ha. Very funny."

Michael smiled and looked away from them, into the dining room. His fortune cookie was decorated with happy faces. It said the yellow sun is pink, when looked at through cupped fingers.

◆

In the weeks afterwards, his cast came off and he used a cane, but he moved so slowly pigeons didn't bother to fly away. They simply cooed and pecked the path around his feet. As he sat on the bench jotting equations in a small spiral notebook, figuring the water resistance on the waterbike's pontoons, trying to calculate which material would be best—a hollow fiberglass shell or aluminum half-shells, or perhaps the answer lay in some totally unheard of alloy, he suddenly realized the other park-goers must think him an oddball. So let them think. He didn't care. He only wished he could get Vienna back, or that he could bring her something she'd never seen before, like the braided rings of Saturn, or Io, the largest moon of Jupiter. But no matter what he brought her, he knew he could never change the time between them, the twenty years of wedge that constituted the space between their parallel lines, never allowing them to intersect.

It was lunchtime in a cold and bluish December—after he'd returned to work—when he last drove to Vienna's school. Snow was falling, and squeaked under his black rubber overshoes as he walked the sidewalk from his car to her playground, where she was out. Vienna ran toward him when he waved, then stopped at the black iron bars of the school fence. Her cheeks and nose were flushed faintly. She wore a dark wool jacket and silver hooped earrings. He lit a cigarette for her and let her take puffs through the bars of the fence, her lips touching the inside of his fingers where he held the cigarette in his right hand, so if anyone saw, they'd think it was his. Her bangs were long. They hung below her eyebrows, and she had to look through them, just so, to see him. She asked about the waterbike, about super-conductivity, if he'd made any quantum leaps since he got back.

A snow-removal machine whined down the street beside them, shooting flumes into the air, its amber warning light flashing, as more snowflakes kept falling, filling her hair, his eyes. Wasn't this storm fabulous? she asked. And Michael nodded yes, yes it was, looking up into the whiteness swirling toward them, and because he didn't know what else to say, he began explaining the relation of low pressure zones to the formation of snow crystals in the upper atmosphere. Miles above us, he said, the air is icy and thin.

WHY YOU?

THE FIRST TIME LOWELL LOST his memory was at sea. He and his wife, Barbara, had got the Landsbergs to drop them off their yacht on the other side of Isla Pajaro, in the Sea of Cortez north of Cabo San Lucas. They were to spend three days there on a survival weekend. In the cabin of the yacht, as Lowell was refilling an aluminum cylinder of white gas for the lightweight stove, Sylvia Landsberg said, "Lowell, you're fifty-eight years old. Isn't that survival enough for one life?"

He shook his head. "That proves absolutely nada."

Barbara laughed and put her arm around Lowell. "Listen to him trot out his español. Just like that Hemingway book, *The Old Man in The Sea*."

"That's *and* the sea, not *in*."

"You wait. If we spring a leak in that raft, it'll be *in*." She winked at Sylvia. When Lowell then tried to convince her steadfastly that everything would be fine if they just carried their own weight—and if they couldn't do that, why go on living?—Barbara laughed off his explanations and patted his cheek. Lowell was so wealthy he could afford to be pompous and eccentric now and then. He had made a killing in the cable TV business by starting some stations in Ohio when cable first became popular, and when he finally sold out to a conglomerate, the stations were worth more money than he had ever imagined. Now he did nothing, except spend his time sailing in Turkey, fly-fishing in British Columbia, and flying his twin-prop Cessna to visit his children and stepchildren; now and then he helped Barbara with fund-raising for one or another of her environmental causes.

Lately he had been on a survival kick.

This weekend he and Barbara planned to hike twenty-five miles across the hilly desert of Isla Pajaro in three days, moving approximately 8.3 miles per day, carrying forty-five-pound backpacks, and would rendezvous with the Landsbergs on the third evening, at a beach on the opposite side of the island. In the meantime, Sylvia and Aaron were going to watch for humpback and sperm whales. "Quietly," said Aaron, "while sipping piña coladas through a straw."

A coral reef guarded the windward side of Isla Pajaro, and since the Landsbergs couldn't get their yacht in close enough, Barbara and Lowell had to paddle an inflatable raft from the yacht to the beach. Lowell took charge of putting the raft in the water and arranging the gear, the orange rubber of the pontoons bright against the blue swells: dressed in his white polo shirt and khaki shorts, with his crisp captain's hat pulled snugly in place, he looked like Gavin McLeod on *The Love Boat.*

It took them over thirty minutes to paddle what had seemed like a short distance to the reef, but by then the yacht seemed abstract and toylike, while the sea was immediate and daunting. The most difficult part of the passage was near shore, when they came in close, buffeted by the waves, and had to pass through narrow and jagged barriers of rocks, black and gray stone pinnacles fluted by the wind and water, encrusted with barnacles. A head wind had picked up and was

working against them, blowing the crest of the waves into their faces
and making it hard to concentrate. The raft pitched and bucked. Barbara could have sworn she saw a barracuda in one of the waves. She
was soaked from the spray and cold—the overcast sky sucked all the
warmth out of them. Barbara tried not to think about what would happen if the raft ripped against one of the jagged rocks or the coral she
could see blooming like crusty orange flowers in the sea beneath them,
visible in the shallow troughs of the waves. The wind filled her ears
and made it difficult to hear Lowell. She shivered, salt spray dripped
from her nose, and the pinnacles of rock were so close that she could
smell the thick fishy odor of their moss. Then she noticed Lowell had
the queerest look on his face. He had stopped paddling. His oar wasn't
even in the water. Without his steering, the raft was turning sideways.

"What are you doing?" she yelled. "We're turning against the
waves!"

Lowell said something in a voice too meek to hear.

"Speak up!" she shouted. "I can't hear you!"

Lowell blinked and rubbed his face, as if the salt spray were cobwebs wrapping him in confusion. "Where are we?" he shouted. He
looked at the island in front of them, the jagged black rocks on either
side, the choppy sea stretching out in a straight and swell-heaved plain
behind them. "I have no idea what we're doing here."

For a moment Barbara was nonplused. "What do you mean? This
was *your* idea!"

"What *is* all this stuff?" he asked, pointing to the backpacks and
provisions in the raft beside him. She noticed how loosely he was
holding his paddle; it seemed as if it would fall out of his hands and
into the ocean any moment, and he wouldn't even reach for it.

Lowell started to cry. He was terrified. "We're going to be bashed
against those rocks," he sobbed. Barbara dug her paddle into the cold
water and refused to look at him. She was on her knees, leaning over
the starboard pontoon, the water inside the raft up to her thighs. The
packs were going to float away if they didn't do something about it.

"Bail!" she shouted. They were so close to the jagged pinnacles that when a wave pushed them near one, she leaned out with her paddle and shoved off, seeing conchs and crabs scuttling in the hairlike seaweed growing on the side of the rocks. The crashing sound of the surf was all she could hear. The raft turned sideways in the breaking waves, sometimes surfing in them, sometimes buckling dangerously, close to capsizing. There was no turning back now; she had to do it herself. Seagulls wheeled and called in the sky above the beach, some of them diving into the wave troughs to spear small fish.

After they passed between the black crags, the waves diminished. For a moment, the raft wobbled in an eddy of currents just inside the wave-break of the rocks. Lowell kept bailing with his hands. His face looked completely stricken, completely unLowell-like, as if he doubted the existence of the universe itself. A gray-headed herring gull hovered a few feet above, pink feet tucked against its feathered belly, at ease in the sky. Barbara's hair was soaked, plastered against her forehead, and still she had to fight the current, which was sucking them back in the eddy against the sharp, guano-splattered rocks. Once more she had to push off with her paddle, until a small wave came by, lifted them gently, and sent them toward the beach. As the wave broke its curl and descended into a foaming roil, Barbara felt the shallow sea floor through the raft bottom with her knees; they bumped and turned backwards, and clumsily, she managed to jump out of the raft, stand up in the waves, and drag the raft to shore by the guy lines looped across the top of the pontoons. Lowell got out and fell on his knees in the surf, stood up, and fell down again when hit by a wave, then finally managed to clamber up and help drag the raft farther up the shore.

Before opening them up, Barbara pulled the bags of gear farther onto the shore. For the most part everything was dry inside, especially the most important things—sleeping bags and clothes—and after looking through the packs, she found her pocket mirror and brush. Lowell sat on the beach, his back now somehow encrusted with dry sand, and stared at the sea. Barbara put a fresh coat of sunscreen on her face, donned her sunglasses, and touched her lips with Chapstick before she even thought about confronting him.

He had lost his captain's hat in the waves. Barbara stared at his bald head with its patch of hair on the sides, and found a spare baseball cap in his backpack. Things could have been worse. They had enough food and water, all the damp things would dry out soon enough, and with the maps and compass they shouldn't have any problem hiking to the other side of the island. She walked over to Lowell, who was now drawing circles in the sand, and said, "Put this on, so you don't bake." He didn't answer, but scratched his calf thoughtfully. When he didn't take the cap from her, she fitted it firmly atop his head and patted it in place. "How are you feeling?"

"I don't know," he said. "I just want to go home."

"What are you talking about? We're on an island, remember?"

"No. I don't. I can't seem to remember anything."

Barbara put one hand on his cheek and turned his face toward her. "Lowell, do you know who I am?"

He shook his head.

"And you don't know where we are?"

"No."

She sighed and considered their predicament. The beach was rocky and rough, littered with seaweed and jellyfish. The sun was straight overhead now, the sky had cleared, and they had plenty of daylight left. Behind them, leading away from the beach, the landscape was brown and dry. Pelicans and seagulls flew above the fields of cactus. A line of hills formed the crest of the island, and Barbara could see these in the distance, and knew from the topo maps they had that it was important they find the low pass to avoid hiking too high up. She would have to lead the way.

"I want to go home," said Lowell, drawing a large circle in the sand at his feet.

◆

They shouldered the heavy packs and hiked away from the beach, up a dry creek bed that Barbara identified from the elevation contour lines on the topo map, which led to a gap in the spine of hills that ran east-west across the island. Lowell hiked slowly and was clumsier than usual. Barbara explained to him that she was his wife, that they'd been married for seventeen years, that both of them had been married before. And that this was a survival weekend that could be dangerous if he didn't obey her.

"Don't waste any water, and be careful where you place your feet. We can't afford a broken ankle or snakebite."

Lowell nodded, his face gloomy as Barbara tightened the shoulder straps and waistbelt of his backpack for him, because he didn't seem to be able to figure it out.

They followed the dry creek bed for several hours, taking breaks every thirty minutes to rest. The path was full of gray limestone boulders, and many round, polished stones as large as a fist or a heart. Lizards sunned themselves on the rocks, and finches flitted through the still, warm air, flying to nests in the towering organ pipe and saguaro cactus. There were no trees, and the only plants beside the cactus were stiff, brittle, fan-shaped things that looked as if they should be growing on a coral reef. Barbara noticed Lowell was wincing with each step, and asked what was the matter.

"Blisters," he said.

After the sun set behind the hills, it became more difficult to see, the limestone boulders of the creek bed turned blue in the twilight, the cactus only visible as spiny silhouettes on either side of them, and with Lowell wincing at each step, Barbara pitched camp. She pumped the white gas stove and cooked a dinner of soup and freeze-dried spaghetti, while Lowell managed to put up the tent, after fooling with the poles for a long time. Barbara rigged up a small candle lantern for light, because there was little wood for a campfire. Lowell's feet felt better after she put moleskin and gauze on the blisters and fresh socks over that, and Barbara felt thankful when Lowell said, "You have a daughter named Misia, don't you?"

She smiled. "Yes. That's your stepdaughter."

He nodded. "And I have two daughters from my first marriage, Glenda and Jan."

The clouds that lingered through the afternoon had cleared off, and that night the moon, stars, and deep blackness of the sky started just inches above their head and belled out to infinity. The Milky Way was so enormous and dazzling they felt overwhelmed in its presence. Venus hung low and bright above the horizon, and Barbara and Lowell crouched, awed and a little frightened, under the immensity of this, of the huge ring of light around the moon, the craters stark and defined, and Barbara reminded Lowell of their life together, how they had met and married, his children and hers, what he had accomplished in his life. Little of it held any significance for Lowell, but Barbara startled him when she said, "We're rich, Lowell. We're in something like the top five percent of wealthiest people on the planet. Of course that's including China and Mexico and Africa, so when I say the *planet*, it's not that great an accomplishment."

◆

The next morning Lowell was even better, and insisted that Barbara let him cook their breakfast of tea, dried apricots, and instant oatmeal. They hiked steadily that afternoon, found the pass through the crest of hills, and that night, when they set up camp on the other side, with plenty of food and water left for the next day, Barbara felt much better. On the third day they reached the beach and saw the Landsbergs' yacht out beyond the waves, its sleek white prow bobbing in the blue sea, Sylvia signaling hello with two bright red flags.

This side of the island had a much deeper shoreline, so Barbara and Lowell waded out until the water was chest deep, and the Landsbergs idled up alongside, then put the ladder over the port side. As soon as Barbara clambered into the boat, dripping wet, Sylvia shouted

"You made it!" and held out a glass of champagne.

"Just barely!" said Barbara, and then began the process of telling the Landsbergs all about their brush with death, Lowell smiling sheepishly.

"For a while there I had no memory whatsoever," he admitted. "I remembered words and how to talk, but I didn't even know my name, much less Barbara's."

He later compared his experience to descriptions he had heard of the Bermuda Triangle, where pilots were lost in the skies, radioing back to Florida that their instruments made no sense, they didn't know which way was north, the sea looked funny. He remembered how they had recently found one of the most famous of the lost airplanes, one that had disappeared after World War II. It was discovered in the Everglades forty years later, the pilot's skeleton at the controls, still wearing his tattered flight jacket, turtles sunning themselves on the bleached wings that reached out from the small fuselage, the salt grass waving in the wind, sunlight gleaming off the water surrounding the rotten rubber wheels. Lowell remembered reading how that pilot had radioed air traffic control that he didn't know where he was, he was scared, the horizon looked odd, he was running out of fuel, he needed to land. Lowell knew the feeling. When he went to see Dr. Gaspard after they got back to San Diego, he told him it had happened suddenly. In the first moments, he felt as if gravity were pulling him down, pulling him into the sea; he had no notion of what had brought him up to that point in his life. He didn't know who the woman was paddling with him in this flimsy rubber raft near a jagged shoreline.

Barbara tried to laugh off the incident, but secretly she was worried it was Alzheimer's, which brought forth the closest emotion to terror she had known in her life. She imagined driving through the streets of Los Angeles late at night, searching for Lowell, who had wandered off and couldn't remember his name or home.

If he forgot who he was and lost his mind, would he still be Lowell?

When he spent the afternoon at the doctor's office, a beautiful twenty-three-year-old nurse took his blood and gave him an EKG. As she applied salve to the pale and loose skin of Lowell's chest, the nurse noticed with a pang of pity that he looked upset. "Are you okay?" she asked, putting one warm hand on his forehead.

"Fine," he said. What else could he say? That her beauty made him feel utterly and undeniably old?

◆

When all the tests came back, Dr. Gaspard called Lowell. He admitted he had no idea what caused the amnesia. "It might have been a ministroke, just kind of little blip in your brain, but there doesn't seem to be any damage." He warned Lowell to start being careful about his physical activity, not to overdo it. "No more survival weekends," he advised.

This explanation satisfied Barbara, but she noticed that as his memory returned, Lowell was not his normal self. He was more thoughtful and pensive. Once she found him in the garage looking at all his scuba gear—mask, tanks and fins, his belt of weights, and his exercycle. He looked at her, almost as if he were embarrassed, and asked, "What is all this junk?"

For some time after the survival weekend, Lowell moved slowly and deliberately. He had to search his mind every morning to find a reason to get out of bed. He enjoyed the warmth of the blankets, the plushness of his down pillow and down comforters, and felt no sense of guilt in lying there happy and warm. In these moments he looked at the ceiling, the soft shadows cast by the sunlight through the curtains, the dresser, the slatted doors of the closet. At first they seemed unfamiliar, but he perceived a certain economy and rightness to the room, and felt it was as it should be.

The rest of the house was another matter altogether. The living room disgusted him, especially one innocent and disingenuous object in it: a large, magenta ornamental vase, with a slim neck, wide mouth, and bulb-shaped body. It was sleek and glossy and had no function

whatsoever. It must have weighed sixty pounds. And what Lowell perceived to be the most ridiculous aspect of it was that in the useless vase
were arranged stalks of a large reed, and among these reeds were min-
gled peacock feathers. The vanity of this ornamental vase repulsed
Lowell. He even asked Barbara if she would mind if threw it out with
the garbage.

"Do what?"

"I hate that . . ." he pointed at the vase, trying to remember the
word for it, "that *thing*. And I want to get rid of it."

"Don't be silly," said Barbara. "We paid good money for that vase,
or *thing*, as you call it." She continued looking at him, and noticed
that the money argument had no effect. "Besides," she added, "I like
it."

The vase wasn't the only furnishing Lowell found repulsive. The
glass-topped coffee table seemed frigid and unfriendly. The leather
sofa immoral, too low, you were almost forced to recline when you
tried to sit in it; the dining room and den were filled with objects from
other countries that seemed homesick and lonely: porcelain masks
from Mexico, pottery from China, wooden shoes from Holland. Lowell wondered what kind of man he had been. He had more money than
he could use, so he traveled to foreign countries to decorate his living
room?

◆

More and more Lowell could not think of a single thing to say to Barbara. He caught himself making statements such as, "There's a forty
percent chance of rain today," or, "I like that sweater."

"This old thing," Barbara would say, pinching it between a thumb
and forefinger, shrugging. "I've worn it a million times." Then Lowell
would realize the emptiness of his remark and grow quieter still. To fill
the silence of their lives, he played symphonies and John Philip Sousa
marches.

Barbara was the kind of woman who skied in Aspen every winter and bought her daughter three-hundred-dollar gold earrings because she couldn't stop herself, yet who also felt a fierce obligation to the environment. At a fund-raiser in Denver, she once made a scene when a woman walked in wearing mink. She wrote congressmen and governors, and believed in conspiracies. She was fifty-seven years old, could hike faster than most women in their thirties, and had finished three marathons (with a personal best of 3:22). At the University of Michigan in 1951, she'd been considered a lollapalooza.

One of her recent projects had been raising money to save trees, to help college kids chain themselves to redwoods. Sometimes she even considered chaining herself to a redwood. She imagined being alone in a gloomy forest, the heavy chain and padlock tight against her chest, the rough bark at her back, the burly loggers waving hideously loud and gruesome chainsaws at her belly, a sky full of ravens visible through a crisscross of branches above.

Barbara and Lowell's grown children noticed this silence between their parents, and worried. Misia was Barbara's daughter from her first marriage, her only daughter, although she also had a son, Byron, the podiatrist. As a child, Misia had almost been too precious for her own good. She had ridden a silver tricycle with blue and white streamers fluttering from the plastic hand grips. Her hair had been fine and blonde, and Barbara marveled at the purity of her scalp, how the hairs emerged from the follicles so perfectly, and she kissed and stroked her daughter like a pet. Now Misia was a restaurant critic for *L.A. Zone* magazine, and chefs and restaurateurs feared and hated her. Barbara remembered once introducing a young environmentalist who was working with her on the EarthFirst! project to Misia. After he left the office, Barbara asked if Misia liked him, because she'd considered playing matchmaker. Misia tucked a flat band of hair behind one ear and considered this for a moment, tapping a pencil against her forehead. "No," she said. "He's too nice. I'd just chew him up and spit him out."

Lowell thought Misia was a beautiful mistake—lovely, but warped and spoiled. He seldom criticized her directly, but he felt there was a sort of ugly glee in her negative restaurant reviews, a pleasure in nastiness. He also never forgave her for the moment when she was still a young girl, at his and Barbara's wedding, when he had leaned down to kiss her cheek and she had jerked away, leaving him puckered in the air, foolish and exposed in front of a crowd of people.

For her part Misia secretly dedicated every negative review to Lowell, and if she'd been thinking of him before she went out for dinner, the restaurant didn't have a chance. When she realized Barbara and Lowell were having difficulties because of the amnesia, she pounced. Misia said if there was a divorce coming, she knew the right lawyer. "You've given him the best years of your life," she said, while they were having lunch at a small art deco café. Misia had ordered a chef's salad, and was picking out the black olives and celery, eating them, and leaving everything else. She avoided the tomatoes because they were part of the nightshade family, the same group that included poisonous toadstools, and they shared some of the same natural toxins.

Misia had said this halfway through lunch, and now Barbara stared guiltily at the half-eaten tomato wedge in her chicken salad. She had always assumed tomatoes were good for you. She wouldn't have wanted to confess it, but this was a basic assumption of her life. What is the nightshade family? Could you be tainted because you were *related* to something poisonous?

"You gave up everything for him," said Misia. "You quit your teaching job. You moved from Columbus, left all your old friends and connections behind, and now he's going to dump you, place you out on the curb for the garbage trucks on Tuesday." Misia sipped her Chardonnay. "You have nothing left."

Barbara nodded pensively, completely convinced her life was fractured and meaningless. "If only he could remember all the good times we used to have."

"I never noticed you guys having any fun," said Misia. "Lowell was *always* a grouch."

As they were figuring up the check, Barbara thought back to the latest argument between her and Lowell. They had been eating lunch on the porch of their Malibu beach house. It was a sunny day; the triangular flags that stretched above the balcony popped in the stiff wind. Barbara had been talking about her friend Lorenzo Camenetti, the chef at Platter Matter, and how he was afraid Misia was going to give him a bad review. "I think he's worried about nothing," said Barbara. "It's all histrionics. He's a Scorpio, you know."

Lowell was watching seagulls land on the railing at the opposite end of the porch, their wings cupping the wind, their feet splayed in front of them, behind Barbara, when this comment caught him. *He's a Scorpio, you know.* How absurd, he thought, and for the first time that morning, he actually contemplated this person—Barbara, his wife—sitting across from him. What a nut. Who am I married to, Nancy Reagan? What did being a Gemini or a Sagittarius say about anyone? Could distant galaxies decide my personality? Orbits make me moody? Violet moons make me frigid? Did the sun decide when I should marry? When divorce? When I should step off the edge of this flat world?

"That's the most ridiculous thing I've ever heard," he said. "It makes absolutely no sense whatsoever."

Barbara blinked and looked wounded. "What are you talking about?"

"That astrology business. It's crazy."

"Not that again." This wasn't the first time Lowell had nagged her about astrology. He was such an Aries. Barbara sighed and picked up an unused coffee spoon from her cloth napkin, placed the broad scoop of it against her right temple, and massaged herself with the cool metal. She had heard it was a good tension reliever. *I will never, ever, ever mention astrology around him again.*

◆

Lowell brooded. It took him forever to get anything done. He took over an hour to get dressed in the morning: he paused and considered each sock separately, each shoe, and eased his foot down his pants leg as if inside it there were land mines. Barbara wondered what happened to the man she loved. She tried to prompt his memory. "Remember our old apartment in Columbus? Remember how we used to sleep on the living room floor all the time, in front of the TV?" Lowell looked up for a moment, focused on the wall in front of him, then shook his head.

"I'm sorry. I just can't remember that far back."

He developed quirks, eccentricities. Often he would blurt something out as if they had been discussing it for hours, although Barbara knew that it was only Lowell discussing it in his mind, in his dark and vocal murkiness. One night during dinner, after not having said a word for most of the meal, Lowell put down his knife and fork, wiped his mouth with his napkin, and placed the fingertips of his hands together in a rhetorical arch. "I understand the inherent emotional advantage in marriage," he said. "That I can get. It's comforting to have someone near you, to stave off the fear of loneliness, the despair of being totally isolated on this sometimes hostile planet. *This* makes perfect sense, this coupling together for mutual affection, loyalty, and support."

Barbara continued eating her pasta salad, not paying much attention to this minilecture, since he had grown so fond of giving them lately.

"And I surmise this bond is what we mean by love, although I'm sure there must be more to it than that. But what I can't for the life of me understand," here he jabbed the table beside his plate with one index finger, "is how this choice is made. Barbara? Do you understand what I'm saying?"

She shook her head, keeping her chin high. "No. Not really."

"Okay, okay, I grant that it makes sense to love someone, but what I'm saying here is . . ." He sighed and looked at her directly. "Why you? Why, of all the thousands or hundreds of thousands of women I could possibly meet, have I chosen to spend my life with you?"

It was, of course, an innocent and philosophically based question, but Barbara took it personally. She flung her cup of Red Zinger tea in Lowell's face. He sat there blinking, the tea drops tumbling down his cheeks. She drove to Misia's house to cool off. There she admitted to her daughter, "The only thing keeping us together now is seventeen years of history, which Lowell doesn't even remember."

Misia frowned. "Have you considered hospitalization?"

◆

Later that evening Lowell found Barbara asleep on the leather sofa in the living room, the television glow illuminating half her face, lovely but troubled. Her cheek was pressed against the pillow, a crease between her brows, as if she were concentrating on a difficult equation of marriage minus love. With sudden clarity, Lowell remembered watching Barbara one spring in Ohio, over fifteen years ago, not long after she had divorced, they had married, and Misia was still a young girl. He remembered an image only. It must have been a custody weekend, because Misia was there, asleep on the sofa, with the blue-white television glow on her face, and Barbara slept with her arms around her daughter, ready to protect her against anything, ready to give up even Lowell, and he had admired and loved her for that fierceness, that blind loyalty. Here, the dim blue light softened Barbara's features, smoothed the wrinkles around her chin and along her neck, and aware that she was a woman who had more life behind her than ahead, Lowell was shaken by a gush of tenderness and melancholy. He struggled with his stiff knees to crouch in front of her on the floor, casting a shadow over her face, and lightly kissed her closed eyelids. She awoke with the warmth and dampness of his breath in her lashes.

◆

A year passed. One afternoon Barbara came home and found Lowell by the swimming pool in his diving outfit. With his wetsuit, mask, and fins he looked like a giant black cartoon duck, and she couldn't help but laugh. "I thought you'd given up diving?" she asked.

Lowell blushed, and as pool water streamed off his black neoprene wetsuit, the white hair above his ears stood out brightly against his pink skin. He sat down at the white wrought iron patio table and worked a squelching flipper off his right foot. "We need to get out more," he said. "Want to go diving off Catalina this weekend?"

"I'd love to," said Barbara. For a moment she wanted to hug him, but he seemed embarrassed about the whole thing, so she simply smiled and carried his flippers as they walked to the sliding glass doors of the pool house, and Lowell shyly watched his huge bony feet leave wet footprints on the pebbled concrete skirt of the pool.

That winter they spent two weeks diving off the Great Barrier Reef in Australia. For weeks afterward that's all they could talk about: the schools of emerald and turquoise fish, the brilliant fuchsia coral, the great white sharks.

Misia resigned herself to putting up with Lowell, her dining reviews took on almost a fairy-tale-like sweetness, and the chefs and restaurant owners of L.A. slept easier. In April, Barbara and Lowell visited his daughters Glenda and Jan in Miami, and from there, they decided to fly their private plane to the Caribbean. At the airport, the twin-engine Cessna sat on the runway, painted a glossy white with red pinstriping. The wide parallel lines of purple runway lights stretched to the north and east, and bands of the purple lights shimmered on the rain-slick tarmac.

"Will we reach the hotel in time for dinner?" asked Barbara.

"I don't see why not." Lowell checked his wrist watch. "We might be in Santo Domingo by eight o'clock."

They took off from the north runway at dusk, with a tailwind of twelve knots, and Barbara admired the view of Miami when they banked and turned to head south. She looked down on the streets of Miami below, the miniature houses and trees resembling a mock-up of some historical scene, like a diorama of some lost time in America. But infusing the city with life were the streaming red and white lights of the freeways and cloverleafs, the bluish haloes of light from mercury vapor lamps on the avenues, until they flew beyond all that and reached the dark blueness of the sea and the twinkling lights of the Keys. They climbed into a band of clouds, trying to get above the worst weather and stay at 20,000 feet all the way to Santo Domingo.

Barbara wondered if Misia would ever soften up, if she would ever marry and be happy. She was such a lovely woman. But so tough and imperious! Typical Leo. Maybe she could meet a nice Libra or Gemini to calm her down.

Lowell was mentally planning their itinerary on the island: *Check plane into hangar. Taxi to hotel. Shower and change. Maybe dinner afterward.*

As they climbed higher and higher into the wisps and rips of the dark gray clouds, the plane began to pitch and sway in the turbulence. Sometimes it felt as if they were plunging over a second or more before the wings caught the wind again, and they continued steadily upward, nothing but a misty grayness visible through the windshield. For fifteen minutes they flew this way, the same inscrutable cloudiness before them, and instead of breaking free into the late afternoon sunlight as Barbara had expected they would, the clouds changed color to white and misty, and she noticed by the altimeter that they weren't ascending anymore, were holding still at 12,000 feet. Lowell held the yoke stiffly.

"Why aren't we climbing?" asked Barbara.

She also noticed from the gyrocompass that it looked as if they were off course, heading SSW instead of SSE. Lowell's face was severe and frightened, fleshier, as if the heaviness of their fate were bearing down on him, pulling down the folds of his forehead, weighing his eye-brows, sagging his cheeks. Barbara stared at him and asked if he knew where he was or what he was doing. For several moments he didn't answer. Finally he said, "I don't know who we are or what we're doing here, but I know we're going to die."

When the sound of his voice ended, Barbara stared at the complex panel of circular gauges and instruments before her, trying to think fast, but all her thoughts collided upon themselves, and as she struggled to form a plan, the roar of the plane's engine grew louder and louder, reverberating off the narrow walls of air.

MOTEL ICE

S HE IS RIDING ON THE BUS the Continental Trailways the
Greyhound Americruiser the window seat for godsakes through
the whirling red fields of Oregon where the wind is always blowing,
blowing, and her sisters—two, Iselle and Lana, the weird sisters—are
near the back lurking, keeping an eye on her, keeping track of the bad
in her, always keeping an eye on her, always on watch, afraid she's
going to speak to a man, afraid she's in league with them, afraid they
might want to touch her (they do they do they do), zeroing in to keep
her in check. She is afraid of falling asleep. She is twenty-seven years
old and knows she shouldn't be afraid THERE IS NOTHING TO FEAR! THE
ONLY THING TO FEAR IS TO FEAR YOURSELF! But she is afraid of falling
asleep. She's been riding for seventeen hours now and hasn't slept in
almost two days in all that time she's riding from Portland to Kansas
City to save the souls the souls that can be saved the souls that will be
saved if they will only listen only she's unworthy she knows that Lana
knows that Iselle especially knows that but she thinks there's a chance

for redemption for hope for change. But she hasn't slept for so long now in all that time on the bus plus more not a wink things are getting weird.

She is afraid to sleep because she is afraid the boy next to her will grope her will put his hands with the warted knuckles beneath her sweater the hirsute hands with the fat blue wriggling veins will clutch and paw her will feel her will touch her his breath is just horrible what did he have for lunch an onion sandwich? but actually he's not bad looking you know if maybe he had a shower and a shave he might be okay. He wears a Notre Dame sweatshirt his hair is cut short and lies in creeping slivers down his nape brown on top and not unattractive actually.

She needs to keep her eye on the road.

The rocking of the bus on the highway in the highway crosswind blowing over the burning fields of Idaho and red moon rising through the smoke makes her queasy. The Notre Dame boy has been fighting fires in Idaho he's told her all about it he wants her to like him he's not all that bad really but she shouldn't fall asleep she should never fall asleep and she is getting so sleepy. The rocking of the bus stirs raises excites the hackles on the back of her neck. What are hackles anyway? she wonders. Are they those hairs on the nice boy's nape sitting next to her the one she wishes she fears she loathes to grope her if she falls asleep here on the bus in Idaho in Oregon where are we now? in Utah? a red moon rising through the forest fire smoke the fire jumpers coming all the way from Canada and beyond the Yukon even to fight the flames the devil's handiwork. Her eyes burn as she closes them and feels the rocking the moon is too much the red sky too lurid she wishes that boy would take his hand out from beneath her skirt her blouse she wishes her nipples weren't so hard it's not good to encourage this kind of behavior buses are not a place for this kind of behavior buses should be safe well dammit that's just not the truth.

As she pretends to sleep the college boy the Notre Dame boy Our Lady boy defiles her uses her thrills her disgusts her with his grubby backpacker fingernails his firefighter calluses his hot tamale breath his teeth caked with peanut butter cheese cracker gunk the orange gunk between his teeth breathing fast and shallow his tongue like an oyster an eel in her ear quick and wet. She is afraid to call out. She is afraid to make a scene. What will Iselle and Lana think? What would they say? He's not so bad really they might hurt him that would not do that won't do you just pretend this isn't happening she just pretends his hand isn't where it is all tight and rough she just pretends his tongue isn't in her ear loud as a mop trapped in an echo chamber. A sack full of otter. She just pretends to feel nothing as he marks her arm with his ballpoint pen as he marks her arm as he initials her with his tattoo name this ballpoint tattoo marking her a marked woman twenty-seven years of virginity and now defiled stained she covers this up she holds this in she quivers with fear and revulsion her teeth chatter as in the morning light the gray light of dawn now in Colorado on the road to Colorado she wakes the Notre Dame Our Lady boy gone the sky as gray as nests the sky the air as thick as cream her pride and glory gone what will Iselle and Lana do? What will they say? As the bus throbs and hums along Interstate 70 heading for Golden Colorado she shivers and quakes with the horror between her legs she rubs furiously at the smear of blood on the Trailways seat the wetness the blasphemy between her legs she rubs the spot out out damned spot but it will never leave will never fade her clothes her blue dress is smeared with a stain the shape of South America of Argentina O God of Brazil Iselle and Lana are not going to like this not one bit they are the brides of Christ she is the bride of Christ she will never be the same again. Christ will not does not will never love her now.

Iselle and Lana discover her loss her filth in Golden Colorado. The bus pulls in and pauses throbbing at a Mobil station the flying horse the Pegasus the sacrilege the pagan sign there before her as Iselle is there before her with her forehead wen and her wraparound sunglasses saying What's the matter, Mary? You've been sitting here so long don't you want to stretch your legs a rolling stone gathers no moss

sloth is a sin now look alive. She follows Iselle to the food mart counter where Iselle is buying Gatorade and cheese crackers complaining
This is not food there is nothing to eat in this hell and shaking her
head at the rows of Bic lighters of key chains of caps and bumper stick-
ers before she begins to stare. Mary? What's that on your dress? What's
that on your dress? My God. My God. She plucks at the cloth with her
fingers. My God girl what has happened to you? Mary shakes and quivers she hides her face. Don't turn away from me everything is Okay I'm
on your side Look at this Lana, something has happened to Mary we
have to help her something has happened to Mary. Iselle kneels down
to peer closer she puts her face in Mary's blood her stain her stigmata.
She touched herself Iselle whispers the clerk begins to stare as Mary
pulls away and tries to run She touched herself and she's punished now
she's ruined the girl our Mary is ruined HOW COULD YOU DO THIS WHAT
WERE YOU THINKING?

She backs against the fountain drink counter she stumbles against
the straws the thirty-two-ounce cups she wishes they would just go
away. They pull her elbows out of shape they stretch her elbows like
putty their fingers leaving dents in the flesh they pinch her the way
the Notre Dame boy pinched her hair as his hand squirmed inside her
as he probed her like a doctor dirty and gone berserk as his tongue
licked the shores of her ear and he whispered something nasty something unmentionable how could he have done such a thing? He
looked so nice yes he needed a bath but after all we're on a bus ride he
thought she was asleep well he certainly didn't seem to care one way
or the other they pull her into the women's bathroom the yellow bar
of soap on the white sink Take off your skirt we're going to clean you
but she'll never be clean she knows that doesn't she she'll never be
clean again. The bar of soap a yellow the color of fear of bananas of
fruit the passion fruit the waiter brings in bananas figs and hothouse
grapes the silent vertebrate in brown contracts and concentrates with-
draws Rachel nee Rabinovitch tears at the grapes with murderous
paws with murderous paws with yellow soap they soak her dress they

scrub they scrub We're not going to hurt you Mary we just want to help Don't baby her Lana she's ruined herself do you hear me in there ruined yourself now what do you have to say? What do you have to say?

There's nothing she can say there's nothing to say she has sinned and must be punished she has defiled herself! The body is a temple and she has defiled her temple. She crouches in the corner of the bathroom the floor sticky and unclean as her soul now filthy as her filthy soul but I didn't do it she thinks well it doesn't matter now she tries to speak Notre Dame she says they say Notre Dame What about Notre Dame? What about Our Lady? says Lana but Iselle stops scrubbing to shout her down You cannot speak the virgin's name you no longer deserve it! Don't be so rough with her Iselle it won't get you anywhere I don't care I feel the anger of the Lord Our Father in my veins.

Maybe that's it! cries Lana. Maybe it was our father in her veins our father's blood his sins have reawakened in her veins her blood is overheated overripe his demon soul is in her. Iselle looms above Mary her wristwatch near Mary's eyes telling the time the few moments she has here her soul swelling with a divine sangfroid as Iselle speaks more calmly now yet frightening more frightening even in its calm she speaks Maybe you're right Lana Maybe it is our father. Our human father. Our mortal father that man that lowly man. You are right I feel him in this room his evil with us impregnating defiling our Mary Our Lamb we must fight him.

What can we do? asks Lana. I thought we were rid of him.

We'll have to make a sacrifice says Iselle and she's right too Mary knows that she's right. It's time to get back on the bus heading east but they don't want to go We can't take her out like this There's a motel across the way Take our things off the bus Lana We'll stay the night We'll work things out bring a skirt for Mary from your bags We'll hide her shame no use telling the world I'll wait here for you Lana hurry now get going It's time to circle our ponies.

◆

Her eyes are pink from weeping her pure green eyes the color of envy
the color of money the color of her father's eyes You've got your
father's eyes her mother always said a complement she meant it as
their father was not always considered a curse that came later after
the fire after the swirling flames engulfed the curtains engulfed the
kitchen splayed skyward against the ceiling blackening the tiles there
him drunk and groggy on the living room sofa while mother rushed
to get them out of the house yanked them by the wrists and rushed
them out the door Just stay here now girls I have to go back in to get
your father get away from the house now you understand get as far
away as you can. Iselle and Lana older but sleepy and not understanding or understanding only vaguely what was going on recognizing unclearly the face of calamity the face of catastrophe as it patted
them on the cheek and said Don't worry now I'll be back in a sec the
yard the air above the yard the air surrounding the house filling with
the invisible smell of burning burning smoke seeping out the second
floor windows now a burst of flames orange and liquid fire and she is
there, framed by the doorway, backlit by the flames her face dark
against the brightness behind her, there is mother passing before the
doorway, disappearing into the orange and rippling glow of the house,
they stand amid the fire ants and the sidewalk cracks of the front
lawn watching for her to return watching for her life to surface watching for her dark form to reappear before the open door of orange
flames the house swirling now the tulips of flames blooming the petals
bursting open the crackle and crack the rush of hot wind Lana and
Iselle running toward the door but stopped by the heat the wind scattering confetti of glowing brands of ash about the yard a scream within their mother's scream another scream as the siren's wail grows
louder and drowns out the dying song the crippled cries the fire truck
barreling up the firemen massive and monstrous in their giant hats
and boots the heat now burning her face Iselle and Lana screaming It
was Papa Papa did it as the fireman tries to pull them away Get her
out She's in there Mama's in there Get her out Please! but no one

seems to listen they furiously connect the nozzle roll out the hoses spray the house of fire with nothing but steam.

◆

You've got your father's eyes they always said well maybe Iselle is right maybe their father is in her maybe the curse is in her on her now that she's defiled there must be retribution Lana in the bedroom of the motel praying Iselle reading the Bible quietly and planning what to do Mary doesn't even want to leave the room just stay here stay inside maybe no one will notice but she's so thirsty she needs something to drink there's a vending machine near the pool I'm going for a soft drink do you two want anything? she asks naturally. They look at her like the deaf leper spoke they look at her like the harlot she is they look at her like they see a black slime across her mouth eyes ears nose and throat. Ice says Iselle. Ice. Bring us ice.

She grabs a handful of coins and buys a Pepsi from the machine the can rocketing down a family of children frolicking in the pool a little boy splashing in the pool and laughing with his water wings and wet black hair You've got your father's eyes they always said her father who drank himself to sleep the night of fire He did it He killed her Iselle said afterwards she's not sure but Iselle is older is wiser is unforgiving and hard as the truth. She trusts no one she loved her mother she will never forgive her father Our Father who art not in heaven unhallowed be thy name.

She fills the plastic bucket with motel ice. What is this glamour this excitement this freshness of motel ice? The ice itself is common common enough frozen water white and wet and hard common as the moon the sea or light but special and holding that special promise of redemption release and forgiveness is this bucket of motel ice you have been defiled it can clean you you have been besmirched it can rinse you you have been sullied it can free you motel ice! Common and special, cold and ephemeral, ready to wet if you close it in your fist, ready to freeze a wound, ready to raise a scar.

She walks back to the motel room dodging shiny black crickets on the concrete path the concrete skirt before the door and parking lot the sky a violet early evening color such a beautiful world so much to see but she's got her father's eyes If the eye offends you pluck it out so much to do so far to go wondering where the Notre Dame boy is now with his callused knuckles and his onion tongue the traffic whining now along the Interstate I-70 eye seventy through Golden Colorado a gift he gave you he took something who did he think he was anyway stealing her bloom in the night-dark of the bus. Why do sinner's ways prosper and why does disappointment all I endeavor end? Carrying the ice back to the room entering there the whoosh of the door throb of the air conditioner Lana still on her knees in the hollows of belief Iselle filled with the wrath of God as she tells Mary what to do how to redeem You will triumph through pain she says There must be a sacrifice to cleanse your soul You can't go on like this you know that don't you?

She whispers to Mary the secret she whispers to Mary the key to redemption to forgiveness to the cleanliness. IF THE EYE OFFENDS YOU PLUCK IT OUT her figure lithe and cleft with hope and terrible fervor she grips Mary's hands squeezing the bones the tendons pinching them together The Lord is our shepherd we shall not want Mary says No, Iselle, I can't don't ask me to do that You must she says You must it is the only way to squelch your father's spirit his taint his curse on you But I can't Yes you can your soul has been smitten by his taint You've got your father's eyes she says you must free yourself You must be clean. But I can't do it myself you will have to help me. I will help you she says.

She wants to be clean. It is the only way. She knows Iselle is right. If the eye offends you. An eye for an eye. She must be cleansed.

I'll do it then Lana hold her down This isn't going to be easy but I'm going to save our Mary.

She squirms she writhes as Lana pins her down a spoon Iselle has a spoon she's holding a spoon You're not going to like this Mary but it's for your own good Don't talk about it just do it she says Beg god for mercy says Lana beg him for mercy we are being merciful in this our pain. Iselle slips the spoon into Mary's face she jerks away something wet on her cheek Hold her still Lana! cries Iselle she pins Mary harder Lana was always the strongest slow and meek but strong and weak beneath the will of Iselle who pins her forehead to the floor and digs the spoon into her face a jerking free Yes! she cries as Mary twists and turns a ball of something wet upon her cheek Now the other! she's back at her again a crow a bird's beak pecking at her buried to her neck in a field she scoops it out the dark Mary blinks the horrible muck nothing there a smear of gore the black slime upon her face no chance to see just the shufflings and noise of a darkened room and Lana trying to stop gap her screams with her wet hand O my God no.

◆

All is now forever night into this nightness she is born her eyeballs wadded in tissue in the wastebasket a bucket of motel ice cooling the blood stanching the flow healing the hurt the wounds that never heal if the eye offends you pluck it out What now? she wonders What other pain is needed? She listens as Iselle and Lana pray she is born into this nightness and waits for her redemption in this dark as we all do as we all shall in the healing murk of time.

For All You Dorks,
Blah Blah Blah

I T WAS AFTER MIDNIGHT WHEN Daolin pulled up to my curb and genius that he was started honking. He had the brains if you want to call them that at least to douse his headlights so when you looked outside (you being some construction guy with The Club locked to the steering wheel of his Firebird and a baseball bat at the ready scratching his nuts at the window) the darkness hid Daolin's car so maybe they wouldn't be able to hunt him down and kill him. All you could see were the white snowy yards the dark street spruce trees heavy with snow, but with all the junkmobiles in my neighborhood it was kind of a pathetic candy-cane scene, like a get-well card for detox. In the car I said, "What's the deal? You trying to get me killed?"

"Find something on the radio," said Daolin as he gunned it down the street. "Those morons sleep too much as it is."

This was Salt Lake City—Mormonville USA. I slipped in Nine Inch Nails and cranked it, imagining murder and mayhem as we drove south toward Provo, deep in burbland. You know the homes—burglar wet dreams on hillsides, with huge yards, mountains on one side and on the other, that stink pool we call a lake. We were on the way to Kooster's, and visiting his place always gave me the creeps. To him we were lowlifes, there to pick up a briefcase, shuttle it to some criminal element we knew, make our lunch money in the process. Kooster was one rich freak with good connections. We had to speak through an intercom to open his driveway gate.

I always felt dirty and misshapen when we visited Kooster. He *made* you feel that way. He did. Really. Like, we weren't supposed to use the front door, but went through the sliding glass door to his den. Daolin once said, "You know what? I hate dens."

Kooster was on his computer playing Doom when we walked in, and didn't even look up—need I say more? There was a mirror on the coffee table with a mound of crystal meth on it. I noticed it. Daolin did, too. He didn't say anything about it, though. Neither did I. What was there to say? Can I have some? What are we, beggars?

Daolin says, "So how's it hanging, Richie Rich?"

Kooster ignored him. He gave us the briefcase and told us how much we were supposed to get for it. We were his middle men. His lackeys. We once made ten g's for him on a single deal. And did he appreciate it? He gave us directions and showed us the door. Here's your hat what's your hurry. As he was letting us out, he pointed at Daolin and said, "I told you not to call me that."

◆

On the way across town, Daolin wouldn't shut up about it. "Who the fuck does he think he is? God? I'll call him whatever I want to call him. And did you see that? He had an eightball of crystal on the coffee table and he didn't offer us any. Not even a taste, you know? So what's that about?"

I agreed. "He treats us like we're his servants."

"Common human decency says you offer friends a taste. Common fucking courtesy."

"Gophers. That's what we are to him."

"Well, fuck that. He's gonna get his."

◆

That's how we ended up stiffing Kooster for six thousand seven hundred simoleons. It was minutes for his life, but hey, for Daolin it was a couple months. Plus the principle of the thing. It never would have happened if Kooster hadn't been so tight-assed. Show us some respect, that's all we ask. So we dropped off the merchandise, took the money and never looked back.

Just in case there was trouble, we headed for Daolin's dad's house, to lay low for a while. He wouldn't mind, at least that's what Daolin said. "Well, maybe he won't be thrilled about it. But, hey, I'm the only son. So what can he do about it? Besides, my half sister sacks out there, like, always. He owes me *big* time."

◆

His half sister, Amelia Ann, was twenty-six years old and still lived at home with her dad. She was looking for a job, supposedly. Daolin told me, "She tried college but wasn't smart enough. So it's back to the drawing board, eh?"

When we got there he introduced me, saying, "Curtis. This is my no-good half sister, A. A."

She was short, *extremely* short, with long, messy black hair, and a face all broken out. Her eyes focused on my mouth when she said Hi, pleased to meet you. Then she turned on Daolin and told him, "That is not my name." She looked at me and tried to keep control. "My name is Amy."

Daolin grinned. "Whatever."

He told his father that his apartment was being painted and I was from out of town and we needed a place to crash for a few days till the fumes blew away. I don't think Dad believed a word of it. When Daolin introduced us, his father said, "Respect our home." When we shook hands, I felt his bones crushing mine.

Then Daolin slapped his hands together and rubbed. "So? What's for dinner?"

◆

Daolin was tall and blonde, but his father was a short, stocky guy with thick black hair and eyebrows that joined in the middle. A male version of Amy. And that unibrow was the thing. It looked like a mustache out of place, and reminded me of a Mr. Potato Head I put together stoned. Daolin called him Papa Throwback. He told me about it before I ever met him. You could tell he was touchy about the whole thing. He said dinner at his house was like Stone Age Europe, when Cro-Magnons hung out with Neanderthals.

"I'm glad I didn't get that gene," he said. "It's like living with something that hasn't evolved as far. You can't hold it against him, but you don't want it to rub off on you either."

Still his dad was pretty smart. He'd been to college. But he was mean, too. He didn't joke around. And he was the only person who called Daolin by his first name, Gerald, shortened to Jerry. I had to keep from smirking when I heard it. Daolin was his middle name, and if anyone ever so much as mentioned Gerald, he'd kick their ass. But around his Dad it was Jerry this and Jerry that. Like, Jerry have you taken out the trash like I told you? It was worth hanging out at his house just to hear that.

At dinner, Mr. York made us all sit down to eat together. On the wall beside the dining table were his degrees, framed and everything. One of them was a master's degree in criminal justice. That was choice. And of all things, he was a parole officer, full time, and part time, a zebra in the NFL. A line judge. His job was watching the side-lines to make sure players didn't step out of bounds. Once they step out, they can't step back in. Or it's illegal, at least.

We were talking about it at dinner that first night. Daolin said, "Okay, Pop. Hypothetically, what if I'm running out for a pass, step out of bounds, and no one sees me. Then I step back in, catch a pass, and score a touchdown."

Mr. York was chewing. We waited till he was finished, which was a long moment, like he chewed each piece eighty-seven times or something. I've never seen such a chewer! Me, I wolf it down. Finally he swallowed and said, "It's illegal."

"But what if you miss the call?"

"I usually don't."

"But sometimes you do, right?"

"Sometimes."

"What then?"

"No penalty."

"Then I score a touchdown, right?"

"So what's your point, Jerry?"

"Well, my point is, breaking the rules is okay if you don't get caught, right?"

"You'll never learn, you know that?"

"Learn what? Why're you getting so hot under the collar?"

Mr. York said, "Jerry? Don't start with me."

Daolin turned to me and made an I'm-innocent face. Like he's not trying to start nothing. "Am I right or am I right?"

Amy had her head down and kept out of it. Her coarse black hair was in her face. Because of her acne problem, she must not want peo-ple looking at her skin, you know.

I laughed it off. "Rules is rules."

Mr. York gave me points for that one. He was glad he didn't have to deal with two assholes at the same time. One is enough. He gave me a look like, hey, you're all right. And Daolin was so fucking stupid he didn't see it that way, the place I was in.

"Thanks a lot, *pal*. See if I ever back you up in a tight spot."

I shrugged. What could I do?

◆

Later in the evening we were playing Monopoly, the three of us, and Daolin was lording it over Amy and me, because he had Park Place and Broadway. He was the Car, I was the Top Hat, she was the Thimble. At first she'd chosen the Dog, but when Daolin said, "How appropriate," she threw it at him.

"You better pick that up."

"Screw you."

She chose the Thimble instead.

I landed on Daolin's property and had to borrow money from the bank to pay the rents. He had hotels on fucking everything. You could tell he thought those red plastic houses meant he was better than us. He gloated. "Looks like you're all washed up, wise guy."

I said, "So what? It's just a game. It's not like I was hit by a car."

He made a face at that, and watched Amy. Then he grinned and said, "Good shot, Oswald."

Amy looked funny for a moment. She stood up and stretched. But it was fake somehow, a fake stretch. "I'm calling it a night," she said. She went back to her room and shut the door.

"What'd I say?"

"Amy was in a brutal fucking car wreck last year. She almost died. Spent months in the hospital. That's why her face is so fucked up."

"How could I know?"

"Didn't notice the scars?"

"I thought it was acne."

Daolin made a dumb-you face. "Acne? Acne is like pimples and stuff. Those are scars, *Beavis*."

"Why didn't you tell me?"

He grinned. "Oh, she's gonna love you for that one, yessir. She remembers fucking everything."

◆

Daolin and I sat up watching some stupid cop movie on TV. The things we do to kill time. About a half-hour after Amy went to her room, her dad walked down that hallway and was in there for about fifteen minutes, then came out and fixed a padlock on her door.

From my place in the living room I had a clear shot down the hallway to her door. I could see the shiny metal bracket that fit on the doorjamb, the Master padlock her dad hooked through the bracket into a metal ring on her door, snapped in place. Then he leaned over, put the key on the ground, and nudged it with the toe of his slipper under the crack of her door.

On his way upstairs, before heading for his bedroom, he stopped to look at the TV for a minute. I didn't know what to say and Daolin acted like he wasn't there. He walked off, and as he climbed the stairs, he said to us, "Keep it down."

◆

Daolin saw I saw the padlock.

"Don't even ask," he said. "It's a fucking madhouse around here."

◆

They had a big place, and Daolin put me in the guest room. I brushed my teeth and got in bed, but the sheets smelled of mildew and air freshener, the pillows were lumpy and had brocade pillowcases. They scratched my face. The way I was tossing and turning, I'd be lucky to still have eyebrows by morning.

I lay in bed for a while thinking about Amy in the room next to me. (Not in that way, get your mind out of the gutter, okay?) Just wondering what she was thinking. What her story was. And I wanted to tell her I was sorry. So I put on my hooded sweatshirt, jeans, and sneakers and climbed out the window. Amy's room was next to mine, so I didn't have far to go, but I had to stand in the snowdrift to reach her window. At first I tapped gently. The curtains were half open, but I couldn't see into the darkness. She didn't come after I'd tapped several times. Finally I gave it a good rap. It almost sounded like I cracked it. Muffled sounds came from inside the room for a moment, then nothing. My feet were freezing. I was about to leave, when her face, pale, like a junkie ghost, appeared in the gap at the bottom of the window.

"It's you," she said.

"Hey." I tried to smile, but I was starting to shiver and it didn't feel right. I wanted to explain what I was doing there, but I didn't know how to put it. For a second I just stood there, dumb. Finally I went, "What gives? Why'd your dad lock you in?"

"You got a cigarette?"

"Sure."

I tapped one out of the pack and she leaned close to take it. There wasn't a screen on the window. I tried not to shake as I flipped the lid on my silver Zippo and struck a flame. She blew her smoke out the window and whispered *thanks*.

Truth was, I never liked Daolin. He was something of a jerk. He learned to play the violin at age six and would never let you forget this. He fancied himself the bad-boy artist and me, just the bad boy. Amy was the reason I'd agreed to crash at his dad's place. He'd told me a few things—about her dropping out of school, about her getting busted in high school. So she kneels against the window, smoking the cigarette, and tells me she sleeps with four cats on her bed and no matter how much her dad tried to stop it, she refused.

"They like my bed. They're not hurting anybody. I don't see what the grief is."

"Me neither."

She said that's why she got locked in every night. "I'm grounded," she said, and laughed softly.

The story didn't make much sense to me. I scratched at white flecks of paint on the windowsill. "You're not hurting anyone," I said.

She nodded vigorously and leaned over. "Hey. Don't scratch that paint off."

"Sorry."

She smiled. "Aren't you cold out there?"

Yes I was, and told her, so she lifted the window higher, told me to get inside and warm up before I got frostbite.

We had to keep the lights out, in case her dad walked by and thought something was up. It was pitch dark in her bedroom. After I took off my sneakers, wet now with snow, she held my hand and guid-ed me to sit on the bed. She left me there and moved about in the total darkness. A cat rubbed its head against my warming fingers. I scratched it and took its furry ears in my fingers, smoothing them and rubbing their backsides. Her purrs seemed to vibrate the entire bed. Amy lit a candle but placed it behind a splayed book, held vertical by its spine. The golden light played against the wall faintly. It was a small flame.

"That must be Rose," Amy said. "She's got the loudest motor."

It was almost as if I were holding my breath. I was afraid of Mr. York. For a moment, I could think of nothing else. Sitting there in the total darkness, I could think only of my fear and of the purring cat, a warm vibrating furry egg in my lap. But once the candle was lit, and my hands and ears and feet began to warm, I relaxed somewhat. In the soft glow Amy looked radiant and angelic. You couldn't see the scars on her face in this light. She wore a flannel nightgown with a collar, sat so close to me our legs touched. She did this, she took her place beside me on the bed, with a comical face, eyebrows raised high, as if to pantomime doing something in absolute silence. As the bed creaked slightly, she pursed her lips.

I knew I shouldn't be there, in Amy's room, in Daolin's half sister's room, with a padlock on her door that her NFL official and parole officer father put there to keep her in place. "He chained me to the bed two months ago," she whispered, her lips touching my ear. "I promised I'd be good."

The cat purred. Somewhere in the misty gold-tinted blackness of the room, I sensed other cats stirring, yawning, or asleep. Amy noiselessly placed an ashtray between us and took another one of my cigarettes, thank you. She whispered, "What are you thinking?"

I was thinking I shouldn't be there, and that there was no way I would leave unless she told me to. That realization of doom and betrayal settled over me like a curse. Some people you don't fuck with. Daolin and his dad were two of them. And sometimes you risk it all.

Amy said she didn't understand why I was Daolin's friend. "You're almost human, you know that?" I was never so terrified as when she put her lips against my neck.

♦

The next day was a Sunday, game day, and Daolin's dad asked if we wanted to go with him to the game he was calling, get in free. We said sure, we don't have anything better to do. We were driving because the game was in Denver. I rode in the back seat with his dad's duffel, carrying the line judge's uniform. The December fields were gray and wintry. In the town, dirty snow covered the medians and was shoved into dead whale icebergs in the parking lots. You couldn't see over them. The road was bleached white by the salt, and Daolin kept asking what lane we were in, because the stripes were all worn off.

His father said, "I know what lane we're in. What's it to you?"

"I don't want to get beaned by some asshole with air bags and more insurance than he knows what to do with."

"You concern yourself with things that aren't your business."

"I'm just saying."

He let it go at that.

◆

I sat in the back seat, deep in a moral hangover. Amy's smell lingered on my lips and mouth. Sweet and sour and salty, too, like something good gone bad. For all I knew she could be pregnant. I didn't wear a condom and she knew. After we did it, she wiped off the goo with the hem of her flannel nightgown, making a grossed-out face. "God," she said. "You were full of it."

Now my head ached. Now I saw Mr. York's eyes staring a hole in me every time I looked into the rearview.

He seemed pissed in general. "What are you boys going to do with your lives anyway? You're not drifting, are you?"

"Yeah, Dad. We've set our sights low. We've resigned ourselves to being drifters now."

"Don't get sarcastic with me."

"You started it."

I kept my mouth shut. There was no winning with these two.

Later, Mr. York told us he thought our problem was a lack of faith. "You two don't believe in anything, do you?"

Daolin sighed and stared out the window at the mountains and trees floating by the interstate highway. "This is going to be good."

"You don't believe in anything. All you do is make fun of things."

"I believe in the tooth fairy. Whenever I lost a tooth as a kid, I'd find a quarter beneath my pillow the next morning." He turned around and smiled at me. For him, this was fun. "I believe that was previous to your wife-choking phase, though, wasn't it, Dad?"

"What you need is faith. But I can't force it in you. You aren't the chosen. I wash my hands."

Daolin made a face. "Well, don't forget to use the soap, *Papa*."

◆

At the game, we lingered in the periphery of the end zone. Mr. York couldn't get us tickets for the stands, but we walked in the service entrance with him and got visitor's passes to the field. "Just stay out of the way," he told us. "No one will give a damn."

"That should be our motto for life," said Daolin. Then he gave me one of those grins. "Well, yours anyway."

It was the Cincinnati Bengals versus the Denver Broncos. I pulled for the Bengals because I liked their helmets. It was funny, though, being on the sidelines of one of these TV games. Everyone—the players, the coaches, and refs—they all looked so small and silly. They were just people running around in special costumes, tossing a ball back and forth. In their uniforms, it was hard to tell one official from the next. Daolin stood with his hands in his pockets and spit on the AstroTurf. When a player spiked a ball near us after scoring a touchdown, he said, "They think they're so fucking special."

Now and then I saw Mr. York running along the sidelines, but he never looked back at us.

♦

We stayed at Daolin's dad's house for several days. "So what do we do here?" I asked. "Just lay low for a while?" I figured it was Daolin's brainchild to pinch the funds, so he must have a master plan.

"That's 'lie.'"

"Lie what?"

"Lie. We're lying low. Get your fucking verbs right? What are you, some kind of moron?"

Back at the ranch, Daolin hogged the channel changer. We sat in the living room watching CNN all day—me, Daolin, and Amy—and he wouldn't let anyone else change the channels. "Let's watch some game shows or something," I said.

"I'm missing my soaps," said Amy.

Daolin made a face. "What is this? Dumb and dumber?"

If he didn't get his way, Daolin would pout. After we bitched for a long time, he changed the channel to *One Life to Live*. Everybody was weeping. There seemed to be a funeral going on.

"Happy now?"

He stomped out of the room, taking the remote with him.

◆

Amy and I barely spoke two words to each other in the daytime, but at night, we took each other as far as we could go, put our fingers to each others scars and tattoos, drank and ate and stuffed ourselves full of each other like our bodies were Halloween candy about to go bad.

On the third night, I squirmed through her window, and instead of helping me to my feet, she took my knees and made me lie on my back on the floor. I said nothing. This was when we had to be mice. On my back on her thick bedroom rug, in the black-hole galaxy of the room, I felt her straddle me, her feet on either side of my chest. I heard the soft rustle of her flannel nightgown lifted, and breathed in her sex as she sat upon me, whispering something I couldn't hear.

◆

That night she told me, "You know, the padlock isn't for me."

Her face was soft and miragelike in the faint glow of the candles. We were on our knees, blowing pot out the window. One of her straps had fallen off her shoulder. Her collarbones were thin and sharp against the skin of her chest, like she hadn't been eating enough.

She was frail. Anyone could hurt her. I knew I could.

And she told me the padlock was not to keep her in, but to keep her father out.

"He's never done anything to me," she said, speaking in a throaty voice while trying to hold the smoke in. "He's never hurt me, really. He spanked me a few times in high school." She made a face, like you know that whole story. "But I kind of liked it. Not in that way, not some psychosexual thing." She shook her head. "I liked it because he'd be really guilty afterward and I could get away with murder."

"I'd never let him hurt you," I said, stupidly.

She grinned and butted heads with me gently, her nose huge and pink-tinted in the tight-focus, cross-eye effect. No, her father had never touched her, but he could and it wouldn't be his fault, she said.

He was a sleep walker. He could get up and drive around the city while completely asleep. He'd been doing it all his life, but in the last few years it had gotten worse. Amy's mother kept waking up in the middle of the night with Mr. York's hands around her throat, choking her. He wasn't quite as strong when he was asleep, but he was persistent. Once, when Amy was sick with the flu herself, he dragged her by her hair. He pulled her down the hallway, down the stairs, banging her bones against the sharp wooden steps. In the living room she fought to her feet, though he still had a hunk of her hair in his grip. She bashed his feet with a heavy ashtray, broke two of his toes.

After that, she got her own apartment. Three years ago. But her dad was depressed, living alone, and when she lost her job at the Fotomat, he convinced Amy to move back in.

"The padlock works like a charm," she said. "I hear him now and then, yanking at the door to be let in."

I didn't know what to say to that. I imagined it—lying in bed while your crazy asleep father tries to get in your locked door and do who-knows-what to you.

"Dad lives in a scary world. All the things he holds inside him seem to creep out at night, and he won't stop it. He doesn't like the medication. I feel pretty safe myself, but the rest of the world, watch out.

"It's like when he falls asleep and then gets up, he could get dressed, talk to you like a normal person for a half-hour, then go kill a schoolgirl or eat a cat or something. No telling what he'd do."

But Daolin was the one who really frightened her. She told me how a few years ago, when her father was away, Daolin tried to kiss her, tried forcing his tongue into her mouth, and she bit it. He walked into the bathroom while she was taking a shower, and wouldn't leave until she came out and threw things at him. And there was more, she said, that she didn't even want to talk about. She once fell asleep in the living room, and when she awoke, her robe had been pulled open and Daolin was sitting beside her, his pants at his knees, his eyes closed. "I felt like one of his old crusty *Hustlers*," she said.

◆

For a few days we holed up in the living room, playing along with *Jeopardy*, Daolin getting them all correct. He started turning sour, though. Daolin was the kind of guy who thought he should be made head of some major corporation, or a movie star or something, and blamed the fact that he wasn't on his lack of connections. He started turning on himself. He was loaded by then. The middle of the day. He slurred his words, saying, "I'll take 'Losers' for two hundred, Alex."

He ranted about how fat he was getting. "Look at me. I'm becoming a tub-o. I'll never leave this house." He passed out and snored on the couch.

Amy and I took advantage of his sleeping.

◆

That evening he told me, "Let's go for a drive." He borrowed his father's car and we drove over to his apartment building. "What's he going to do to us anyway?" he asked, talking about Kooster, whose six thousand seven hundred dollars we still had. "He's not with the mob. He's just a rich fuck who likes to hang with dopers and make some easy investment cash. So he snubbed the wrong guy, right?"

"I hear you."

"He isn't going to try anything with me, because I know who's coming up on the short end of the stick there."

"He's a nobody. But still."

"Still what?"

◆

I played lookout for Daolin as we crept down the hallway to his place. He held his father's gun inside his jacket. I could tell he thought this was a TV show. He the star, me the sidekick. He grinned at me and said, "Yea, though I walk through the Valley of the Shadow of Death, blah blah blah blah blah blah blah."

If somebody was coming, I was supposed to whistle, though I didn't whistle worth a fuck. I watched as he walked down the hallway. All I could do was make sure no one was behind him. He opened the door with his key and went inside. My mouth was dry and chalky. He was in there for a minute. I started walking toward the elevator in case someone I didn't know came out the door, or in case I heard gunshots. Hell, I didn't know what would happen. And I was half inside the elevator before Daolin was there in the hallway, giving me a look.

I told him, "I was just keeping it on the floor."

"Wussy."

◆

Inside Daolin's place, it was obvious no one had broken in and ransacked it. That's what we supposed. Why not? That's what they do on *The Rockford Files*. Daolin seemed disappointed. The answering machine had Kooster ranting on it. He kept saying, "This is not cool, you know. This is *not* cool."

Daolin shook his head and grinned at me. "You don't have much of what they call 'courage,' do you?"

Daolin's apartment was extremely neat. Cold, too. Like a model home for upwardly mobile social outcasts. He sorted his mail and I checked the refrigerator for something to eat, but it was all old. The answering machine played on. Kooster became threatening, repetitive. "You're going to pay for this! You're going to pay!" Daolin made a flapping motion in the air with his hand, gab gab gab. One of his girlfriends sounded peeved, wondering Why don't you call? Are you out of town or something? Someone from a corporation wanted to set up a job interview with him. He frowned at the machine. "If they want me to start at the bottom, they can just forget it."

I asked if he was ready to go.

"What's the matter? You scared?"

"Let's not push our luck."

Daolin did a thing with his face, scrunching up his forehead and eyebrows. He was doing his best Sean Penn. "*Our* luck? No. No. I have my luck. You have yours. There is no *our* luck."

"Whatever."

"You know you are so *snide*. It's not good for you. And catch this. I don't want you fucking my sister anymore. Got it?"

"Half."

"Pardon me?"

"Half. Half sister. Amy is."

"Half, whole. Different eggs, same sperm, okay? And I don't want yours in there anymore, okay?"

I poured a Diet Pepsi from his refrigerator and stared him down. I could sense he didn't know where he was going with this. He was Jupiter, the big planet. Anything in his orbit got sucked in. I said, "All you need is a badge, Jerry, and you can run for sheriff."

◆

I had no pride or dignity left. I was in the shadow of this monster, my friend. One afternoon he told me, "I wonder what it would be like to kidnap someone. A woman. You know, follow her in a parking lot. Make her drive out in the woods. Tell her you won't hurt her if she cooperates." His eyes were far off and mistylike.

"I don't know. I mean, ransom is, like, impossible."

"Who's asking for ransom? Not for that." He grinned at me.

Then he told me he was just joking. But I knew when he was lying, and when he was telling the truth.

If Daolin were picked up by the police on murder charges, I

wouldn't have been surprised. I could see him following some guy who had tailgated him into a parking lot, getting out and shooting him in the face. He surrounded us with debts that would be collected painfully.

Listening to Kooster on the answering machine, I could feel the hole Daolin was digging for himself getting deeper and deeper and deeper and deeper and deeper.

◆

Driving back from his apartment, Daolin was giddy. He kept slapping the steering wheel, making a flat rubbery sound when his hand hit the curvy plastic, a vibration. "We did it," he shouted. "We got away with it. I can't believe Kooster didn't see this coming. He just didn't take me seriously."

I didn't say anything. I was thinking about Amy. It would be harder to drive over to her dad's house in the middle of the night and sneak in her window. If he was awake, he might shoot me. If he was asleep, he might join me.

Amy was drowsy when we returned. She could barely keep her eyes open, sitting on the couch, wrapped in blankets. A cat in her lap. "Where have you been?" she asked. Her voice sounded watery and dim, as if she were at the end of a long distance line, but she was there, right there, and soon I'd have to leave her. Tomorrow was a game day, and Daolin's dad had gone to bed early because he had to catch a flight to Seattle in the morning, to work the Seahawks game.

"I wanted to stay up, so someone has to lock me in," said Amy.

There was a bottle of wine on the table. Amy had sucked it all down.

"This is our last night," said Daolin. "We're going to blow this joint before you know it."

I said, "Maybe we should celebrate."

Daolin thought that was a great idea, and said since Half Sister

here had guzzled all the vino, let's make a run for the liquor store. All
he had to do was take a piss and we'd be ready to roll.

"You just got here and you're leaving already?" said Amy, slurring
her words across the room.

Daolin kept the money in his sock drawer. The door to his room
was always open, so I waited till he went to the bathroom before I
made my move. His room was silent and incredibly neat. The rug
aligned with the slats of his hardwood floors. The curtains were just so.

He reminded me of my stepfather, years ago, who scared everyone
but who lived without fear himself.

I slid into Daolin's room as the splashing sound of his urine in the
toilet bowl filled the hallway. The money was in a green vinyl bank
deposit bag behind his socks. I took it and was passing the bathroom
when he flushed.

"I need to call somebody," I told him when he came out. "I'm
gonna see if I can set up something tasty for us later."

"What? Not happy with dead-fishing Amy tonight?"

I used the phone in Amy's room, called Kooster. I told him where
we'd be, and that his money would be in Daolin's car if he wanted to
come get it. Just leave me out of it is all I ask. He liked the idea and
said he had some friends over just then. He said he'd bring them to
help out.

◆

There was only one state liquor store near his father's house, and
Daolin drove straight there. He kept going on and on about how lucky
he was. I was thinking, speaking to him in my brain. You *fool*. You
moron.

At the liquor store, I held the door open for him and saw the car
pull into the parking lot behind us, the headlights cutting white.

"I forgot," I said. "I'm supposed to call Judy back."

Who was Judy? Just a name. Four guys got out of the car. They carried baseball bats. Kooster with them. They ignored me as I walked to the phone booth, got inside and dialed. Kooster said something and two of them took the bats and stepped into the shadows, out of the light. I dialed Time. Daolin walked out and Kooster was there, in his face, two of the guys grabbing Daolin as he struggled with them, his jacket suddenly over his head, one of them slugging his guts. They dragged him to the side, at the edge of the darkness. I saw the baseball bats flashing in the light. I tried not to listen to the muffled sounds and voices.

I was making a change. I was in the right.

I would take Amy for a drive into the mountains. And when we awoke, we would put this time in our lives behind us.

That's what I was thinking. I was thinking things like that, honestly I was, when I walked back to their house. (I mean, I couldn't drive. Daolin had his keys.) So it took me a while to get there, an hour, hour and a half. Like at Kooster's, I went in the back door.

In the living room, Daolin's father was sitting there, watching TV. He didn't react when I walked in. He was sitting there, staring at the screen, looking happier than I had ever seen him before. Watching the David Letterman show with Joy all over his face. His pajamas were torn and ripped open to show his gray hairy chest. On TV, Dave was doing his Top Ten list. TOP TEN SIGNS YOUR WIFE MAY HAVE BEEN ABDUCTED BY ALIENS.

Amy was lying face up on the living room floor, her mouth and eyes open, her black hair spread out like a puddle of oil. You could smell her. You could tell she was gone and there was no bringing her back.

Dave read from his cue cards. "Number Five. She goes out to get a dozen eggs, comes back three days later naked and covered with lime Jell-O." I stood there and listened, trying to know what to do. The studio audience laughed. "Number Four. Her tuna casserole is out of this world!"

Daolin's father looked up at me and smiled. "Watch this, Jerry." He pointed at the screen and said, "This is good, this is really good."

THE DECLINE
OF KING FABULOUS

A FTER HIS HEART BEGINS skipping beats, begins lurching and stumbling, begins pausing as if it has forgotten something, as if it's uncertain whether to continue, Neal waits months before calling Dr. Garcia's office and making an appointment, hating the idea of having anything wrong with him, the idea of being sick, and vaguely hoping that if he just makes a point of running four miles every other day, as he has for years in the past, it will cease this flip-flopping and get back to its rhythm. He is forty-two years old and a little wear and tear is to be expected, yes? His hair is thinning, he's gained a little weight, so what else is new. There's nothing unusual about an irregular heartbeat, is there? He's sure all kinds of people have jerky hearts. Longshoremen. Accountants. Plumbers. Even Bill Bradley, presidential wannabe, had to cancel a few sessions of baby-kissing for it.

In the waiting room Neal reads a copy of *People* and listens to his heartbeat, hearing it constantly now, only vaguely remembering a time when he was able to ignore it. He realizes this is not a good sign.

Today it seems okay. Maybe there's nothing wrong with it after all. Maybe he's fine. He also has tinnitus and besides his heartbeat, hears a constant ringing in his ears, enough to drive a weaker man bananas. Neal believes in the virtue of strength and perseverance. Yes, the constant high-pitched ringing not unlike the proverbial nails down the chalkboard is irritating, maddening, even, but there's nothing to be done, no cure, no way to shut it off. He coaches himself in the philosophy of No Nonsense. Get over it. Life is tough. When the going gets tough, the tough get going.

An anonymous nurse appears and leads him down a long hallway toward what Neal fears will mark the end of life as he knows it. After weighing him and asking him to urinate into a small plastic cup in a small bathroom, she tells him to wait in the second room on the right down the hall. Neal wanders vaguely in that direction and is about to open the wrong door when the nurse reappears, guides him by the elbow to the right door, opens it, then motions him inside. As she begins to leave he asks, "Aren't you going to take my blood pressure?"

Without answering she closes the door.

In the small room is an examining table, a small chair on which Neal sits, a sink, shelves of medical supplies, and a poster of New Year's in Aspen, Colorado—peaks clad in blue snow, fireworks bursting fiery red and jade green in the sky inky black above, the light trails of skiers carrying torches swooping back and forth on the downhill course. Neal wonders if the doctor is going to require that he drop his pants. He doesn't think that will be necessary. It's his heart, after all, that's the problem. He wonders if the man will want to poke a finger into his anus. That is totally uncalled for. What is this? An alien abduction?

He squints at the poster and wonders if Dr. Garcia actually likes to snow ski or if he simply thinks this is the appropriate pastime for doctors to pursue, the right image to put forward for his patients, golf being stereotypical of course, passé of course, but that never stopped anyone did it? Still, skiing, now there's the sport of the greedy and vain. Dr. Garcia is a heavyset man from California who rarely says much. Neal thinks he looks like a butcher but knows he's probably just being prejudiced. Dr. Garcia will probably suggest that Neal keep his cholesterol down, get frequent exercise, and stop drinking too much coffee.

Neal used to believe his life was blessed, but now he's not so sure. In high school he was nicknamed King Fab after starring in a comedy called *The Frozen Dumpling War* as King Fabulous the Less-Than-Enthusiastic. He wore a red velvet cape and jeweled red velvet crown. It was one of the top ten moments of his life. He made everyone laugh, heard the roar of applause, and kissed Daphne Dupree, later voted Most Beautiful.

Now that all seems so long ago. For years he struggled to be a comedian, doing physical, zany antics to emphasize the oddball quality of his body, how his head and hands seemed too big for the rest of him, giving him a comical, Pinnochio quality. But nothing came of it. He was funny, but he wasn't quite funny enough. For a time he actually made a living doing television commercials. He had that kind of face, the kind of face that sells cars and detergents and pain relievers, not terribly handsome but able to smile on cue, to show off his Pepsodent teeth. Otherwise he struggled as a stand-up and managed to land a few acting roles, appearing twice on *The Bob Newhart Show* and once on *Silk Stalkings*. In his early thirties he began doing video production work to make ends meet. He quit scrambling to audition—such humiliation wears down the soul.

At some point he realized the life in showbiz was not for him. Oh, well. It hurt, but life sucks then you die, right? To friends he made a joke of it. Success is overrated. Look on the bright side. "If I made it big, I'd probably get expensive drug habits and have to put up with all those horrible seminars in rehab." And it's lonely at the top, right? "Failure isn't so bad," he added. "Ever call up an escort service and they send over your mother? Now that's bad."

He's now a photographer who operates video surveillance equipment for divorce lawyers and corporate private detectives. The pay is disgustingly good. To Neal it feels like blood money or the wages of sin. Blowing the cash recklessly is how he copes with the guilt. He's returned to live in St. Louis, where he grew up, and has fallen back in with his best friend from high school, Lawrence Boon, whom he caught up with at their twentieth reunion, and whom he still refers to by his last name. Boon manages a rock group called The Spazmos. They play at local rock and roll clubs. Neal gets high with them back-stage, snorting coke and smoking pot as if he's back in college. He sus-pects this is what's causing his heart to skip, but dodges the issue by telling Boon, "Da Nile is more than a river in Egypt."

◆

Finally the door opens and a woman enters, a woman in a white doc-tor's coat, who apologizes for making him wait but this is just one of those days. She shakes his hand and introduces herself. She is Dr. Cimino and she is new. "Please call me Olivia," she adds. "Now, what seems to be the problem?"

Her dark hair is pulled back with a white headband and hangs to her shoulders. Her throat and face are milky white and her eyebrows thick and dark. She is maybe Neal's age, maybe younger, but not much.

"Well, I guess it's my heart." Neal tries to affect an unruffled atti-tude, tries to pull off an air of Hemingwayesque sangfroid, but it does-n't work. He tells her everything, even how it's been happening for months and that he realizes he should have come in earlier but he doesn't want to be sick. He can't stand the idea, actually. Maybe she should know that his ears are ringing, too. Constantly. He's seen a doc-tor for this and the prognosis was not good. No one ever used the world incurable, but he got the point and is used to it by now. Still you can't stop modern medicine. New advances by the minute. Prozac. Zo-loft. Propecia. Zyban. Biotech stocks making millionaires overnight. He's read about this, he's up on things. He stares at her throat and says, "Please tell me there's nothing wrong."

She watches him closely for a moment and asks if he's having any problem with his vision. "No," he says. She keeps looking at him and Neal shakes his head. "No. I mean, yes. Yes, I do. Sometimes it's fuzzy."

Olivia nods and reads over his file on a clipboard, smiles faintly. She leans close to him and puts the stethoscope against the skin of his chest, slipping the end of it inside his shirt. Her face is close to his as she listens to his heart. When she speaks, she pitches her voice softly, almost a whisper. "Are you married?"

"Yes. Well, no. I was."

"Are you sexually active?"

Neal blushes and doesn't answer.

He can hear his own heart beating wildly. Through the stethoscope it must sound like a kettledrum.

"Do you use any recreational drugs?"

Again he doesn't answer. This time, still pitching her voice softly, almost conspiratorially, she says, "I take that as a yes."

Neal frowns. "I suppose I'm not the best person in the world."

When she leans away, Olivia appears as a fuzzy vision of dark hair and white skin across from him until Neal blinks several times and she comes into focus, writing something in his files. She then tells him the plan: She's going to schedule an EKG, a cholesterol test, and she will now take his blood pressure. She doesn't think there's anything seriously wrong with him, but don't quote her on it. She gives him a business card and jots her home number on it. "Feel free to call me if the symptoms persist."

◆

Years ago Neal's father killed himself. For what? Who knows. It happened when Neal was three, so had no more effect on him than the sinking of the Lusitania or the kidnaping of the Lindbergh baby. What did affect his life was that his mother remarried a public relations director with two children, the upshot of this unholy union being

Neal has a stepbrother, Jack. He and his wife are the only married people Neal knows in St. Louis. Jack is a vigorously healthy high school football coach, who insists he's this close to getting an offer to be the offensive coordinator for the University of Maryland. But he doesn't know if he'll take it or not. He has to weigh the pros and cons. On the one hand it's a great spot at a Division I NCAA school. But their mascot is a turtle. "That's a hard thing to live down," he says, laughing.

His wife, Anna, is a dental assistant from Croatia. She is almost pretty, with an olive complexion, thick lips, and lustrous hair, but her face is a bit too wide, squashed-looking. She is meek in the presence of Jack and says very little. This is not surprising or unusual. It's hard to carry on a conversation with Jack. He always seems to either overreact or fail to let you finish your sentences. When Neal tries to tell him about the heart problem, Jack says, "You must be kidding! You're too young to have a heart attack!"

"It's not a heart attack," he insists. "It's arrhythmia."

"A what?"

"The problem is my heart has been skipping beats and—"

"I know. You think you're going to die. Well, I have news for you, Bud. It ain't that easy. You can live with a bad heart for years. Decades, even!"

"Well, it's not that, really. . . . But I mean what I hate is—"

"You think we're all going to look down on you for being sickly, is that it? For being feeble? Hell, lots of people are—"

"—going to the doctor."

The phone rings and Jack jumps to answer it, says, "Speaking," then gives Anna and Neal a wink to signify it's the Maryland university people. He leaves the room, booming, "Of course I'm interested."

Alone with Anna, Neal asks what's new in her life.

She shrugs and says, "New? There is never anything new. How you say? Same ol', same ol'."

"It's the weather," says Neal. "It's not cold and it's not hot and it's not anything. I wish it would snow." Neal notices Anna staring at his mouth and becomes self-conscious, stops speaking.

"I am taking poetry class at university."

"Really?"

She nods.

"How's that going?"

"I love it. I absolutely love it. But Jack does not approve. He does not like poetry. He calls it flaky." She frowns. "I do not care. What does he know about art? Nothing. I do it anyway. I am not slave."

◆

The mirage of Dr. Olivia shimmers on the desert horizon of Neal's life until he can't stand it anymore. He calls her house, and when she answers and he hears her soft voice, he gets nervous and says she probably doesn't remember him but he is one of her patients and she said he could call so. . . .

"Is this Neal?"

"It's me."

"How's your heart?"

He can feel his pulse pounding in his throat and his fingers feel numb. "It's beating like crazy."

"Why?"

"You tell me," he says. "You're the doctor."

She gives him directions to her house and asks if he's eaten. She pauses for him to answer and he doesn't. If he's hungry, she'll fix him something to eat. "Are you hungry?"

"I don't know," he says. "I just want to see you."

◆

Olivia lives in a one-room flat in an old wooden house divided into six apartments. When Neal arrives, he presses a buzzer at the door. She comes down to meet him. Inside the ceiling is high, the bright hallway light on the flaky paint of the walls makes it look old world, European. The stairway is scuffed, a newspaper lies outside Apt. 1B like a welcome mat. Olivia wears faded blue jeans, a black wool sweater, and lipstick. Her white skin is shaded a faint pink tonight, her lips glossy red, her hair black as charcoal. She looks straight into his eyes and speaks, smiling, but it is as if Neal is under a highway overpass with trucks whining on the bridge above and he cannot hear clearly, though he thinks she says something about pasta. "That's fine," he says.

She tells him she's glad he came, but he thinks she said, "I don't remember your name."

"I'm Neal," he says.

She takes his hand and squeezes it. "I know." She leads him upstairs.

Her apartment has a large living room, a small bedroom off that through a doorless opening wide enough for French doors, and down a long hallway, a bathroom and kitchen. In the living room is a sofa, a small TV, books on leaning crowded bookshelves, a picture of Jesus and the Virgin Mary, photographs. There are no curtains on the windows and no coffee table. The air smells of a woodsy incense stick burning in an ashtray atop the television.

"How is your heart?" she asks.

"Beating."

She pours him a glass of red wine and insists it's good for the circulation. He sinks into the sofa and is overwhelmed by a sense of extraordinary luck and good fortune—knock on wood. His luck must be changing. All is not lost. Olivia folds her legs beneath her and sits close to him, her body in the shape of a Z. In his mind Neal thinks of her as O. He considers the letter to have a lovely shape. A lengthened circle, a rounded oval.

She begins to tell him about her day, about a patient who came in complaining of a persistent cough but who smokes two packs a day, and a woman who insists she can't be pregnant but she is, and at some point she stops, puts her wine glass on the floor beside the sofa, leans very close to Neal, and says that he is not listening to her, not one bit, he hasn't heard a single thing she's said.

"You have the longest eyelashes," he answers.

Olivia kisses him, putting one hand against his right cheek and leaving it there. Neal closes his eyes. When she stops and takes another sip of her wine, he opens them and puts down his glass of wine and waits while she puts her glass back on the floor, then he takes her face in his hands and kisses her nose. She pulls off her sweater and places her nipples in his mouth. Her breasts are heavy and point down and their nipples are as wide as the rims of their wine glasses. Neal is aware that with the lights on they must be visible from the street through the windows with no curtains. The world is a blur of blood vessels and skin and soft breasts and the sound of voices of people walking on the street below and in the distance the wailing siren of an ambulance.

In the middle of it all, Olivia stops and says she has to turn off the sauce or it will burn on the stove. Neal sits there confused as on a parking date in high school. When she returns, he watches as she walks down the hallway wearing only the faded blue jeans, her arms folded over her breasts. She turns off the lamp behind the TV and the room is filled with the silver light from the moon outside falling in a square block from the large window onto the Persian rug and part of the sofa.

"That's better," she says.

He pulls her close, kissing her navel as he unbuttons her jeans.

After they make love, when they are lying in the moonlight of the bedroom, Neal's heart, as it does every night, begins to stumble and pause. Olivia holds his wrist and takes his pulse, then she puts her ear to his chest and listens. She says, "This is not good."

Neal sits up, propping himself on pillows, and tries to breathe calmly and evenly. Olivia tells him he should see a cardiologist. He should get that thing checked out by a specialist. EKGs are highly ineffective. Dr. Garcia is no heart expert and neither is she. "I know you like playing the funny guy, but a bad heart is no joke."

Neal confesses that for years he tried to make it as a comedian. "Wouldn't it be ironic if I died laughing?"

◆

Within days Neal is thinking he's in love with Olivia, although he often thinks this with women and often actually it's merely an advanced stage of infatuation. He was married once before, to a beautiful and kind woman, Mary, but their sex life was dismal and Neal, being something of a sex addict, ended up making love to other women in cars, in hotel rooms, in public parks. Eventually he and Mary divorced. He still speaks to her on the phone often and sometimes still refers to her as his wife when it seems too confusing or awkward to say 'ex.'

Mary still loves Neal and wishes they could get together again but neither of them will ever change so she realizes it won't happen but there's no harm in dreaming or hoping is there? At least they never had children. After the divorce she told Neal, "Now I'll never have a family of my own. We were supposed to stay together and have children and be good to each other. Till death do us part, remember?"

"Does anyone believe that?"

"You ruined my life."

"I did not."

"Yes, you did."

"No one ruins anyone else's life."

"What about Hitler?"

"That's why we didn't have a good marriage. You're always comparing me to Hitler."

"I am not."

"You are too."

"You've just got a guilt complex, that's all it is. As you should. I mean, when you go around ruining other people's life it's hard to—"

"To begin with, your life is not ruined, but if it were ruined, which it's not, it would be your fault alone. You're always telling me to take some responsibility, right? Well, it works both ways. We're all the masters of our fates. We're all the captains of our own ships."

"You really believe that?"

"No." Neal stared out his window, the phone hot and cramped against his ear. The sky outside was totally white. "But still."

◆

He calls Mary and tells her about Olivia.

"What do you know about this woman?" asks Mary. "She sounds fishy."

"You don't trust anyone."

"Maybe not. But let me get this right. You knew this woman for how long? Fifteen minutes? And she slept with you? You don't find that fishy?"

"Not at all," he lies.

◆

For the next few weeks, Neal's heart seems to fall into a steady rhythm and the cardiologist cannot find anything wrong with it. He tells Neal to cut back on the café latte and puts him on Cholestyrine, a Tang-like orange drink he takes nightly to drop his cholesterol. The cardiologist also suggests a beta blocker to calm him down at night and to stop his heart from skipping, but the fine-print side effects described in the promotional literature include impotence, unusual tiredness or weakness, slow heartbeat, heart failure (swelling of the legs, ankles, or feet), dizziness, breathing difficulty, bronchospasm, mental depression, confusion, anxiety, nervousness, sleeplessness, disorientation, short-term memory loss, emotional instability, cold hands and feet, constipation, diarrhea, nausea, vomiting, upset stomach, increased sweating, urinary difficulty, cramps, blurred vision, skin rash, hair loss, stuffy nose, facial swelling, itching, chest pains, back or joint pains, colitis, fever, sore throat, and liver toxicity.

Neal chooses not to fill the prescription.

For these first few weeks, his obsession with Olivia fills his world and that itself makes him less conscious of the faltering rhythm of his heart. There is much about O. that he does not understand. She seems to be married to a trucker or an airline pilot, someone often out of town. She won't be seen in public with Neal and will only let him come over twice a week. She says it's a rule she has. To keep from getting her heart broken.

"If I see you more than that, I'll become dependent on you and then you'll break my heart. I just know you will."

"No, I won't."

"Yes, you will. It's happened before. You've done it before, right?"

Between the nights he spends at her apartment, Neal cannot stop thinking about Olivia. He wonders what she does on other nights of the week. Mary insists that no doubt she's doing who-knows-what with other men and are they practicing safe sex of course they aren't no don't tell me anything about it I don't want to know. Really. But tell me this. Do you want to die of AIDS? If that's what you want, fine, but if you don't, if you want to live, then you better think twice about this woman, because she's bad news.

◆

The next time Neal visits Olivia he wants to have a talk. He's not going to touch her, kiss her, no lips, no tongue, no nothing, but is going to be honest and tell her he thinks this can't go on. They end up immediately making love on the kitchen floor, which hasn't been swept in a long time, and as Olivia swivels on top of him Neal can feel the grit of crumbs beneath his back. When they're finished, he feels his heart pounding wildly as he works up the nerve to say, "Olivia, I think we have a problem."

She dabs her naked thighs with a paper towel. "Which is?"

"Why can't we see each other more? I want you all the time. What is it? I feel like I don't even know you."

She walks away from him naked through the rooms of the curtainless apartment for all the world to see and returns with a bottle of wine. One thing he realizes that he does know about her is she's got a bit of a drinking problem. But from the look on her face, he figures this is probably not the best time to offer this observation of her character flaw.

"You want to know who I am? Okay, I'll tell you. You're right. You don't know me. Not the real me. Well, no, that's not true. You know the new me. Not the old me. The real me is somewhere in between that."

Olivia told him she had another life in another town that she has left behind. In her other life she was, say, Marjorie Ellis (not her real name) of Youngstown, Ohio (not her real home), married to Brad Ellis. She was fifth-grade teacher at Ralph Waldo Emerson Elementary and she hated her life. At some point she couldn't stand it anymore. She went shopping one afternoon, and when she didn't drive home they retraced her steps and found her car locked and abandoned in the parking lot. The police suspected foul play. Perhaps she'd been kidnaped and murdered.

Olivia relates all this in a husky voice, little more than a whisper. When she's finished, she cries fat tears, blinking quickly, rubbing her long lashes.

"How did you get away with it?" asks Neal. "Don't you miss your husband?"

She dabs her eyes and nose with a Kleenex. Well yes of course she misses her husband. Brad was a good man, just a little dull. "He's better off without me, anyway. Isn't that what you said about your ex?"

Neal agrees Yes that's true but really he doesn't know what to think. He's always suspected it's impossible to know people, to truly know them, and know their hearts, but he didn't expect his suspicions to be confirmed.

"And I'm not a doctor," adds Olivia. "I just learned enough from Vincent, one of my lovers who was a professor at a medical school who helped me to get by and later I faked a diploma and Dr. Garcia, what does he know? He's easy to fool."

"Me, too," says Neal.

Olivia draws his head to her breasts and pats his back, rocks him gently. "Now do you see why we can't see each other more? I can't be trusted. If I get too close to you, I'll break your heart. One day I'll just up and leave. I'm not normal. I'm sick and I can't help it. I can't stand routine. I always want different. I want new. If we become an everyday thing, it won't be like that anymore. It will be old and tired and I can't stand old and tired."

"But how could you do such a thing?"

"How are you so different? What a hypocrite! Didn't you leave your wife and start a new life? Didn't you want a second chance?"

"Yes, but—"

"But nothing. It's called reinventing yourself. People do it all the time."

◆

When Neal leaves the next morning, Olivia asks if her secret is safe with him and he tells her not to worry. He would never dream of telling another soul. This is not true. He wants to do the right thing, but he's not at all sure what that right thing exactly is. It's a matter of deception. Of fraud. Olivia/Marjorie has deceived her ex-husband and family into thinking something horrible happened to her. No doubt the police have spent countless hours investigating her disappearance, when they could have been pursuing real criminals who committed real crimes. And her family, think of the anguish! Plus she's practicing medicine without a license!

For two weeks Neal avoids Olivia and tries not to imagine her misdiagnosing ruptured appendices for stomachaches and headaches

for brain tumors or, worse yet, failing to catch an outbreak of the next
Ebola-type virus mutation by pegging that fever and nausea as "only a
flu." With his stepbrother Jack out of town, he has dinner with Anna
to keep her company. During dessert she complains about being bored
and asks if they can do something different. He doesn't see why not.

They go to a neighborhood bar called the Aquarium Lounge, a
make-out place whose lighting is provided by only the virid glow from
its many aquariums, where couples canoodle on sofas and easy chairs
in various states of murky abandon. The dim lighting suits Anna well,
and her Croatian voice sounds like a seductive Eastern European spy
in a James Bond film who will do anything to get the microfilm. The
lounge seems an odd place for a heart-to-heart, but the gesture is not
without its Diary-of-a-Mad-Housewife allure. Anna has had it with
Jack. All he cares about is football. It's not healthy, is it? For a thirty-
nine-year-old man to watch videotape of his high school games and to
invite the players over afterward to party? "He is phony," she whispers.
He gets his hair permed. "Plus now he tells me he wants to get his
thing made bigger. He wants surgery for this! Penile implant! Can you
believe such foolish thing?"

Neal laughs.

Anna does not want to move. What does she know about Maryland? Nothing. Who does she know there? No one. She likes St. Louis.
She has friends here and a good job, and that means nothing to Jack
because he is selfish man. Neal agrees that Jack can be rather bull-
headed at times, but basically he means well in his fourth-down-and-
goal-to-go kind of way.

After two drinks Anna asks, "Would you kiss me? I need to be
kissed really really really badly right now. This minute." Neal drives
Anna to his place, his radio tuned to a country/western station playing a No. 1 hit titled "You Called It Love But I'm Thinkin' It's Only
Like," one of Neal's secret favorites. Near the front door he asks non-
chalantly how her writing is going. She leans against him as he searches in his pockets for his keys. "I want to read for you new poem."

In the TV room she makes him sit close and listen, forbidding him to make any comment afterward, good or bad. "Close your eyes," she commands.

He does as she asks and experiences a moment of sensory deprivation. In the internal night of his closed eyes a flash of light streaks by, as if a falling star were shooting across the sky of his eyelids. Anna reads the poem in a hopeful and enthusiastic voice, a poem filled with metaphors comparing love to chocolate, hate to football jerseys, and sex to self-service car washes with really good water pressure. When it's done Neal says, "Wow. That's something else."

She puts a finger to his lips and says, "No no no! The rules, remember? You are to say nothing."

He takes her hand and kisses her fingers, one by one. She closes her eyes, and when his lips reach her neck she whispers, "This is different."

As they make love, his pelvic thrusts rock her liquid-filled belly, making a sound as if someone were skipping rope on a waterbed. She orgasms while Neal's head is between her legs, and tugs on his hair. He panics for a moment, fearing she might uproot his remaining vulnerable follicles. When she stops panting and crying out, Anna tells Neal he is without a doubt absolutely the greatest lover she has known in all her life. He has the distinct impression she has said this same thing before to other men.

Though she insists there's not chance of them getting caught, they both agree it's best that he drive her home. As hard as he tries to seem cool, Neal can't help feeling decidedly like a defendant. If Jack found out, sitting down and having an understanding talk would be out of the question. Most likely his response would involve a baseball bat and Neal's blood spurting in slow-motion droplets from his face, a la Jake LaMotta in *Raging Bull*.

That night, alone in his apartment, lying in the sheets that reek of Anna's perfume, roll-on deodorant, sweat, saliva, and sex, Neal cannot sleep. His heart lurches and pauses as if it has a case of hiccups.

◆

At three in the morning he calls Olivia for the first time in over two weeks and there's no answer. He lets the phone ring and ring and ring. The next day he drags blearily through an assignment to video-tape and tail a public school superintendent from Morgantown, West Virginia, attending a conference titled "No Tolerance Means No Problem: Classroom Discipline in the New Millennium." At a high-class topless club, he tapes the man smiling wickedly while a gorgeous blonde writhes before him seductively, slowly removing her Catholic schoolgirl costume of white shirt, black tie, tartan skirt, and knee-high socks.

After getting enough footage for thorough incrimination, Neal calls Dr. Garcia for an appointment. The receptionist puts him on hold. While waiting with the phone crooked against his shoulder, Neal rewinds his camcorder then erases the 8mm tape of the busted superintendent. The time to change is now. Who is he to point the finger? So far he's been on the lucky end of the camera lens. That won't last forever.

When the receptionist gets back on the line, she informs Neal the earliest date Dr. Garcia can see him is in three weeks.

"But I see Dr. Cimino."

"She's no longer with us." The receptionist explains this happened over a week ago. Do they know where she is? The receptionist won't say. She's not allowed to divulge such information.

Unable to shake the feeling that he has made a tremendous blun-der, Neal visits Olivia's apartment house. He waits on the porch, in the shadows, for a half-hour, until another renter, a pale woman, arrives and opens the door with her key, then he catches it just before the door closes and climbs the stairs to the third-floor landing. At her door he knocks and listens, hearing, across the hall, someone playing guitar. She doesn't answer the doorbell. From a pay phone outside he calls the landlord and is told Olivia no longer lives there.

On the drive home he cannot concentrate, cannot focus. He is having difficulty with his vision, squinting furiously. The road is mackled and weavy. He leans forward to keep from running things over. He's struggling to prevent ruining not only his life but some poor defenseless animal's as well. Mary said he had ruined her life and that if he didn't turn over a new leaf he was going to ruin his own next. Maybe she's right. Olivia could have made him happy and now she's gone forever. So she's not completely honest. So what. We all have our faults.

When he returns home, the phone rings and it's Anna wondering when they can see each other again. She misses him and can't get him out of her mind. She wants to tell Jack she will not move to Maryland and that's final. She says she has made her pubic bone sore from masturbating too much while thinking about him. She thinks she falls in love, yes? What about Neal? Does he fall in love?

He tells her yes but can he call her back later. He's not feeling so good right now actually. His heart feels funny. His left arm is aching and he can't breathe right. The faint thump of his heart seems too fast and tight and he needs to sit down and be calm. He listens as Anna says okay but don't call me back here because I think Jack suspects something. He is acting . . . how do you say? Fishy? She will call him. Later. She hopes he feels better. What he needs is a good night of sleep, yes? Before hanging up she whispers that for him she is longing very much.

◆

Neal decides if he can just sit here and catch his breath, everything will be fine. His heart lurches and stops, lurches and stops. Sometimes it feels as if it's buzzing, as though the buzzer of a joke handshake were being pressed against it. His arm aches as if he's been tossing footballs for Jack's high school team, his chest feels as if a crushing fluid weight were draped over it, as if he were pinned beneath the flabby hulk of his own waterbed mattress.

He realizes there is a number to call for this, but the phone now seems so very far away. He tries to catch his breath and waits for everything to pass. If he can just hold on until the appointment next week, he'll be fine. He knows what Dr. Garcia will say. He's going to tell Neal that it's time to change his life. No more alcohol, no more butter, no more cigarettes, marijuana, methamphetamines, cocaine, Ecstasy, Xanax, Valium, Darvon, or women in trouble. Constant exercise. He'll join a gym. That's what he'll do. Become a regular. A regular Joe. No more fooling around. It's time to change. As Mary said, he has to grow up and start telling the truth.

When the phone begins to ring, he figures that's her, that's probably Mary, checking up on him. It's been awhile since she called to see how he was doing. The machine answers and it's Boon asking if he wants to see The Spazmos tonight at Club Foot. Boon sounds loaded. "Come on, Grandpa," he calls from the machine. "Get off your ass and join us. Whatever happened to the King Fabulous I used to know?"

Neal remembers images from the video his mother taped for him of *The Frozen Dumpling War,* clowning about in his red cape and crown, sweeping Daphne into his arms, but things speed up quickly. The action sequence hurries as in a Keystone Kops film. Dimly he senses this must mean it's time for his life to flash before his eyes. *Arrivederci,* nightclub people. The days of King Fabulous are past. That was long ago and far away. The King is dead. Long live the king.

The phone rings again and this time it's Anna. She wants to meet him at the Aquarium. She wants to rendezvous. How perfect. The French have a word for everything. Maybe he'll just meet her for one drink. One last drink. No harm in that, is there?

He frowns and closes his eyes, willing his heart to quit galumphing, quit this nonsense. Failure is bad enough, isn't it? He's not actually going to die, too, is he? After all, there's nothing seriously wrong with him. Nothing that a good honest sweat can't cure. He wants to answer the phone but the outlook is doubtful. Perhaps it's time to throw in the towel. Perhaps he just needs to answer it and give the word, spill his guts, tell the truth, because by all indications it must be time to tell the truth, time to get on the horn and say Sorry. Really. He's sorry. So sorry. He doesn't want to let anyone down, but it may be too late. It looks like he's running out of time, actually. And truth be told, he's probably not going to make it.

FATHER TONGUE

T HE LAST TIME THEY WERE PLAYING the Would-You-Still-Love-Me-If game, Tina had asked, "Would you still love me if I hurt you really badly?" Roy said Yes of course I would and five minutes later she slammed the car door on his hand. Now his left ring and middle finger were in splints. Tina said she was sorry about a zillion times and swore on her mother's grave it was an accident they happen all the time don't they but still sometimes Roy wondered. Some people you never know.

Two weeks later at ten P.M. in the dining room of the Holy Mackerel Café in Tallahassee, Florida, Roy's french fries were striped with ketchup. Tina had hardly touched her salad and it was her turn, so she said, "Would you still love me if I had one of those colostomy things because of colon cancer like my Aunt Nancy and carried my intestines around in a purse? Would you still love me?"

Roy wrinkled his brow. "Yes, of course I would still love you."

"Would you still love me if I spilled sulfuric acid on my face and looked like that guy in *Phantom of the Opera?*"

"You betcha."

"Would you still love me if I used to be a prostitute?"

Roy arched one eyebrow. "Is that the best you can do?"

As Tina chewed Roy's challenge, he sipped his Bloody Mary and secretly retreated to his past. He still loved his ex-wife Nicole, and no matter how hard he tried to get away from it, from her, she was still there, sitting at a table in his mind, lithe and brainy and good-hearted and gorgeous. Bloody Marys had been her choice of poison before she quit drinking and became serious about everything. And now she was married to someone else, a doctor for Chrissakes. Roy wondered where he went wrong, why he always wanted what he couldn't have, and Tina asked, "What are you thinking?"

Roy chewed a french fry and bought a tiny plot of time. "I'm thinking you never eat. Look at that salad. What do you live off of? Air?"

"I eat," said Tina. "Lots." She popped half a deviled egg in her mouth and chewed, then opened her mouth to showcase a mix of paprika and yolk. "See?"

"How about this one," said Roy. "Would you still love me if I was like Jeffrey Dahmer?"

"But you wouldn't be you if you did that."

"What if I had multiple personalities? One minute I'm Jeffrey Dahmer and the next I'm Mr. Nice Guy."

Tina pursed her lips. "I don't know if I'd go that far."

"Well, what about Mr. Right?"

"I'm thinking maybe Mr. Right Now." She grinned. Tina the Kidder.

Roy slumped in his seat. "I feel so special."

"You're not fooling me one minute, Bucko." She pointed her fork at Roy. "I know what's in that dusty photo album you call a brain."

"Oh, yeah?"

She chewed a piece of lettuce and drew the moment out into a fine-tipped point. "No, it's no photo album. It's a video store. Your mind's a Blockbuster Video, but inside the store, the shelves are filled with all the tapes of you and Nicole. Famous couple and their famous life together."

◆

Women could always read Roy's mind. He struggled to control his thoughts, but it did no good. His wayward thoughts got in the way of his happiness, and he wanted very badly for Tina to make him happy. He thought she was his one big chance. But his best friend, Otto, had recently said, "Tina can't make you happy. Only *you* can make you happy."

Roy didn't know what to make of that. He didn't even know how to think of that. Like when someone says, My mind drew a blank. Roy's mind = a blank. That's what Roy thought about making himself happy. He had no idea where to start. He doubted that he would recognize happiness if it came up and bit him.

After mulling it over for days, Roy called Otto late one night and said, "Okay, pal, this is what I think. I think happiness is like a tropical fish. You can go to a mall and buy it and bring it back to your tank in a wobbly plastic bag full of water, but invariably it dies after a few weeks. And all the pretty orange coral and topless round-breasted mermaids and ceramic castles in the world can't stop it from going belly up on the surface."

Otto asked, "A topical what?"

Roy didn't pause to answer the Q.

"Like a tropical fish, the fins of happiness are fragile and lovely. They are not to be touched. If you feed it too much it will die."

After silence at the other end of the line, Otto said, "You know what I thought you said at first?"

"What?"

"Happiness is like a *topical* fish. And I was lying here at two in the morning thinking, What is a topical fish?"

Roy complained that he was beginning to fear that nothing would make him happy. He wasn't happy with Nicole and he wasn't happy with Tina. Both of them were wonderful women who loved him deeply.

He heard Otto yawn at the other end of the line, then offer this advice. "Pick one and stick with her and be good to her and you will be happy. Next caller, please."

Otto returned to sleep, but Roy went on with his life. He could not sleep, he could never sleep. He could remember happy moments, but they were all in the past. He remembered falling asleep at night next to Nicole. Every night as they fell asleep, he and Nicole would lie on their backs, stretched out comfortably in their queen-sized bed, and Roy would rest his left foot against Nicole's right foot, his foot under hers, and every night this is how they would fall asleep, just their feet touching, but linked together like that, wonderfully, beautifully, gently. Sometimes they would rub their arches and nuzzle their toes, and it was a gentle poignant moment of grace and understanding at the end of each day.

After he left Nicole, Roy could not sleep, but when he could sleep or when he tried to sleep, it was like a mental patient—nightmares on a cheap mattress, the sheets twisted and tangled. Alone he slept curled into himself, tight as a fist. Except when Tina came over and fucked him silly, after which he'd usually pass out on top behind or beneath her.

But Roy knew this was not going to last. He was ten years older than Tina, and he knew that difference would eventually come knocking on the door and deliver its wilted roses. He told himself to concentrate on The Moment a kind of be-here-now idea, but the problem with humans is looking forward backward all at once if you never thought about your approaching doom perhaps it wouldn't matter and Roy in particular knew Tina would soon be history not as in dead but as in another man's arms hairy thighs fellatio you name it.

Tina was in the last year of law school when they met, though Roy hadn't thought much about it, other things on his mind—Nicole for one—but now that she was about to take the bar, things were different.

He felt like washing his hands after touching what would soon be a lawyer. Roy had little room to talk himself, being the sales rep for a liquor distributor, but at least it was promoting good honest alcoholism and not the distortion of truth.

"Truth is a matter of taste," said Tina. "State of Colorado vs. Alferd Packer."

Roy figured Tina would pass the bar, sell her soul to the devil and how do you say That would be that. Meanwhile Nicole love of his life fire of his loins his sin his soul lolls in her new doctor's arms like Queen of the Nile. Roy resented the doctors lawyers professionals of the world. He dribbled the clumsy ball of an amateur among professionals. They hit every free throw as his palms sweated and even his passes flew out of bounds.

When Tina and Roy first met, they made love within a few hours. Tina said, "I'm not sure we should be doing this," right before Roy rolled her over on her stomach and slowly peeled down her Be-My-Valentine underthings. After that, they slept ate bathed danced fucked laughed talked together for an entire dizzy four days. They drew tattoos on each other's bodies with ballpoint pens. Roy had a huge *T* high on his arm, above his bicep, while Tina had an encircled *R* on the left cheek of her bottom. It was all quite romantic and giddy and both of them knew it would never last.

Ten restaurants and eight orgasms later, Roy landed on his feet in a world that noted Tina was not his wife and thus his behavior was Wrong. For the next few months, he woke in the morning and brushed his teeth staring in the mirror at the Bad Guy. Nicole knew everything immediately if not sooner. She was intuitively psychic and not averse to reading Roy's mail. She was sweet and forgiving for three weeks, then slugged him in the throat while he was asleep one night and thanked God later there wasn't a gun in the house or he'd be one fucking dead wife cheater.

At first Roy would not introduce Tina to his friends or go out with her friends because he was still married. Tina said it made her feel like something to be ashamed of, like an embarrassment. It made her feel mediocre, and she did not like to feel mediocre.

"I feel like I'm dating Snuffleupagus."

"Who's that?"

"He's Big Bird's imaginary friend on *Sesame Street*."

"After my time," said Roy.

"At first no one believed Big Bird that Snuffleupagus even existed, but now everyone can see him."

"Oh, I like that. That's sweet. Maybe someday I won't be imaginary anymore either. Then I'll just be The Friend, not imaginary."

"Aren't you serious about anything?"

"Okay, okay. I'll be Sears, you be Roebuck."

Tina stared at him without batting an eyelash, then said, "Before my time."

After a few months Roy was right. He wasn't imaginary anymore. Everyone knew about Tina by then. The men imagined her naked body and said, "Lucky dog." The women predicted stretch marks for Tina and spiritual bankruptcy for Roy. "Just you wait," they said. "Things are great now, but how long have they known each other? Four months? Hell, the first two years don't even *count*."

Otto the accountant and best friend described his problem as a mathematical equation: Beauty/Youth + Ambition − Guilt = Trouble. "And you left Nicole for this? Are you blind or something, buddy? This baby's headed for the big time. D.C. The hill. The house. And you? You are an accessory not included."

◆

After finishing another round of Would-You-Still-Love-Me-If, Tina ordered a bowl of lime sherbet and, watching the table closest to them being served a cauldron of gumbo, remarked on the barbaric practice of boiling live crabs. "What is that?" she asked. "The Spanish Inquisition?" Roy paid the tab, and as he signed the credit card voucher, the table wobbled slightly, provoking another memory of Nicole to rise from the murky sonar depths of his mind. Whenever they had dined out Nicole would check the tables for a wobble and slip a book of matches below the offending leg if necessary to fix the problem. She liked the taste of butterscotch but could do without peppermint thank you very much. Tina continued to worry the bone of gumbo crab torture, while Roy tried to keep his feet as the whitecaps of life with Nicole crashed over him. He knew there was no point in nostalgia. She was something he had lost and would never find again. He shouldn't be thinking of her he knew this it would not do to burst into tears at the Holy Mackerel Café with Tina thinking Enough is enough but no matter how hard he tried his mind filled with the grace and whirl of Nicole the way she told him I don't care about the house or the car goddammit I want you can't you see that can't you get that through your thick skull?

Before he moved out, Nicole tried to persuade Roy to stay, tried to solve their problems and figure a way to start anew again. Roy complained that they never made love anymore, while Nicole deconstructed his definition of "never." He complained that she was always saying No to him, pushing him away, refusing to touch him. They talked about how they never had anything to talk about. Roy said she didn't talk to him anymore, she only argued. He said she disagreed with everything he said. "I do not!" Nicole shouted. He said she didn't know the rules of polite conversation.

"What rules? Where did you get these rules?"

"You don't get them from anywhere. You just know them. Or you don't. And *you* truly don't. Talking to you is a job. It's like work."

Nicole pointed out how they'd been together for twelve years and things change with that time. "Of course we're different people than when we first met. You've told me all your stories. I know all about you, your life, your family, everything. What do you know about Tina? Nothing. Don't you see? You've got to get through the ups and downs. A good marriage isn't easy. It's work."

"You shouldn't have to work at love!" said Roy.

Nicole shook her head. She gave up. "Fine. Do whatever you want."

"Don't be that way," said Roy. He reached for her hand and tried to kiss it, but Nicole jerked it free.

"You make me sick," she said.

Now she was with her doctor a surgeon for Chrissakes a surgeon who smoked Cuban cigars sailed racing yachts for kicks made killings in the stock market while Roy maxed-out his credit cards and called Nicole too often. The last time he called she didn't have the time to talk. She said, "I think I have somewhere I need to be."

◆

Roy sensed the whole iceberg of their past together floating just beneath the surface of his life, and realized that too often he became the Titanic, moving forward slowly but inexorably and feeling that whole past beneath him ripping a gash in his side but powerless to stop it.

◆

As they were waiting for the waitress to bring them a to-go container, Tina asked, "Would you still love me if I sprayed insecticide on my father's food and poisoned him?"

"I'd love you more than ever."

"He didn't die or anything. He just got real sick, and now he's paralyzed because it attacked his nervous system."

"Even if he died I'd still love you."

"I'm not kidding. I poisoned my father. I can't believe I'm telling you this. I never tell any of my new friends this. Just you. I don't want us to hide anything from each other, okay? I think it's because with you I can be totally honest."

Roy wondered if 16 percent was enough of a tip. "It's called the best policy."

Tina was giving him a weird smile, so he asked, "Are you pulling my leg?"

"Jesus. Your skull *is* thick. This is real, okay? I poisoned my father. You want to meet him? He lives here in town now. I take care of him, kind of. He has a day nurse and all, but she's always reminding me she's not a maid. For the last few days I've been meaning to go over to his place and clean it up. He doesn't get around very well."

"You poisoned your father. Right. And I strangled my mother while having sex with her."

"Roy? I'm not going to say it again." Tina stared at him, her eyes pink and misty. "I almost killed him. I almost spent the rest of my life in prison."

"Wait a second. You said you hadn't seen your father in years, that he ran off and left your family when you were a little girl?"

"I lied."

"How do I know you're not lying now?"

"Trust me."

"Then let's go see him. Prove it."

"You promise you'll still love me?"

"Tina? Give it a rest, okay?"

"You have to promise."

"Okay. I promise."

In the oyster shell parking lot, a white mist swirled past the street lamps like television snow. Roy could smell catfish and regret in the damp air. He unlocked Tina's door first, wondering what other sins were up her sleeve. She'd once mentioned being the star of an orgy, but when he seemed shocked, insisted it was a joke, jeez, you'll believe anything. He dropped the keys and had to kneel beside the door and palpate the shadows to find his way, while Tina held the white Styrofoam to-go containers of all the food she would never eat. After he managed to get the door unlocked, she kissed him on the cheek and said, "You are such a gentleman. I'm never going to let you go, you know that, don't you?"

◆

On the way over to her father's house, Roy drove carefully on the shiny and slickened streets, counting the traffic lights and turns because he had a horrible sense of direction, was always taking the wrong turn, and wanted to know exactly where he was at all times. Once they were moving, the mist grew thicker, mixed with fog. Amber yield lights glowed like Van Gogh's sunflowers. Even the street noise was hushed, the hissing of their tires like a mean whisper, as Tina explained how she almost killed her father. It had started out as a joke, sort of. True he was always yelling at her and her mother. He drank like a fish and hated his salesman job. So what else is new? But she loved him she guessed. She certainly didn't mean to kill him though the thought had crossed her mind that if he weren't around she and her mother would be much happier carefree even but that was just serendipity she wasn't serious about that she wasn't a cold-blooded killer for Chrissakes she had a conscience just as much as anyone still he made her life hell.

"How'd he do that?"

Roy missed a left and Tina directed him to pull into a parking lot and turn around, reverse direction, and take a right. She quit talking until they were back in the right direction. Paused at the next intersection, Roy felt the world closing in on him. He tried to get a glimpse of the sky above through the wiper beats of his windshield, but only glimpsed a misty patch of white space tangled with power lines and broken kites. To Roy the fog seemed mystical and otherworldly—the aftermath of some cataclysm, the drifting muffle of volcanic ash. Once they were back on track, he asked Tina again how her father made her life hell.

"He was an asshole. Always yelling at me to clean my room and do my homework and clean out the car and about a million other chores. I called him Commandant Klink."

"Wait a second. You poisoned your father because he made you do your homework?"

"No, I didn't poison my father because he made me do my homework. There was more to it than that. He was always bothering me. It started when I was little. He did things to me."

Roy rubbed the fogged windshield with the palm of his hand. He asked what kind of things.

"Disgusting things. I don't want to talk about it, okay? All I know is I remember taking this creativity quiz in high school one day. It asked *If you could witness any event, what would it be?* My best friend Shanna said she wanted to see the liberation of Paris. I said I'd like to see my father's death."

Tina stopped talking. She rolled down her window, fished in her purse for a cigarette. As bands of light from the street lamps crossed the car, Roy tried to read her face. He reached out and squeezed her left leg.

"And that night he was loaded to the gills, shouting at my mother about how the house was always a mess, and it was my turn to fix dinner. I was sick of listening to him, so I took this can of Raid out from beneath the sink and sprayed his plate with it, then put the macaroni and meatloaf on top it.

"You see he had this horrible habit of always licking his plate clean. It was creepy. Every night I had to watch that gross, disgusting tongue of his. He said it showed how he didn't waste anything, but really, I think he just liked to lick things.

"I wanted to get back at him, so I sprayed his plate with Raid. But I never thought he would eat it. I figured he would take one lick and say What the hell? That's what I was waiting for, that look on his face as he tasted the bug spray on his plate."

Tina paused in her story to give more directions, while Roy was having difficulty keeping his mind on the road. In this part of town the houses were drab and boxy, the street curbs packed with parked cars.

On a dark side street, Tina pointed out her father's driveway. Roy pulled in and quickly got out of the car, needing to catch his breath. Although the yard was flat, he was dizzy, seemed to have trouble keeping his feet, as if the world were spinning too fast. And even the sidewalks here looked like earthquake damage. They were clotted with weeds, the concrete buckled and broken, as if something were surging up from below. The house was a small bungalow with the fuzzy shadows of palm trees in the yard and scallop-shell wind chimes on the front porch. There were several newspapers heaped on the steps. The lawn was overgrown, and in the center of the driveway, the brown glass of a broken beer bottle glistened.

Roy said, "So your father licked the plate, right?"

Tina leaned against the car and scratched a fleck of something on its hood, pouting. She refused to look at Roy. She didn't like the tone of his voice she knew this confession honesty thing was probably a mistake maybe some stones are better left unturned but it's too late now and if you love someone they forgive you everything, right?

Roy said, "Come on, now. Don't start moping."

"You don't like me anymore, do you?"

"Tina."

"Don't 'Tina' me."

"Would you just finish the story?"

She kept scratching the hood and said, "Well, I was sitting there watching and waiting for him to say something about the food tasting funny, but then the phone rang and it was for me. I didn't know what to do, so I took the call. It was my friend Shanna and she was crying because her boyfriend Ted Kay had just dumped her, so I had to talk to her and try to make her feel better. By the time I got off the phone, my father had licked the plate clean. He didn't notice anything! Thirty minutes later he went into convulsions."

Roy and Tina stood in the front yard, the fog drifting by like a flurry of ghosts, as she explained about the investigation. She insisted she never lied, really. She more or less told the truth. But the law people couldn't decide whether it was attempted murder, assault, or a screw-up, so the grand jury didn't indict her. "The prosecutors didn't know what to do with me. One of them said I was The Bad Seed and the other said Girls will be girls. You know, that's when I first got the idea of becoming a lawyer. They were so cool and powerful. I wanted to carry one of those briefcases and look important."

As they stepped up the porch, the only comment Roy could manage was, "Well, at least you didn't end up in the Big House." It was a stupid thing to say. He knew this. He stared at the palm trees and wondered if he'd stumbled into some twisted version of an ABC *After School Special*. Tina found the key in her purse and unlocked the door. She called into the house, saying Daddy! Are you decent? You've got company!

Inside the house, the cluttered rooms were dimly lit, and everything was brown. Brown paneled walls, brown carpeting, brown sofa. Even the telephone was brown. Roy could not remember ever seeing a brown telephone. The ceiling was low and the living room dominated by a large aquarium full of tropical fish. Tina immediately went to tap on the glass and say Hi Vincent! Hi Mia! Roy didn't know what to do with his hands. He followed as Tina left the fuggy living room and walked down a hallway to where her father lay in a rumpled bed, propped on pillows. He was watching TV and did not react to their presence.

"Daddy, this is Roy. He's a friend of mine and he's going to help me clean the house for you tonight."

Tina's father nodded at them and blinked his eyes. His face was mottled and stubbly, his bald head the yellow of old newspapers, his jowls fleshy and slack. Roy could barely force himself to look. He was coming to believe that nothing could be gained from this experience. It was beyond the realm of his understanding. After such knowledge, what forgiveness?

Tina chatted about how she and Roy had met and told her father things were pretty serious between them, but that Roy hadn't popped the question yet. The old man kept his eyes on the television, channel surfing with his remote control, the sound blaring, while she continued talking. "Well, okay, Daddy, we're going to get to work then!" Tina said loudly. The old man nodded and set down the remote. He closed his eyes and seemed to be waiting for them to leave the room.

Roy emptied the garbage cans and Tina vacuumed the living room. As he was moving around the house, Roy struggled not to peek in her father's room. Whenever he walked by it, he heard screaming. It seemed her father had found a horror movie. He also heard the old man talking to himself, but couldn't catch exactly what he was saying, the words like a mumbled act of contrition. When cleaning the bathroom, Tina noticed her father was out of toothpaste and Kleenex. Roy said he knew of an all-night drugstore nearby and offered to make a quick run for it. Tina said, "Okay, but hurry back."

Outside the house, Roy breathed deeply, trying to suck fresh air into his lungs. On the way to the drugstore he had an impulse to keep going, suddenly felt that he needed space, but controlled himself. When he returned, Tina was washing the dishes. To kill time, Roy sat on the brown sofa and flipped through the only magazine on the coffee table, an outdated issue of *Popular Psychology*.

After a few minutes he called out, "Are we almost finished? I need to get some sleep tonight."

"Roy? Would you behave? I don't like you rushing me." She said she'd be done soon, though they couldn't leave until they changed her father's sheets. Roy would have to pick up her father while she peeled back the sheets and slipped the new ones beneath him. Roy would have to reach his arms under her father's back, under his legs, and lift him in the air.

In his bedroom, Tina's father had his eyes closed, though his purple lips continued mumbling. A vampire hissed on TV and cowered in the shadow of a crucifix. Tina and Roy positioned themselves on opposite sides of the bed, as if visiting a dying relative. She explained what they planned to do. Her father opened his foggy eyes and nodded. His lower eyelids drooped, showing a crescent of pink skin.

Roy stood there and tried to just get through the moment. He did not enjoy being this close to suffering. Nicole would never have sprayed insecticide on her father's dinner! Not even as a joke.

Tina asked her father if he was ready, and he said Let's get it over with. Roy worked his arms beneath the man and struggled to lift him up. It took all his strength to get him in the air. He could feel the warmth of Tina's father through his pajamas and could not help but be repulsed by this. Roy's face flushed red as he held his breath and tried to keep from dropping the man. Tina pulled the sheet down quickly and said they were doing great, just a few more minutes and they'd be finished. Roy lowered him back on the bed but kept his arms in place as Tina flipped out the clean sheets. Hunkered over her father, Roy listened to the old man's raspy breath. When he glanced up, he saw her father looking at him with those milky eyes. They seemed to focus on the center of Roy's forehead.

"She did this to me, you know."

"I know."

The old man nodded and curled his fingers on the stained bare mattress. He said, "I forgave her."

Roy knew Tina was giving him a look, but he concentrated on ignoring everything around him and waiting for his moment to lift. He listened to the relentless sound of the poisoned father's breathing. When Tina was ready with the sheets, she motioned for Roy to lift.

Her father said, "Now look at me."

"I'm sorry, Daddy. It was an accident, right? I didn't mean anything by it," said Tina.

Roy struggled to hold the man aloft as Tina worked on getting the sheets in place. Her father leaned his head against Roy's shoulder and spoke: "Lawyer said she was temporarily insane, but I never believed that."

"I was just a crazy kid."

"What's your name again?"

"Roy."

"Well, Roy, what do you think? You got an opinion on this?"

Roy could feel father and daughter waiting on him. "What do I know?" he said. "I wasn't there."

Tina finished putting the sheets in place. "I think forgiveness is the best thing you can do. No use holding a grudge now, is there?"

"I guess not," said her father. "I deserved it anyway."

Roy lowered the man back on the bed, trembling with the effort. He stood back and rubbed his hand as Tina straightened the top sheet. "Roy?" she asked. "Could you tuck in that side?"

"Oh, sorry." He had to use his bad hand to tuck in the sheets, and winced as he jammed the splints between the mattress and box spring. When he looked up, rubbing the knuckles of his broken fingers, Tina's father was staring at him.

"Who did that to you?"

Roy shrugged. "She did," he answered, nudging toward Tina. "Accidentally, of course."

Tina's father nodded. "I understand. The world's a funny place, isn't it?"

Roy continued rubbing his hand, staring down at the old man's wrinkled and bony yellow fingers. "You can say that again."

"No, I wouldn't do that." He dropped his head back on the pillow and closed his heavy eyes. "Once is enough."

There's Nothing The Matter With Gwen

S HELBY SAYS THE MATTER with Gwen is that her breasts are too large, and this makes her feel self-conscious, leading her to be alternately shy or outrageous, on the one hand insecure and on the other overcompensating for it. He suggests breast reduction surgery. A little nip here and there and her outlook on life will be healthier. "It'll be like Prozac," he says, "only different."

Gwen does not agree, and she's no dummy. She teaches fifth grade, though Shelby does not respect this, how difficult it can be. On this particular day at her elementary school, Brian Gish stands before her desk, his hair matted in dreadlocks and, since he shaved off his eyebrows the week before, his face frozen in a cartoon expression of surprise. "Miss Tremain? I have the hiccups." He wants a drink of water. He wants to be let loose in the hall.

Gwen is an extremely short, lovely young woman with a heart-shaped face, pale skin, and slightly discolored teeth. Her black hair is streaked with silver and cut in a shag, so that she resembles a coquettish skunk. She notes that hiccups can be fatal. In fact she knew a man who hiccuped for fifteen years straight.

"Fifteen years?" Brian frowns. "No way."

"He died of hiccups. True story."

"Miss Tremain . . ."

"Tell you what," she says. "I'll let you go get a drink of water. If you'll hiccup for me." She points one brightly painted fingernail straight at his mouth. "Now."

Brian stares at Miss Tremain and blinks. After several moments, Gwen smiles and suggests Brian return to his desk, and be thankful his hiccups are cured.

♦

Technically, Gwendolyn Tremain is Mrs. Shelby Batch, but the subservience and scratchy rasp of that moniker rubs her the wrong way, so she chooses to withhold that information—her marital status—from the underage busybodies otherwise known as her class. On her drive home that day she retrieves her wedding ring from the glove compartment, slips it on with one agile hand, where it feels as comfortable as the heavy iron manacles kidnaped Africans were shackled with on barbaric nineteenth-century slave ships and on which human beings were forced to eat worm-filled gruel and wallow in their own feces. She's heading home. A three-bedroom, two-bath in Tacoma, Washington.

The house is Shelby's idea. Shelby's silent baby. Shelby's dream vision of a garage full of golf clubs, closets full of skeletons, and medicine cabinets stocked with denial and relentless, blank-faced repression. It cost $237,000 of Shelby's money. The mortgage payment is so high they cannot afford a second car. An extremely resilient and civic-minded person, Shelby does not mind taking the bus to his job in Seattle. They also cannot afford furniture. In this respect their home is extremely dreamlike. *I was in a house with no furniture or curtains and the phone was ringing. . . .* No matter. They can adapt. Every marriage has its rocky beginnings. Years later they will look back and laugh laugh laugh. They sit at the breakfast nook and watch TV on the kitchen counter. The other six rooms of the house are empty, carpeted, and vast. When Gwendolyn is home alone, the electric sockets eye her suspiciously. If she stares at the blank white walls too long without blinking—which she does more often than she should—they begin to swirl with ripples of the palest yellow, blush the faintest pink, like a deceptively festive, Hallmark-card version of the Rothko Chapel.

The backyard is large, fenced, and stripped of every naturally occurring blade of grass. In its center stands a rapidly rusting swing set left by the mysterious former owners, who had no children. The tall privacy fence shuts out the neighbors and creates, along with the swing set, an aura of abandon. On evenings when Shelby is gone, Gwendolyn swings in it wearing nothing but the cool lingerie of the night air. At the apex of each swing, for a moment her hair floats free, as if immersed in an inky sea, silvered only by the fingers of moonlight.

Deciding to pick up a film to watch that evening, Gwendolyn pulls into the parking lot of the Movie Magic video store in Tacoma, but before she steps out of the car, she squirms off the wedding ring and plops it in the ashtray.

In the Adventure aisle, a tall disheveled man smiles at her, and she smiles back. She wanders by him three times, half pretending she can't find a film to rent. "I've seen them all," she imagines explaining, if asked to defend her indecision. She only half pretends. Really. She doesn't have a clue what to get, but then again she isn't really trying. She fingers several femme fatale VCR sleeves, covers emblazoned with sex goddesses in lingerie and shadows, lipstick in one hand and a pistol in the other. Finally settling on a sugary piece of foreign silliness that will stymie Shelby, she isn't surprised when, as soon as she takes her place in line, behind her looms the smiler.

Gwen will talk to anyone. People like this about her. The gift of gab. She meets new people all the time and makes new friends. In line at the video store, she begins chatting with the disheveled man, an attorney named Sean. He makes a face at her selection, a romantic comedy with big-shot actors about falling in and out of love in Paris. She wants to know why he made that face.

"France," he scoffs. He's seen that flick, that's why. He comes across as an extremely confident person, maybe a bit pleased with himself, but oh well.

"You want my opinion?" he asks.

"Absolutely."

"It sucks."

"Okay," says Gwen. She nods triumphantly. "Thanks for that advice. I won't rent it." She plops it atop the microwave popcorn display and marches back to the Drama aisle, then reverses herself halfway there and returns to Sean in line. "What should I see?"

He shrugs. "What I'm seeing?"

"Okay."

His house is full of books and birds. Cages of parakeets and exotic finches. A white cockatoo and a blue-throated mynah. After several drinks, Gwen tells him about Shelby's plan to reduce the size of her breasts via surgery and asks what he thinks.

"I think that's the craziest thing I've heard in a long time."

Pretending to be absorbed in her glass of Chablis, Gwen smiles and flushes faintly. When he asks if he can take a Polaroid of her, she says, "I don't see why not."

After several glasses of wine, Sean does not have to twist her arm to get Gwen to unbutton her blouse. If they're going to be reduced, perhaps there should be some record of them in this state. Of grace. Of nature. A *Before* picture, you might say. "Okay," she says, and removes her blouse.

She watches as the Polaroid develops in her fingers. In the photo, her eyes are pink and glowing, her breasts seem well-shaped and oddly matter-of-fact.

She's never done this before: Is that what a *Before* picture means? A picture of something you've never done before?

"No," he says. "I think it means a picture of something before it's going to change."

"Not necessarily."

Gwen says the weirdest Polaroid she ever saw was of her neighbor actually being eaten by his pet python. True story! It's a little-known fact that many people who buy exotic reptiles such as boa constrictors, pythons, Komodo lizards, and anacondas are actually eaten by their own pets. It's more common than you think. Somehow the thing freaked out and attacked him, getting his whole arm, right up to the shoulder, in its mouth before the firemen could yank it off. During the hubbub, another neighbor who heard the screams snapped the photo. "Was that a Before picture?" she asks.

When Gwen's glass is empty, Sean offers to freshen it. "You're too kind," she says. She follows him to the kitchen and watches as he mixes them. "You don't have anything stronger, do you?"

"Stronger?"

She nods and puts one finger to her lips. "I don't know. I guess I'm just dying to be bad."

Sean produces a vial of powder and a mirror, a razor blade, and a short plastic straw. They snort several lines while watching the Cartoon Channel. In Gwendolyn's opinion, an occasional romantic/amorous dabbling is not actually cheating if the spouse in question does not give a hoot. When Sean describes a Democratic party fund-raiser he was at the night before, Gwen interrupts him to confess that in high school she grew up in Bethesda, Maryland, and used to date Walter Mondale's son. Sean laughs. "Aren't you the name dropper?"

She smiles and laughs, touching his knee with one hand lightly, her black and silver bangs slipping over her eyes.

◆

At some point Gwen realizes she's home. She's in the driver's seat of her car, and the engine is running and there are no small children impaled on her hood ornament. To all intents and purposes she has made it home safely. She remembers not a thing. That night, the next day, or years later. It is as if she experiences the "lost time" phenomenon common to victims of alien abductions. Perhaps she actually has been abducted. You never know. Stranger things happen.

It's raining. Her first clear awareness of her world is that the windshield wipers are driving her bananas. Something must be done. Action must be taken. She stares forward at the windows of her garage, briefly considers trying to use the remote control device to raise it, but the contraption spooks her when sober, and in this condition, forget it. The light glares in a reflection of the garage door windows, like the evil face of the house in *The Amityville Horror,* and she rubs her neck, tickled by the feet of a horde of hideous fantasized houseflies.

Wait. Here we go. I know. There.

She turns off the headlights, stops the maniacal back-and-forth, back-and-forth of the windshield wipers, a motion that makes the glands in her neck swell and produces a metallic taste in her mouth. She kills the engine. A horror-movie silence plops into the seat beside her like a poisonous toad.

Attempting to carry herself with the mien of Grace Kelly, Gwendolyn sways across the flagstone walk to the front door, scratching her arm on the pesky shrubbery and losing one shoe. There then begins the problem of the keys. She checks the five separate pockets of her overcoat at least four separate times, finding only a book of wooden matches from the Sweet Dreams Café, a dime, and the wrinkled, shiny foil wrapper of a chocolate after-dinner mint. Her hair is getting wet. The speed of the earth's rotation increases as she stands there, flinging raindrops down with pointed vehemence and, as Gwen struggles to search her purse, pinning her back to the door. Giving in to the centrifugal force, she slides into a stable if less-than-ladylike position on the welcome mat.

Using the flame of a butane lighter for illumination, she stares into the black hole of her purse. What are her underthings doing in there? A whimper of guilt wriggles free, as if a movie star has stepped onto a hand mirror in her bare feet. Holding the flickering flame like a fallen woman penitent, legs crossed swami style, Gwen becomes aware of a decidedly gooey sensation in her inner sanctum as the bright metallic fish eye of her key ring flashes in the trout stream of the purse.

Once inside the house she realizes something is wrong. She wonders if she's wearing the wrong feet on the wrong shoes, and does not realize that Shelby has not yet returned from his softball game. The rooms are totally dark, velvety and rich and airy, with only the digital clocks on the VCR and atop the oven glowing, though the ice maker hums as if the restless spirits of Native American dead are chanting a seriously pissed-off ghost dance. Gwen tries to reach the bedroom, but the hallway entrance spins away from her, the living room passes by in its wake, and it takes all her concentration to attempt a beeline for the breakfast nook, which swoops away, tumbling her into the empty cavern of the den, where her head bonks against the carpeted floor. Ouch! She laughs and sits up, rubbing the goose egg on her noggin.

Where is Shelby? Shelby is where? Where is Shelby? Shelby is where? Where is Shelby? Shelby is where?

She unzips her skirt and unbuttons her blouse, deciding he must be gone and she will seduce him as soon as he walks into the house. While she waits, she can't resist the erotic eeriness of the moment— the Fiona Apple, bad-girl allure of being wasted on shag carpeting, her slightly wet hair—so she touches herself. When Shelby arrives a short time later, the front door is open, exposing the innards of the house as dark as doom itself, broken only by a parallelogram of streetlight that splashes into the entry hall. He stands there for a moment, clutching a cluster of bats and a cardboard box of softballs. Arming himself with a Louisville Slugger, he inches forward, ready to bash out the brains of any burglar dumb enough to try to steal this home plate. It isn't until then that from the fugitive darkness of the den, he hears a plaintive whimper.

◆

The next day Gwendolyn physically appears at school in room nine, as usual, standing before her class of thirty-two eleven-year-olds, two of whom are absent, lecturing them on the mysterious lives of birds. She begins the slide show with the exotic: the ungainly stork, the triumphant swan, the nelly flamingo. In the darkened room, the children grow sleepy and listless. And Gwen finds her mind drifting, her consciousness floating away, as if her mental self, the loci of her thoughts and feelings, were a canoe adrift in the overpowering current of the Columbia River, a famous waterway first successfully navigated in 1804 by the party of Meriweather Lewis and William Clark, aboard rafts made of rough-hewn logs lashed together with the ponytails of Native American maidens. Halfway through the slide show she turns off the machine and flicks on the overhead lights. The students fidget suddenly, rubbing their eyes and turning to her for guidance or merely out of curiosity. Sherman Keeler tickles Cynthia Schnobel's ear with the tip of his No. 2 pencil. She flicks at her earlobe and tells him to cut it out or he'll get it.

Gwendolyn says, "I have an idea. Instead of sitting in this stuffy room staring at pictures of birds, let's go outside and see the real thing."

The students stare at her dully. "Outside?"

"Come on," she says. "You know. A field trip!"

Impromptu field trips are discouraged, of course, at this elementary school. Such activities effect too much risk, and will likely result in unforeseen circumstances such as drownings, bear attacks, poisonous spider bites, and broken ankles. All of which could entail lengthy and costly litigation proceedings and considerable unpleasantness. This policy, however, is not known to the students. For her part, Gwendolyn cheerfully tosses those paranoid considerations aside as so much hooey. If you're afraid to experience life, if you're afraid to breathe, to live, to walk in the woods or swim in the sea, you might as well be dead. And her class, thank god, is very much alive.

Marching en masse past the baseball diamond, at eleven A.M. the entire class is thick in the middle of one of the great rain forests of the Pacific Northwest, or the closest they can come to it. Although once inside the deep blue shadows of the fir and spruce the little varmints scatter like commandos in Cambodia, Gwen does her best to identify various species of birds—by their common names, of course—to whoever scurries within earshot.

"These rain forests are filled with birds," she says. There is not a feather or a beak in sight. "Look up there!" Gwen points vaguely toward the higher branches of a pine. "Isn't that a hairy woodpecker?"

"There's no such thing," says Ellen Demarest. "Birds don't have hair."

"It's just a name. And feathers are like hair, aren't they?"

She pats Ellen on the back, who is now climbing rather awkwardly over a fallen tree trunk. On field trips, Ellen always shadows Gwen, and is afraid of everything. "Are there ticks in these woods?" she asks.

"Not a one," says Gwen.

"My father always warns us to be careful of ticks. He says we can catch Lyme disease from them."

Gwen assures her there's nothing to worry about.

"My brother got that last summer," says Jeffrey Ang, appearing to crawl out from under a large rock. "He's dead now."

"You've got one on your neck, Ellen!" shouts Annie Grotz, the Tomboy. "RIP, Ellen. RIP."

"Look, everyone!" Gwen points toward where she hopes a bird will appear. Miraculously, as if on cue, one does. A flash of red against the sweeping black lines of the drooping spruce branches. "What was that?" She squints her eyes, now authoritative. "A scarlet tanager?"

Benjamin Doost, who knows everything, exclaims drily, "That was a robin."

"No way," says Gwen. "I know a robin when I see one. They're a dime a dozen. But that bird up there was rare." Without glancing in Benjamin's direction, she says, "Maybe it was a western kingbird—"

"Robin," says Ben.

Gwen is about to snap at Benjamin, when Bradley Tufts points ahead and asks what's that one. She peers into the verdure as Ben scampers forward in excitement. "I don't know," she says. "Lord Benjamin the Heavy-Footed scared it away."

All the children nearby laugh, except Ben.

"I did not!"

"And that was," says Gwen, going on, "if I'm not mistaken, a female large-breasted throat-smasher."

"Way to go, Ben!"

◆

In the parking lot of the Sweet Dreams Café, Gwen performs an act of oral love on Sean and really, they barely even know each other. When she returns home Shelby is in the living room, practicing the guitar. He's improving himself. He's not your average Mr. Stagnant Pond. No sirree. What a catch this one is. He learns something new every day, and the rest of his life, he won't get older, he'll get better. Gwen knows that Shelby will age well. Like cheese. Like Gouda or Muenster. Rich and dusky he is. He'll be. He was.

Later that night, Gwen and Shelby eat dinner at Bennigan's. Shelby orders appetizers of jalapeno peppers and buffalo wings.

"Why do they call them buffalo wings?" asks Gwen.

Shelby shrugs.

"Buffalos can't fly."

"It's chicken."

"Pardon?" asks Gwen.

"It's chicken," says Shelby. "Chicken wings."

Gwen looks at him—her husband, the man she chose to marry, the lord of her manor—then says, "I know."

He eats the contents of the entire basket. Gwen is hungry, but does not manage to eat a single one. He looks overly pleased with himself and needs to use his napkin more often than he does. He says, "So it doesn't matter if buffalos can't fly."

"Yes, it does."

"Why?"

"Never mind."

Shelby smiles. "You just don't want to admit I'm right, do you?"

◆

On the weekend, Shelby's friends invite them for dinner and drinks. When everyone is soused they play the game of I NEVER.

"It's a game of confessions," says Jim.

"Oh, goody," says Gwen. "I could use some spice in my life."

Jim's wife, Georgia, has hair the color of Tang. During their dinner of spinach tortellini, Gwen drinks too much Chianti and begins to obsess that this isn't right, you know, none of this is right. Men wanting to shrink their wives' breasts, women dyeing their hair the color of powdered breakfast drinks. This ship is going to sink. This sun is going to set. This stoolie is going to sing.

"Your turn!" Georgia overturns a card with a flourish, her eyes doing Jackpot before she reads aloud. "For Gwendolyn. I've never been part of a menage à trois."

Gwen pauses dramatically, making a great show of struggling to think, to search her memory. Finally she says, "Well . . . ."

Shelby smiles vacantly. He trusts his wife. There is nothing to fear.

"Sorry to disappoint ya," she says. "Never. Not even once. Close, maybe. But that doesn't count."

◆

On the ride home, Shelby is silent as an empty birdcage. Gwen asks what's on his mind. He says, "Nothing."

They pass the Movie Magic video store. They pass the parking lot of the Sweet Dreams Café. Gwen tells Shelby this is not how she imagined her life to be.

Shelby uses his turn signals expertly. He says, "What did you expect?"

Warmth, she says. Kindness. Passion. Lust, even. Not deadness. Anything but this. She says, "Sometimes I feel like I don't even know you. I mean, like, I don't even know your favorite color."

Shelby sighs. He looks as if his son has just handed him a report card crazy with Ds. Really, he says. She shouldn't use "like" so much. It makes her sound childish. It's bad enough being a schoolteacher, but to talk like a—

"What is it?" asks Gwen.

"What is what?"

"Your favorite color?"

"I don't have one."

Gwen realizes her head is nodding overemphatically and that this is never going to end. "See? That's exactly my point."

◆

Shelby is a fine man, a decent and responsible citizen, and a tedious daily companion. He is suspicious of complex reasoning, homosexuals outside the closet, and the phrase "perception is reality." He nominally believes in god but does not like to talk or think about it. To him the very idea of sex toys is revolting. All his clothes are slightly too small, as if his mother were still buying for him (to a great extent she is) and has frozen his age-fifteen, good-boy size requirements in her brain and never bothered to update. His khaki pants are slightly high-water, never touching his Hush Puppies, exposing his enormous ankles, a tuft of leg hair, and creating a dramatic space between pants cuff and loafer.

In his normal attire Shelby most resembles a box with feet.

Although he has the appetite of a Marine, Shelby does not like to eat onions, tomatoes, or any variety of ethnic food, pizza not included. He enjoys television, the funny pages, and team sports. Sex is a healthy function twice a week, but no funny stuff. After two years of marriage, Gwen can't remember why it ever happened, what possessed her. Still she loves him like a brother. But of the many kinky fantasies she entertains regularly, none involve psuedo-incest.

To please Shelby, Gwendolyn drives a no-frills white Ford Taurus. No CD players, no radio, no power steering, no air conditioner, no cigarette lighter, no digital clock in the dash. It is the height of anonymity. On several occasions Gwen has tried to fit her key into the door lock of someone else's white Ford Taurus, mistaking it for hers in the personality void of a supermarket parking lot. Her husband chose the Taurus for perfectly valid and positively wooden-headed reasons. Air bags. Antilock brakes. Zero-percent financing. *Consumer Reports* named it Car of the Blah Blah Blah. But when it comes down to the vinyl shoulder-harnessed truth of it, driving this white cow is like reading a statistical report concerning crash test dummies.

So the car is Shelby's. The things in the glove compartment (a blue Bic pen, a solar-powered calculator, an instant oil change receipt) are Shelby's. The trunk is filled with Shelby this and Shelby that. Shelby's spare tire and Shelby's lug nuts. Shelby Shelby Shelby.

The mysterious stains on the passenger seat, however, did not involve Shelby.

♦

On a soggy gray October 12th, Gwendolyn celebrates her thirty-first birthday by calling in sick to work, telling the principal, Dr. Hoffmayer, that it's female troubles. "These cramps are killing me," she says, talking into the cordless phone while standing naked in the empty shag-carpeted field of their den, the curtains open wide. She wonders if anyone can see in and moves closer to the window, until her skin is almost touching the cold panes. A damp draft chills her, rippling her arms with goose bumps, hardening the bronze circlets of her aureoles. The front yard is hazy. Brush strokes of brown and yellow cover the lawn like thick splashes of oil paint. The leaves of the Japanese maple have now turned and are falling, blanketing the ground beneath its branches like a crimson shadow, while branches of the white poplar beside it are still leafy and full, shimmering green and yellow in the misty light.

A noisy flock of black birds and starlings seethes in the poplar, stark and bright against the white pillar of its trunk. The mailman crosses Gwen's yard to the door, wearing a pith helmet and the uniform of the U.S. Postal Service, blue slacks with black stripes down the legs. After he drops off the mail, he sees her standing there. His face is indistinct as he nods to her.

Gwen needs the day off. Being a teacher, there is so much pressure to know things. To have knowledge. The capital of Ethiopia (Dar es Salaam.) The capital of Delaware (Dover.) The number one export of Brazil. There is too much to know and feel. For an entire year, spanning twenty-nine and thirty, Gwen sees Sean three times a week in the afternoon and on more than one occasion has three orgasms, so three times three equals nine and nine times fifty-two equals 468 but he was gone on a business trip at least three weeks and then there was their two break-ups minus another week so six times nine equals fifty-four subtract that from 468 equals 414 well let's just round it off to four hundred even then contrast that number to her total number of orgasms with Shelby (two) and it adds up to a life of misery, deception, hurried guilty fumbled pleasures, and schizophrenia.

◆

Sean is sick of being an attorney but resigned to the necessity of making money. He spends most of his time researching cases, writing briefs, and watching films. Though gifted with discerning the weaknesses in complex tort litigation and with finding convincing legal precedents, aided by an astounding ability to memorize case histories, the ordinary chores of life stymie or repulse him. There is rarely anything edible in his refrigerator. Supermarkets intimidate him. All the happy shopping couples! All the choices! Tubs of butter or sticks of oleo or Squeeze Parkay. His voice is often hoarse, his eyes are often bloodshot, and he always insists that next week he is going to quit drinking by god and get in good shape. When he has too much wine, his cheeks and nose become pink as Santa Claus, and he can't keep his hands or tongue off Gwendolyn, whom he calls Monkey Girl for no apparent reason.

That afternoon, Gwen's thirty-first birthday, Sean mentions he has some good news and some bad news. "Good news first," says Gwendolyn.

"Okay," he says. "Good first. Then bad."

The good: He has been offered a new job. More money. A major firm. Swanky offices and lofty perches.

"And the bad?"

He smiles in a way that takes her heart out and replaces it with something else, touching the bright red box of the birthday gift he has for her distractedly, touching the bright red bow of the birthday gift he holds in his hands.

◆

Making love to Sean that afternoon is the closest Gwen has ever come, or ever wanted to come for that matter, to necrophilia. It is as if he has already moved to Miami, as if he has already bought that wretched white stucco townhouse, with its art deco gate, its crowded tennis courts, with its palm trees, its ferns in clay pots, its violet tropical dusks, and its swimming pool in the shape of Gwen's broken heart. He will not do well in the heat. He will sweat unpleasantly and become known for persistent body odor. His brain will mildew. His exceptional mind will pop like a blown fuse from too much air conditioning. Soon, very soon, he will be dumb as pizza or wax lips, overcompensating by being arrogant, smug as Don Johnson. If *Miami Vice* is what you want, be my guest.

That afternoon, as they indulge in one for the road, Sean becomes a nonperson. Wheezing and grunting like a piano mover, his body swells to the girth of a rhinoceros, crushing the air from Gwendolyn's lungs, streaking her neck with his viscous spittle. The devil has already collected his soul. Only the corpus remains—birthmarks with hairs protruding from them, the keratotic scars of dog bites and bad acne.

The moment after he finishes, Gwen squirms out from under him, mops herself with his down comforter, and hurriedly pulls on her sweater and dress.

"What are you doing?" he asks.

She will not look his way. She stands for a moment looking about the room. "I can't find my shoes."

"Gwen? Don't be this way."

"Where are my shoes?"

She leaves the bedroom, walks down the hallway, and stands in the center of the living room. Every wall is stacked with books. She sees through this, of course. It's all an act. The sensitive book lover. Ha! Where is her purse?

"Gwen!" he shouts. "Don't leave!"

God forbid he should get dressed and run after her. Don't trouble yourself. I'll let myself out.

◆

On her thirty-first birthday, Gwen walks in the rain the six miles that separate Shelby's house from Sean's place. It always rains in Tacoma. It never stops. At home Shelby is waiting in front of the TV, channel surfing, with a white chocolate birthday cake bought at D'Agostino's on the dinette in the breakfast nook.

"You're all wet," he says.

"I know."

He wipes the sodden black and white bangs out of her eyes. "And barefoot."

She pulls off her sopping wet sweater and drops it. Unzips her skirt and lets it fall to her feet, then heads for the bathroom. Shelby follows her. He's worried. My god. Cover yourself up, for Chrissakes. You'll catch your death. He wraps thick soft towels around her. When she sobs, he says, "There there. Everything's okay. You're home now."

He rubs her hair dry and buffs her back. "It's not the end of the world, is it?" he asks.

Yes, she is home. On the imitation marble of her bathroom counter there is her basket of potpourri. There is her scallop-shaped soap dish. Her yellow balls of scented soap. Her seahorse and starfish decorated shower curtain. Yes, she is home. It's foolish to be anywhere else. It's not the end of the world. The world will never end. She will. But it won't. Shelby is the Saint of Softball. When she tells him how Marcie met her for a drink after work and then she wanted to leave early because she missed him and it was her birthday and everything, he believes her. When he gives her a coffee table book on Japanese gardens because she once mentioned how they should build a Japanese sand garden in the backyard, she thanks him. She kisses his cheek and tells him it's perfect. She starts to cry.

◆

By the weekend her temperature is 104. It's hard to convince her there are no moths in the room, and she keeps asking why the ice cream truck won't stop at their house. If it's going to make all that noise circling the neighborhood, can't it stop at their house? Can't she have an Eskimo Pie? The substitute in her class, Mr. Beatherd, stays for two weeks and the students despise him. When Gwen returns, this makes her smile. She's frail for almost a month. The doctors say she has walking pneumonia. Gosh. She feels almost special. She never had an ambulatory disease before.

◆

A month later she's all better. And she tells Shelby they need to talk.

"Do we have to?" he asks.

She stares at a sack of groceries on the countertop. "This isn't a good thing," she says. "This should stop."

Shelby puts the world on pause for several breaths. He does not freak out. He does not scream, turn red in the face, or slug her in the kisser. He takes her hand in his. It's okay. Nothing is set in stone. But he wants to know the reasons why.

"I haven't always been truthful to you."

He rolls his eyes and laughs. "I know that."

Gwen's bottom lip quivers. When she speaks, her voice barely makes it to the outskirts of Whisper. "I've done things."

"What kind of things?"

"With other men."

Shelby nods vaguely, starts to speak. Stops. Scratches the birthmark on his wrist. "I know that, too."

◆

The divorce is to all intents and purposes a civilized, hostility-on-simmer parting. Gwen gets the car, her clothes, and an ugly, denunciatory letter from her ex-mother-in-law. Her own parents are crushed flat. Devout Lutherans now married for thirty-two years, they are fearful for Gwen's future. She will work the rest of her life as an inadequately paid public schoolteacher with a reckless libido and too much credit card debt. At the rate she's going, God will never forgive her. You can bet on that.

The first few months after the divorce she wears Little House on the Prairie dresses in the classroom and in the nightclubs and bars, black-leather jackets, scooped-neck blouses, too much makeup and too much denim. She dates another lawyer, a hardware store employee, a part-time bartender who wants to be a cellular phone salesman, and a software designer geek who, when listening to any of his favorite Top 1000 songs, cannot refrain from playing air guitar.

At a PTA meeting, Gwen meets a coach of the local high school and agrees to play tennis with him. His Adam's apple is too big and his hands and feet are too big and his eyebrows too bushy but still there's a certain burly Bunyanesque charm to the man. When he burps, Gwen can recognize what he's had for lunch or dinner, and he seems to burp an inordinate amount of the time. This lasts for three weeks. Then it stops.

She joins a health club and is treated for chlamydia. No matter how juiced or giddy the moment, her destitute, lonely, and misbegotten Golden Years stretch before her like vigilant parents waiting up for their bad-seed teenage daughter, but it's long past curfew and the worst they imagine is not half as bad as it really is.

Two years of this and Gwen begins to consider professional help. "Maybe we should join Skanks Anonymous," says her friend Marcie, who has just confessed to her third affair in a five-year marriage.

◆

One Friday Gwen hooks up with the junior high school teachers crowd and has margaritas at a Houlihan's in downtown Seattle. They are as exciting as watching highway repair. But the bar is crowded with sailors, fresh off four months on a training mission aboard the USS *Nebraska*. They are dying to party. Gwendolyn stays on her best behavior while accompanied by the other public schoolteacher deadbeats, but after all of them traipse out together, she returns on the pretext that she forgot her purse. She somehow then becomes the star contestant in a drinking wager. When the bar closes she ends up in a room at the Marriott with an ensign named King who, after ejaculating onto her earring and the collar of her denim jacket, proposes marriage.

During breakfast the next morning she says she'll think about it, okay? And can she have another cup of coffee, please?

◆

The day before what is scheduled to be her second wedding, Gwendolyn stuffs her one piece of luggage—a pale pink Samsonite box made of space age plastic, square, short, and squat, shaped remarkably like a cube of Pepto-Bismol—full of jeans, lipstick, lingerie, and CDs, and drives through Tacoma to Seattle and through Seattle to board a ferry to cross Puget Sound heading west. Once the car has bumped aboard and is parked, Gwen gets out and walks around, watching the churning wake from the rear deck. It's windy there, the sky full of seagulls, her hair getting blown into her mouth. The boat has such a fish odor problem you'd think they were trawling for tuna.

At the concession stand on the mezzanine, the clerk asks, "Do you want something?"

"Yes." Gwen stares at the list of soft drinks, coffee, and tea.

The clerk waits, mannequin with half-smile, expressing a hint of confusion. "What?"

"Everything."

On the top deck there are flags popping in the wind, children pointing at the water, and enough scenic vistas to choke Walt Disney. Gwen chain-smokes in the briny air, delirious with the smell lingering on her palms and fingers. She is a bad person and will pay for it. She watches the ocean swells of gray water and sees a pod of killer whales, all slick and sleek and black and white, their spumes frothing white against the gray air, like dairy cows taken to the sea, blowing farewell kisses to all those farmers and barns.

◆

Once across the Sound, she takes the highway north to Port Ludlow.

Why? She's never been there before. In her room that night at the Seafarer's Inn, she sits on the bed and reads. She is alone and she can handle herself. She is alone and this is not a bad thing. In the mirror she watches her reflection, her black hair with its silver highlights, her white wool turtleneck, the gold locket at her throat. In the mirror she also sees a painting above her. A framed watercolor of docks and seagulls, seagulls and docks. Like Henry James said, "Cats and monkeys, monkeys and cats. All human life is there." She is a good woman who has made many mistakes in her life. People do learn, don't they? Tomorrow she will be better.

DARK MATTER

WHEN JULIE FEIN'S BOYFRIEND CAME home from work one afternoon and announced that he had named her the beneficiary on his new life insurance policy, she squinted her eyes at him and asked exactly what did that mean? She had glasses but she refused to wear them. So what if her focus was a bit fuzzy? She could see through things. That was what bothered her about this blood money. "I don't like it," she said. "It means I get paid if you die, right? That's not life insurance. It's death insurance."

Hart told her don't count your chickens before the eggs are hatched, okay? But to Julie it was no joke. She feared being a hex. Things died around her. She wouldn't go so far as to say that everything she touched died, but sometimes she wondered. She did not have a green thumb. Her plants tended to wilt and wither. When she was little she had a hamster named Tickles. One day she came home and her dog Puffer had chewed the wooden door of the hamster's cage open. There was just a little hook that fit into an eyehole screw on the outside, and she thought Puffer had hit the door until it popped open and then he ate Tickles.

Julie wept and wept and her mother said, "Don't worry, Julie. Everything dies." Two weeks later Puffer was chasing cars on Snow Goose Road and a truck ran over him. Julie's brother Garth saw it and said the sonofabitch didn't even stop, just ran over Puffer and kept going. But Puffer wasn't dead yet. He yelped and ran home and died under the house. The neighbors asked if they wanted a kitten. Their orange tabby had just had a litter of five and they were looking for good homes for them. But when Julie asked her mother if they could adopt one, she said maybe we shouldn't get any pets for a while and Julie said I guess you're right. When she was sixteen her Aunt Sarah and Uncle Rod moved to Fairbanks, where Julie's family lived. They wanted to get rich by working on the trans-Alaskan oil pipeline project, as Julie's father did, although it had never seemed to work for Julie's family. If they were so rich, why were they always eating moose meat? Julie hated moose.

Aunt Sarah and Uncle Rod had one teenage son named Collin. Julie loved him more than anything else in the world. Collin was fearless and dreamed of becoming a professional trapper, although Julie did not like that part of his personality. He insisted he was going to teach her how to skin a beaver and cure its pelt, and said that the fur was so soft and warm you wouldn't believe. Here. Feel this, he said. And she said, No, thank you. She figured this trapping thing was just a phase. He'd grow out of it. Sooner or later. He went to spend a two-week stint in the Yukon, trapping muskrat, lynx, and beaver, and said that by the time he got back he should have enough money for a down payment on a snowmobile.

Collin never returned. Uncle Rod feared he was most likely killed by a grizzly bear. Or that he was somehow injured and unable to hike out—a broken leg, ravens croaking in the looming fir branches, his voice growing hoarse from shouting for help. Over time it came to be an almost mythic death, Collin's Mysterious Disappearance, and Julie felt even worse. She became convinced that everything she loved died quickly and too soon and too young.

So she wouldn't let it go. She insisted Hart name someone else as his beneficiary. His sister, his mother, his Uncle Roy. She didn't care who. Just anyone besides her. And he said Okay, whatever.

Later they broke up. He wanted to get married and have a baby and she said No. She was afraid. Somehow she sensed it was the wrong thing to do. So she moved away and he started seeing someone else.

◆

Two years later, a dream of white birds prompted Hart to remember how Julie had believed in ghosts. By then he was professionally known as Dr. Lissom, though he frowned on that sort of lofty title thing. He certainly didn't believe in ghosts himself, but he wondered half seriously if they were the answer to dark matter. Being a physicist, Hart often puzzled over this mystery. According to the implications of various gravitational phenomena, 90 percent of the mass of the universe is invisible. Cosmologists term this "dark matter." Could the solution to this mystery lie in the spirit world? An entire universe of ghost people—and ghost birds and bears and whales, for that matter—that inhabit the air we breathe, that pass through us, that intermingle with our very blood?

Hart's reflections on ghosts and death was a sign of the seasons and the times. It was late winter and the news was full of shootings. A six-year-old child shot and killed a classmate, and the next day wondered why she was absent. A newlywed shot his wife because she wouldn't stop drinking and afterward killed himself. It seemed that everyone who was short-tempered, disgruntled, physically unattractive, and resentful owned a gun and didn't think twice about using it. It was America.

That morning Hart's live-in girlfriend, Twyla, was silent and a bit gloomy and he was late for work, but somehow that didn't seem to matter as much as it should. He had a funny feeling, as if he'd forgotten something.

He asked if Twyla wanted to have dinner at Ortega's that night. She shrugged. She was tired of Ortega's, their hangout in the gentrified section of New Brunswick, New Jersey, where they lived, tired of salty margaritas and greasy chips. But she had appointments scheduled all afternoon and that was something. She was a hairstylist, and after standing all day touching other people's hair you'd be surprised at how weary you can get. Too weary to cook. She said it didn't matter and asked Hart what he wanted for his birthday.

"It doesn't matter," he said, imitating her.

She gave him half of a smile. She would be hungry later and the quesadillas would be good and then she would be cozy and they would make love with her on top of him and a mirror placed strategically so he could see her behind. Hart was a visual person and liked that kind of thing. And later after their orgasms they would fall asleep in a tall soft bed with an iron bed frame in a room of hardwood floors and wooden ceremonial masks. Theirs was a pleasant life.

She told him she was sorry for being a putz and that sounded like a good idea, dinner at Ortega's, at seven. She didn't know what was the matter, nothing really. She picked up her car keys, kissed him, and left for work.

Hart stepped onto the back patio in his socks to check the weather. He taught at Rutgers University and didn't need to be on campus for an hour. Behind him the door clicked sharply. With a sinking feeling, he realized he had just locked himself out of his house. Not the first time. His keys were inside and if Twyla had locked the front door after her, to get inside he'd have to break a window. Again.

The backyard resembled a woodcut illustrating a poem by Edgar Allan Poe. Everything was damp and black. The maple and birch branches were leafless in the early morning light, the sky white with gauzy clouds. Through the trees walked a pair of slouchy teenage boys in floppy oversized clothes and backwards caps. They were both smoking cigarettes and one of them spat as he cut through the yard. Hart considered spitting repulsive, the disgusting squirt of it.

He walked toward the two boys and asked what were they doing there? A flock of crows crackled in the upper branches of the maples, the huge black bodies hopping from branch to branch, croaking raucously, the noise of them drowning out Hart's voice. One of the teenagers ignored him and the other glanced in his direction, both of them hunched over, as if their bodies were being twisted by the petty guilt of all the windows they'd broken, candy bars they'd stolen, and spray paint they'd sniffed. Hart asked the question again, moving toward them to block their way through his yard.

"What?" said the one who now stared at him. "You say something?"

The other one flicked his cigarette into the leaves.

"What are you doing, cutting through my yard? And pick up that cigarette. What's the deal?"

"What deal?" asked one of them. Up this close, Hart struggled with the blurry sameness in their faces, both pale and stupid, both ugly, both slightly distorted. One of them had his mouth open, and the other had eyes that looked slightly crossed. They had stopped walking and now stood as if that was where they were supposed to be.

"Get out of my yard." Hart realized his voice didn't sound quite right. It came out forced and tinny. Too Don Knotts, higher at the end than the beginning, quavering with fear and outrage. "And pick up that cigarette butt. What do you think this is? Huh? What do you think this is?"

"Go fuck yourself," said one of the teenagers. The cross-eyed one.

The other laughed. "We're not doing anything," he said. "Who said this yard belongs to you anyway? I don't see a sign."

The cross-eyed one nodded. "Where's the sign, Shithead?"

Hart said he didn't need a sign and if they knew what was good for them they'd get the hell out of his yard NOW.

The laughing teen quit smiling. He glanced at his friend. "Are you threatening us?"

The cross-eye pulled a gun out of his jacket and pointed it at Hart.

"Who the fuck do you think you are?"

"I live here," said Hart. "This is my yard. This is my house."

"Fuck your house," said cross-eye. He shot Hart twice in the belly. He kept pointing the gun at him. "What do you think of that?" His friend pulled him away by his jacket. The backyard seemed tremendously still after the gunshots, the rustlings of their feet in the dead leaves loud and crackling. At first the cross-eyed one seemed to want to hang around to watch Hart bleed, but after the other kept tugging his jacket, both of them took off running.

Hart winced and clutched at his belly, but he did not fall. He walked back to the patio, his hands trembling as they held in the warmth and wetness of his blood. Woozy and weak, he struggled with the locked knob, leaning against the door for support, watching his blood drip onto the gray concrete at his feet. He sat down on the hardness of the patio and retched for a moment, then spat a mouthful of blood.

◆

After work Twyla was angry with Hart for having stood her up at Ortega's. She called and left a message on the machine, sarcastically thanking him for being so considerate. She came home and changed clothes, then watched TV for a while, waiting for him to arrive home and make excuses, waiting to tell him how she didn't like being taken for granted. She began to worry. She called a friend and asked what she should do. After she'd been home for over an hour, she happened to turn on the outside light. Hart's body was slumped on the back patio, already stiff with rigor mortis, his face frozen in a grimace. When the ambulance people came, they had to place him on the gurney in the curled, awkward position of a giant fetus.

◆

Months later Julie Fein came home tired from her job as a teacher at a Montessori school in Twin Forks, Colorado, and there was Rory, her roommate Peggy's loser musician friend, sitting naked on the couch, talking on the phone. The acoustic guitar across his lap kept him from totally grossing her out, but still she hated the thought of his wrinkled scrotum rubbing itself all over her couch. He waved and smiled weakly as she began straightening up the living room. Rory was a folk singer wannabe. Though his wiry black hair was noticeably thinning on top, he wore it long and wild, his beard salt-and-pepper scraggly. He smelled faintly sour. He was painfully skinny, his ribs sharply visible, resembling a poor man's Jesus Christ Superstar. He didn't believe in restrictive clothing, bathing more than once a week, or making a living. Though he ranted against the evils of technology, he always seemed to be on the phone.

"The problem with you," he said into the telephone, "is that you've had it too easy all your life. You don't know what it is to suffer. To struggle. You'd be more forgiving if you had, believe me. I mean, all I'm asking is a second chance."

That would be his ex on the phone. He wasn't good at letting go.

"You still love me. You know that, don't you?"

Though she had grown up as a Jewish girl in Alaska, there was a softness, a smoothness about Julie Fein's features that seemed almost British and usually produced the effect as if she were being glimpsed through a veil of mist. For the moment the mist had cleared. Without looking in his direction, Julie said she'd appreciate it if he could please put some clothes on or go into Peggy's room because it was her apartment and call her crazy but she really didn't like strange men sitting naked in her living room, even if he did happen to be covering his dick with a guitar.

Rory held the phone away from his mouth and asked, "Since when am I a strange man?"

As she carried away the dirty dishes from his lunch, Julie mumbled, "Taken a good look in the mirror lately?"

"I heard that."

Julie didn't care. Rory never listened to what anyone else was saying, but he loved to criticize. He also didn't work, so Julie had the feeling that the only thing he did all day was sit around the house watching television and eating and putting his slimy fingers all over her underthings when she wasn't there.

Julie was a pretty girl, famous for those pale gray eyes and for her hair, the color of autumn leaves, which always seemed to twist and turn in the shape of softly unwinding spirals. But there were times when she flinched under the constant attention and looks she got, and she was sick of the way Rory, in particular, often stared at her. While she was changing clothes, he walked into her room unannounced. She had to hide behind the closet doors and say, "Do you mind?"

"Peggy had to go out of town, and she wanted me to ask if you would feed her fish."

"Why don't you do it?"

"I'm not good at things like that. You know that." He smiled ingratiatingly. Rory was under the mistaken impression that all the world loved him and thought he was funny. "It's too much responsibility."

"Would you leave? I'd like to finish dressing."

He stepped into the hall and spoke to her from there. "Are you going to my gig tonight?"

Rory performed now and then for tip money in Twin Forks at Stinky's Saloon, a loud, smoky place that in the summer nights filled with local drunks and tourist kids whose families were there for the many guided white-water rafting outfits. He covered Eagles' hits like "Witchy Woman" and "Peaceful, Easy Feelin'," and on his best nights could get the whole boozy bar crowd to join him singing "Desperado."

Julie asked if he'd found anything yet.

"Found what?"

She sighed and opened her door. "A place to live? You said it was only the weekend at first, but that was weeks ago."

Rory made a helpless face. He nodded and thumped on his guitar. "Not exactly." He sang softly, "But I ain't never gonna find / What I'm lookin' for."

Stifling the urge to grab his scraggly beard and drag him out of her house, Julie went to the living room and smoked a bowl from her favorite pipe, which made her brain feel fuzzy and vaporous. She turned on the TV to the network news. There was replay footage of teenagers shooting people in the cafeteria of Columbine High School in Littleton, Colorado. Encased now in baffled, tragic nostalgia, the homicidal teenagers lived on only in the grainy, pixilated images of video surveillance cameras as they fired semiautomatic weapons. They appeared triumphant.

Curling up beside her on the sofa, Rory asked Julie if she wanted a back massage. He said she seemed tense and that's not a good thing. He picked up her pipe and helped himself to her pot. "Only a crazy person would turn down a good back massage." He smiled at her.

Julie sorted through her mail and began opening envelopes. The last thing in the world she needed was one of his disgusting back massages, which always felt as if he were transcribing porno into braille on the skin of her back. She said, "I think it would be a good idea if you could find a place by this weekend."

"Maybe I can get a special deal," said Rory. "I'm good at bartering with people." The truth was that all the money Rory had to his name was fifty-five dollars and seventy-five cents, in a fringed pouch around his neck.

While Rory continued jabbering about where he might live, insisting that he didn't need much, really, like a basement or a garage or a spare room, a place with roommates, although he supposed it would be nice to have his own pad, do the solitude thing, he could get into that, Julie stared at the letter in her hand. She reread it twice to make sure she understood it.

Finally she looked at Rory and frowned. "Hart died."

He said he was sorry to hear that. Bummer. Who was Hart?

"My ex."

Rory nodded and took another toke from the pipe. "You still love him, don't you?"

Julie admitted that yes, actually she did. She did still love him. Her eyes were turning pink and shiny. She still loved him and now he was dead.

"I knew it," said Rory. He put his arms around her, and though she didn't like the bony feel of his arms and chest or the scratch of his beard, Julie let herself be hugged by him and cried against his shoulder. When she quit weeping, she said she never imagined Hart would die so young, wouldn't be around to talk to her when she was down. He had such a sweet voice. It always made her feel better.

"And you want to know the really weird thing?"

"Life," said Rory.

"Pardon me?"

"Life is the really weird thing."

Julie stared into his face. "The weird thing is I'm getting money from him. From his life insurance."

She put the letter in Rory's lap. He read it through and looked back at her.

"Two hundred and fifty thousand dollars?"

She nodded. "I guess so."

Rory loaded Julie a bowl and handed it to her. "Lucky you."

◆

Rory wasn't really in the mood to party, his lack of money and generally meager prospects working like a major buzz-crusher on his wobbly ego, and he didn't really know any of those people, but when his gig was over and the raucous crowd at Stinky's were all filing out and a blonde with long braids and a fringed leather vest asked if he wanted to come trip with her, he said, "If you're pulling out of the parking lot, I'm already there."

"Then hop in, Stringbean. The night is young and ain't nothing I like better than a young night!" She winked and swaggered across the parking lot, whooping at the top of her lungs. She offered to let him ride with her as long as he brought his guitar, promising he'd have a place to sleep, no problem. She drove a four-wheel drive minitruck with bad shocks and took so many twists and turns Rory had no idea where they were, not that he ever did to begin with, but the truck's bad shocks rattled and pounded the cab when they followed the dirt road for what seemed like far enough to reach Utah or New Mexico or Kansas or Wyoming, whichever direction they were heading from central Colorado.

On the drive they got to know each other. Rory learned the driver's name was Vicki Las Vegas and she liked to party. She was several years of drinking and drugs past pretty and slightly chunky, with large breasts and a dark mole on her cheek. She purposely did not mention that Las Vegas was not legally her surname or that she was the stepdaughter of television actor Frank Weaver, who played the comic sidekick to a cowboy-detective on *Saddlebags*, the long-running TV series in the Seventies. That was her business and nobody else's. With her cassette deck blasting The Grateful Dead she drummed on the steering wheel and said, "So let me get this straight. You're a singer, right? How cool! Do you write your own songs?"

He did and promptly sang one for her. When he was finished with "Rattlesnake Rita," she let go the steering wheel to clap a short round of applause. He asked if she'd like to hear another one and she said well not right now but maybe later.

By the time they reached the nondescript ranch house smack-dab in the middle of nowhere, Rory had already decided he was spending the night with Vicki Las Vegas and maybe this would be the right move to put Mary Katherine, his yearned-for ex, behind him. They walked down a dirt road lined with Jeeps and four-wheel drives. At the house the driveway was packed with bikers on their choppers, drinking beer and shouting at everyone.

"That wouldn't be Miss July now, would it?" shouted one biker, weaving and squinting at her. She stepped up and said she was sorry to disappoint him, but her name was Vicki Las Vegas. He grinned and said, "Well, give me a kiss anyway."

He was a big man and she hopped onto him, planting a big tonguey one in the middle of his stubbly kisser, until he stumbled backward, his friends shouting catcalls, and Rory faded toward the open door of the party house. The place was packed and someone told him to try the punch. No one mentioned it was spiked with cat tranquilizer.

A half-hour later he was so high he couldn't stand up. He sat on the floor of the back deck, shivering with cold. His blue-jeans jacket wasn't warm enough, and he was freaking out on all the stars in the sky.

"It's like Lucy in the sky with diamonds, man," he said aloud. "I see it now. I know what they meant, man. It's all so clear."

One of the bikers belched and stared down at him. "Who is this pussy?" Several people laughed.

Rory clammed up. He was shivering badly and knew he should go inside and get warm, but he'd have to pass the biker, so he stayed where he was. After a while Vicki Las Vegas appeared and leaned over to look at him. "How's it going, Fogelberg?" she asked. "What in the world are you doing down there?"

Rory struggled to stand up, clutching the rail to keep steady. "I don't feel so good."

She gave him a pill. "Don't worry, that'll set things straight right quick."

He swallowed it and closed his eyes, a shiver passing through his body violently.

"Where's your guitar?"

Rory didn't know. And that was the last thing he remembered.

◆

Hours later, in the Sunset Motel's parking lot, Bob the Biker asked Vicki Las Vegas to stand lookout while he jimmied the door open. He used to work maintenance there and claimed one well-directed fart would open the doors.

"Why are we doing this?" she whispered, standing in his shadow but facing out so she could see if anyone drove up.

"Why not?"

"That's not a reason."

"Reason? Who needs a fucking reason for anything?" Bob jimmied the door lock for a few seconds, until it popped open. "I just want to rattle his cage."

She smoked a cigarette in the coolness of the Colorado summer night air, standing in a patch of moonlight that made the motel look like it was the set of a low-budget horror flick shot in black-and-white. Bob carried Rory's unconscious body over one shoulder and into the hotel room. Vicki sat down on the bed and flicked her ashes on the carpet as Bob laid the singer down on the bathroom floor. Write the note, he told Vicki. But don't turn on any lights.

She watched as he yanked off Rory's clothes, then looked up at her and grinned. "This is going to be cool."

"How am I supposed to write it? I don't have pen or paper."

"It's a motel, Stupid. Look in the dresser. Use your fucking head."

"Don't call me Stupid."

"Don't act it and I won't call you it."

She wrote the note, squinting in the dim light, and tied it around Rory's neck with a piece of string she found in the wastebasket. She thought the scheme was idiotic. Who would fall for such an old trick? But she held her tongue and rubbed the note with the cuff of her jacket, realizing she needed to smear her fingerprints.

Bob flopped the singer's body in the tub, his head conking loudly against the porcelain. Then Bob unzipped his own pants.

"No, Bob." Vicki hurried into the bedroom, shaking her head. "Really. Don't do that."

"What's it to you?" He pissed loudly into the tub, sighing. When he was finished he zipped up and asked, "You got a thing for him? Is that it?"

He stumbled into the bedroom, grabbing her by a belt loop and pulling her close. "You got a thing for folk singers? Is that your type?"

"Let's just get out of here."

Bob undid her western belt buckle and kissed her belly. He asked if she was in the mood for doing a couple of lines and she said okay, but let's be quick about it.

"Where's the fire?" He took a crumpled envelope out of his wallet and opened it, pulled out a straw and razor and a small plastic bag of crystal meth. "You want to split, go right ahead." He sat on the bed and began chopping up the chunks of powder on the nightstand. "It's a free country."

She knelt on the bed beside him and licked his neck. "Who said anything about splitting? I'm with you, Cowboy."

They snorted the powder off the glass top of the nightstand, the speed burning Vicki's nostrils and creating a bitter taste in the back of her throat.

"You know," said Bob. "When I used to work here, I was always tempted to break in here some night and fuck somebody."

♦

When they were finished, Vicki lay staring at the ceiling, spacing out, the bluish-gray light of dawn seeping into the darkness of the room, creating a pointillistic effect, so that the light of the world seemed only a series of fuzzy dots and shadowy splotches. She knew what she had done was wrong and that she would undoubtedly be punished for it somehow but she forced that thought from her mind Don't go there and simply concentrated on breathing, telling herself that there was no real harm done now was there. The silence distilled the taste of Sunday morning in it. When Bob took a drag off his cigarette, she heard the tobacco and paper cracking faintly as it burned. Her stomach loosed a faint, high-pitched squeal, like the song of a blue whale.

A while after dawn Bob pulled on his jeans and said, "Party's over." He took one last look at Rory in the bathtub and laughed softly. Vicki Las Vegas couldn't find her panties and was crouched beside the bed when Bob walked to the curtains and peeked out. He said, "I don't know what you're doing but it's time we get the fuck out of Dodge." She told him she was looking for her panties and he said, "Don't bother."

She was getting sick of all this and was about to let him know good and loud that she didn't like being told what to do, but when he added that it was a crime to wrap up a lollipop that sweet she decided he wasn't so bad after all.

Bob opened the door cautiously and looked out. The parking lot was quiet, only the neon light in the shape of a red sun with yellow rays shooting out from it still buzzing above the office. He said, "I'm hungry."

"Me too."

"You got any cash?"

"No," she lied.

"Me neither. But I got an idea."

He dug around in the leather saddlebags he'd brought with him after leaving his chopper at the ranch house and getting the ride with Vicki. He fished out a plastic mask, a kid's Halloween thing, the face of a red devil with horns. It had eyeholes and a rubber band to hold it tight. Bob winked at Vicki. "Won't be the first time this thing came in handy."

Sitting on the passenger side of her minitruck, Bob directed Vicki Las Vegas to drive to a convenience store on the edge of town and park on the side, where they couldn't be seen from the glass front of the store. Once there he pulled a pistol out of one of the leather saddlebags and told her to sit tight and leave the engine running. Vicki Las Vegas didn't like this, she didn't like this one bit. He told her, "Don't go pulling that shit on me now. We're a team, right?"

"If you don't put that gun away, I don't know anything about any team—"

But he was already out of the minitruck and leaning down to look through the open window, his eyes wickedly bloodshot as he told her,

"Everything is fine. I'm just going to pick up a little cash. No big deal. Don't get your panties in a knot. But if you aren't here when I get back with the money, money to buy you your goddamn breakfast, I swear to God I will fucking hunt you down and rip your heart out with my bare hands."

Before Bob disappeared around the corner of the building, he gave one last wave, then slipped the red devil mask over his face. Vicki Las Vegas felt as if all the blood had been drained from her body. Her heart was racing with adrenaline and amphetamines and fear so sharp she could taste it, like the odd discomfort you get from a glass thermometer beneath your tongue, a metallic ugliness in your mouth. A few moments passed. She tried to light a cigarette, but her hands wouldn't stop trembling. She had to pee. Speed always did that to her. Finally she managed to hold the glowing orange tip of the minitruck's cigarette lighter to the tip of her smoke long enough to get it going. She smoked the entire cigarette and was telling herself that as soon as she tossed it she was out of there, when a series of gunshots split the silence of the parking lot. She started whimpering and put the car into gear, but hesitated. She expected Bob to come running around the corner any second, ready to hop in with the loot. That's how it happened in movies. She felt her urine leak out warm and wet between her legs. This wasn't happening to her. This was not her life. She was a good person. She was being punished for all the evil that she'd done in her life. She was going to jail do not pass go do not collect $200.

♦

The only living man that Julie loved, the only man who came close to stirring up what she had felt for Hart, the only man who could possibly break her heart, who made her ache and made her come and made her lose sleep at night, was Billy Kraub, whose claim to fame was being the stepson of a famous heart surgeon. He owned a horse ranch in Huerfano County but had a violent phobia of being trampled and refused to ride. He was a diabetic with a speech impediment, a stammer, which made him sound timid and clumsy if you didn't know him. But if you knew him, as she did, it made him sound charmingly modest and self-effacing.

The night Julie learned Hart had been killed in a shooting incident and she had inherited a quarter of a million dollars, Billy grilled garden burgers with fried onions and served her tossed salad in wooden bowls and wine in tall, clear glasses meant for iced tea. He hugged her and kissed her forehead and tried not to say the wrong thing. He had his telescope set up on a platform on his back deck and told her about the sixteen moons of Jupiter, how three of them are bigger than our own moon—Europa encrusted with ice; Ganymede large as the planet Mercury, its surface cratered and striated; Io covered with volcanoes.

He thought this might distract Julie and looked at her hopefully, but she only blinked back tears. He wanted Julie to marry him, but had not asked her yet because he was afraid she'd say Yes. Though a female friend said he was a real catch and though he had a beautiful house with a hot tub, still he felt useless and unnecessary. He considered himself without natural gifts. He knew he was basically a good person, but that wasn't enough.

The only real talent he acknowledged in himself was the uncanny ability to hypnotize total strangers merely with the sound of his voice. But at best that was just the ugly cousin of the talent world, hidden away somewhere in a dusky attic while the stunning and beautiful siblings held the stage like Mozart composing symphonies at the age of nine or Picasso teaching the world a new way to imagine the human figure. The best Billy could do was to put someone he'd never met to sleep and persuade them to meow like a cat or pretend to deliver the Gettysburg Address in French when they didn't even know the language or Lincoln's actual words.

Julie ate only a few bites of salad. Chewing seemed like more trouble than it was worth. When Billy put the garden burger in front of her, she asked for a doggy bag. She apologized. He'd gone to all the trouble and it was sweet, really it was, but her appetite seemed to have fallen off a truck or a boat or a cliff. She drank several glasses of wine, and even though he really didn't want to hear it and part of him couldn't help but be jealous of Julie's dead ex-boyfriend, she told Billy about Hart. How he slept with his arms around a pillow and called it "riding the donkey." How as he fell asleep he would repeat the word "donkey" with eerie contentment. How he was oddly fascinated by froufrou knickknacks and thingamajigs, like commemorative Eiffel Tower paperweights or key chains with plastic aliens dangling from them, how he thought shopping malls were obscene, and had once said potpourri is like Muzak for your nose.

After too much wine on an empty stomach, her face grew flushed and she started sobbing, asking the questions people always ask when a person meets his death too young and in an unseemly and insulting manner. She had to lie down in the grass. Things were spinning. She feared she was going to barf. She thought barf was a funny word. She apologized for making a fool of herself. Billy told her not to worry. "You know me," he said. "After a few drinks I become, like, Mr. Id."

Julie's face was eerily pale in the moonlight, while her eyes were inky black, streaked with smudged mascara. She told Billy that she believed in ghosts and that in fact she believed Hart was here with them at that very moment. Not the movie version of ghosts. No sheet-ed spooks or shimmering, diaphanous specters. Spirits are much more diffuse than that, insisted Julie. Picture the tiniest, most infinitesimal particle of a living thing. Millions of them. Not cells or molecules or atoms. But you're getting warmer. The tiniest. And each of these is a piece of a person's spirit and each of these lives on, only it/they pass into the invisible world that moves through us, that permeates us. An increate world without which ours, this flesh-and-blood dynamic of monstrosities, could not exist.

"He's here," said Julie. "I know it. I feel it."

"Stop," said Billy. "You're freaking me out."

"Don't be silly. The dead are like air. That's why we never actually see ghosts. They're everywhere, in us, moving through us, but invisible."

♦

The next day Rory found himself alone in a cheap motel bathtub, lying naked in a puddle of what he hoped was his own urine. A dirty gauze bandage covered his left side, and a note, scrawled on a piece of hotel stationery rolled up like a tiny diploma, was tied on a string around his neck. It said that he had to call 911 immediately or he might die. It said that one of his kidneys had been removed and he needed to get to a hospital, like, pronto.

When the EMS people arrived, they found him whimpering, his naked body wrapped in a bedspread, whining about getting his kidney back and how it wasn't fair, he never did anything to anyone. But for his whole life nothing ever went right for him. And now this. The medics urged him to calm down and strapped him onto a gurney. One of them peeled back an edge of the gauze. He told the other medic to check it out. She peeked inside it as well and shook her head.

Rory asked how it looked. Was he going to die? Please tell him he wasn't going to die.

The female medic patted his head. "You're going to be fine."

The male medic said, "It's just someone's idea of a joke." He pulled off the bandage and there were only red patches where the tape had irritated the skin.

"False alarm," said the woman. "Mr. Kidney has not left the building."

♦

That same morning Julie Fein awoke with a crushing headache, a pasty film on her tongue, puffy cheeks and bags beneath her eyes. Billy had her swallow Ibuprofen but she said what she really wanted was a Slushee.

Coming right up, said Billy. "If anything can cure a hangover, it's an icy slush full of sugar-sweetened carbonated beverage."

On the drive to the nearest convenience store, Julie said the sky was all wrong. It was disgustingly blue and beautiful. And she hated the trees. They were too straight and graceful. For a day like this, for a day after she had learned the man she once loved more than anyone else in the world had died, she wanted a bleak white sky on a windswept plain.

In the Loaf-n-Jug they bumbled around the Slushee machine, tasting each flavor, trying to get the mix just right. Eventually Julie bought a thirty-two-ounce root beer flavor and Billy a sixteen-ounce banana, mainly because he loved that perfectly artificial coloring shade of yellow. They lingered in the candy aisle and argued over whether Three Musketeers or Almond Joys were the most decadent chocolate bar.

As they were about to step toward the cash register, a big man in scruffy clothes and a child's plastic Halloween devil mask burst open the door and pointed a gun at the clerk. He didn't see Julie or Billy and shouted at the clerk to give him all the fucking money in the fucking cash register or he was going to blow his fucking head off. The clerk was stunned and, at first, didn't react. He was a fifty-something man with white hair and a fleshy, sad-dog face. Julie knew he actually owned the store and was a nice person, even though he'd voted Republican in the last election.

"What's the problem, Grandpa? You stupid?" Bob neared the counter, holding out the gun in front of him until its muzzle was only a few feet from the clerk.

"I'll give you the money, but point that somewhere else." He opened the cash register. "You're twitching so much you're liable to shoot me dead from sheer nervousness."

"Hurry your ass up. I might do it just for fun is what I might do."

As the clerk scooped all the money in the register into a white paper sack, Bob glanced around the store and saw Billy and Julie standing stock-still in the candy aisle.

"What the fuck is this?" He pointed the gun at them. "Get the fuck over here where I can see you."

They moved forward, Billy stepping between Julie and Bob, who pointed the gun right in his face and asked, "What's your problem, Fatface?"

"I don't have any problem . . . I mean, well, I do, but I don't think that's what you mean. You know what I'm saying?"

"You want to be a hero? Is that it?"

"Well, no, uh . . . not really. I mean, um . . . yes, I do want to be a hero. But not if it means, um, get, getting shot at and I think that's what it means. Or I think that's what you mean. That's, that's, well, what you mean by that, isn't it?"

All the while Billy talked he moved closer to Bob, who seemed completely absorbed with what he was saying, and somewhat confused. He aimed the gun at Billy's forehead and told him not to try anything funny.

Billy spoke evenly and softly, the way you might talk to a snarling rottweiler, assuring Bob that he had no intention of trying anything funny. He wasn't actually a funny person to begin with, he said, and now wasn't the time to start but again that's probably not what he meant by funny was it?

Bob didn't reply. He didn't say anything at all. He seemed to have forgotten where he was and who he was and what he was doing.

Billy kept talking softly and timidly, stammering, "Well, the problem with me as far as being funny is concerned is that I just have no natural talent, no gift for witty putdowns or even simple comic timing, the right moment to give the punch line or the right tone of voice to narrate the setup. I mean, I don't know, I can't even tell jokes. Like did you hear the one about the snail that got mugged by a tortoise? 'It all happened so fast,' he said." Billy smiled. "You see what I mean?"

For a torturous impossible stumble of heartbeats, Bob kept the gun pointed at Billy but seemed lost in a trance, and then the clerk reached beneath his cash register, lifted up a large pistol, and said, "Hey, Cowboy!"

Bob turned and the clerk blasted him three times in the chest. He stumbled back and fell against a soft drink display, a large cooler filled with ice cold cans of Mountain Dew and Pepsi and Mug Root Beer, knocking it over, loosing a gush of water and ice across the white tile floor of the Loaf-n-Jug.

The clerk stood trembling, still pointing the gun at Bob. "Lord Jesus have mercy," he said. "Oh Lord Jesus."

For several seconds, in a silence interrupted only by the hollow sound of the wobbling cooler as it came to rest and the ringing in their ears, Billy and Julie stared at the clerk and at dead Bob the Biker. They looked outside and saw Vicki Las Vegas speeding away in her battered minitruck.

◆

If you had asked her, years later, Julie would have admitted that the best thing about her marriage to the goofy rancher who raised horses but never rode himself wasn't the wedding that took place on a pavilion atop the cliff overlooking Lost Dog Canyon, with the dazzling white plash of Smith Creek Falls in the background. That was beautiful, but that was one afternoon. No, the best thing about their marriage was that it lasted, that they lived long and reasonably happy lives. And often when she came home from work, if Billy was upstairs she would hear her man bark like a dog, happy at the sound of her closing the door and being delightfully home.